Easy Errors

Books by Steven F. Havill

The Posadas County Mysteries
Heartshot
Bitter Recoil
Twice Buried
Before She Dies
Privileged to Kill
Prolonged Exposure
Out of Season
Dead Weight
Bag Limit
Red, Green, or Murder
Scavengers
A Discount for Death
Convenient Disposal
Statute of Limitations
Final Payment
The Fourth Time Is Murder
Double Prey
One Perfect Shot
NightZone
Blood Sweep
Come Dark
Easy Errors

The Dr. Thomas Parks Novels
Race for the Dying
Comes a Time for Burning

Other Novels
The Killer
The Worst Enemy
LeadFire
TimberBlood

Easy Errors

A Posadas County Mystery

Steven F. Havill

Poisoned Pen Press

Copyright © 2017 by Steven F. Havill

First Edition 2017

10 9 8 7 6 5 4 3 2 1

Library of Congress Catalog Card Number: 2017938961

ISBN: 9781464209222   Hardcover
      9781464209246   Trade Paperback

Poisoned Pen Press
4014 N. Goldwater Boulevard, #201
Scottsdale, Arizona 85251
www.poisonedpenpress.com
info@poisonedpenpress.com

Printed in the United States of America

For Kathleen

Acknowledgments

Special thanks to Barbara, Robert, and the Poisoned Pen Press staff, who have kindly allowed my use of their time machine.

Author's Note

Easy Errors springs from a reader's request, as did *One Perfect Shot*. The Posadas Mysteries have been around for more than twenty-five years, and at one point several years ago, after many titles in the series, a reader asked if I would write the story covering the day that Estelle Reyes-Guzman joined the Posadas County Sheriff's Department. That's how the prequel *One Perfect Shot* came to be. Chronologically, that prequel's action happens two or three years *before* the adventures in *Heartshot....* the book that started the series back in 1991.

"How about Bobby's history?" was the next question. Well, why not? Prequels are fun to write, so how about a pre-prequel? *Easy Errors* is the result of that exercise.

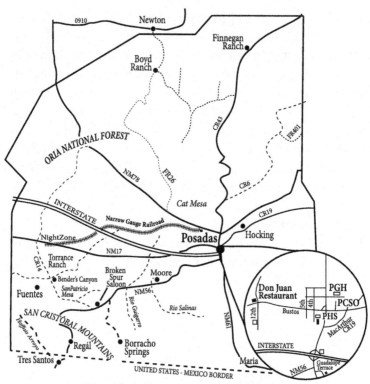

Posadas County, New Mexico

Chapter One

At 9:17 p.m. that Wednesday night in early June, cradled deep in the leather of my reading chair, I turned to page 107 in Peterson's *History of the Single-Shot Cartridge Rifle in the United States Military.* I settled in and opened to where I'd left off reading three weeks before. I half expected the damn phone to ring, because that's the sort of day it had been—myriad little interruptions, this person and that wanting a slice of my time. But that's what I was paid for. If I didn't respond to each request, legitimate or oddball, I had no reason to be carrying the badge as undersheriff of Posadas County.

For days like this one, my hundred-year-old spreading adobe was a perfect hideaway. I wasn't a social animal. My eldest daughter, Camille, is fond of referring to me as "the Badger" because of my habits. I liked a dark, deep burrow. My adobe, with its two-foot-thick walls, small windows, and the forest of surrounding weed trees, was just the ticket. I couldn't hear the voices of children playing down the street at the mobile home park. I couldn't hear the whine of tires or the loud flutter of jake brakes up on the interstate.

What drew my attention to the clock this evening was the distant shriek of tires tearing rubber and the loud, dull *whump* that followed. Two lesser contacts and a final ground shaker followed. *Whump,* then *bang, blang, BAM.* Just like that, with a pulse or two between each concussion. The clock jerked to 9:18.

Sounds have a way of wandering when they're out of context. The collision might have been up on the interstate behind my adobe, the concussion filtered through the five acres of undisciplined overgrowth that obscured my property. Or even out on Grande Avenue, the main north-south drag through the Village of Posadas, two blocks west of my home.

The concussions were so massive that not for one second did I think that my nearest neighbor, Ennio Roybal, had once again backed his aging Buick into the side of his own garage. They weren't those sorts of almost delicate sounds.

Still listening hard, I placed the bookmark and gently slid the slender volume onto the end table beside my chair. The window in my bedroom was open, but I heard no voices, no screams. Maybe that was a good thing.

I picked up the phone at my right elbow and punched in a string of numbers, and waited for the circuits to connect.

"Posadas County Sheriff's Department, Beuler."

"Chad, this is Gastner. I just heard a hell of a crash that sounded like an MVA. Has anyone called you yet?"

"Been quiet, Sheriff. Really quiet." That's the way Beuler liked it, I knew. He worked part-time, sharing dispatch with us and the village PD, and made do with his pension from the railroad and the nickel-dime salary we paid him. Tall and gawky with a receding chin line that damn near blended with his Adam's apple, he had no ambition to advance higher up the ladder within either the Sheriff's Department or the Posadas PD, even though we'd made the offer several times.

Still, Beuler was absolutely dependable, and that's all that mattered to me. He cheerfully agreed to take any dispatcher's shift—days, swing, or graveyard—at any time.

"Okay. I'm going to see what I can find. Keep the numbers handy. Payson is on?"

"He is, covering swing for Baker. And complaining about having the new guy as a ride-along."

"That's good for him. Builds character." Sergeant Lars Payson loved to hear himself talk. He was an endless font of bad jokes, critiques of the latest proof of the public's stupidity, or his own biased take on the politics of the day. On the other hand, the "new guy," fresh out of the academy and taciturn as a rock, was Payson's opposite. If rookie Deputy Robert Torrez needed three words to get a thought across, he'd try to do it in one or two.

The new guy's reticence wasn't because of laziness. Coming from a large family that included sisters as well as brothers, perhaps he just had grown weary of trying to slip a word in edgewise. He was scheduled to start his tour on the day shift in the morning. But here he was, an informal ride-along, during the swing shift—that odd time at the end of the day when people were most apt to do something stupid fueled by job anxiety, family friction, too much alcohol, or a dip into other recreational drugs. Swing shift was where the action was.

For now, Torrez was assigned to working days, the standard procedure that gave rookies the chance to learn the county and its people—all seven thousand of them. Having been bread-and-buttered in Posadas, Torrez was as local as they came. Anyone he wasn't related to, he probably knew. And I had been delighted when Sheriff Salcido slid Torrez' application across my desk. The sheriff didn't need my approval, but he was good about that sort of thing.

I had known Robert Torrez, eldest son of Modesto and Ariana Torrez, since he was in middle school. I knew his older sister, who worked over at the Motor Vehicle Department. I knew the other five siblings, from nineteen-year-old Ricardo, now serving in the Navy, down to eight-year-old Ivanita—and all the others in between.

"Have Payson head this way. This was more than somebody just knocking over a trash can. In the meantime, I'll be out and about. Let me know. Stay sharp."

"You got it, sir." Even as he said that, I could hear the phone in the background. I didn't tie up one of the phone lines waiting. Boots, gun, hat, and handheld radio, and in two minutes I was out the door into the cool fragrance of that June night.

The Crown Vic started easily, but that was its only virtue. The power steering squalled as I swung out of the driveway, and the transmission held first gear far beyond normal range, finally up-shifting with an unhealthy lurch.

Out of Guadalupe Terrace to Escondido Lane, and I saw Ennio Roybal's Buick parked right where it should be, with no fresh dents in the garage siding. A few yards farther on, no one stirred at the Ranchero Mobile Home Park. With all the patrol car's windows down, I could hear the sporadic traffic up on the interstate to the north…it didn't sound as if anyone was pausing to rubberneck a crash scene.

At the intersection with Grande, I slowed for a moment. North or south? Pick one. I turned north just as the radio lit.

"Three ten, PCS." The crappy radio reception almost blanked Beuler out.

"Go ahead. And ten-one." Beuler responded to my numerical complaint about radio reception and slowed his speech accordingly, upping the volume as well.

"Ten forty-five with probable injuries right at the interstate overpass. Three oh three is in route. ETA two minutes."

"Affirmative. I see it." Just to the north of my secluded neighborhood, State Highway 56 angled in from the southwest from Regál, then swung north to enter the village. It immediately widened to become four lanes as it joined State 61, the route connecting the village of Posadas with the tiny hamlet of María to the southeast. The two routes, 56 and 61, merged to form Grande Boulevard. Those four lanes ducked under the interstate. Four concrete pillars supported the center span of the super highway, growing out of the littered carpet of the gravel median.

Debris now covered all four lanes of Grande, both north and southbound, with the explosion of wreckage scattered under the overpass. I stopped the county car in the middle of the street, trying to think of a way to block both sides of 56/61 and the two interstate off-ramps as well. I needed about five of me, but the decision was made when I saw to my left a form crumpled on the pavement not far from the stop sign of the exit ramp. A foot clad in a tennis shoe jutted upward. This was not just an old coat discarded by some vagrant.

I bolted out of the car, leaving it crosswise in the center of the highway, lights ablaze. The mangled remains of a victim lay just off the pavement on the shoulder, face crushed into the oil and stone, his skull split open. One leg was twisted up over his back until his right foot touched the back of his left ear.

Even as I palmed my handheld radio, I knelt and touched two fingers to the youngster's bloody neck, trying to find the pulse amid the mangle of flesh. Nothing. I heard the howl of a powerful engine and saw the bloom of emergency lights approaching, southbound on Grande. Sergeant Lars Payson reached the northern-most support pillar of the overpass and stood on the brakes, stopping the patrol car crosswise to block Grande's southbound lanes.

My first inclination was to sprint over to the wreck, but Payson and his ride-along would beat me there. The dead youngster at my feet needed protection from traffic. I took a step away, trying to take in the whole picture. After cartwheeling two or three times, the wreckage of the boxy Chevy Suburban had folded itself, passenger side first, around one of the massive highway support pillars. Other than the pinging of cooling metal, the place was silent. No cries of pain, no groans.

In cruel irony, the smashed truck had taken out the *descanso*, a white cross and religious souvenirs, marking the spot where the year before Freddy Sandoval had lost his bout with the same interchange buttress. The drunken Freddy had been northbound on NM 61, and his aging Plymouth wagon had strayed—like a homing missile—straight into the interstate support pillar.

Sergeant Payson and his ride-along got out of the car, and I saw that it had been the rookie, Deputy Robert Torrez, who had been driving. And I guessed, from the look on the young cop's face, harshly illuminated by the one functional streetlight, that I wasn't the only one who recognized the crushed Suburban.

I keyed the radio, trying to watch five places at once, including the immediate threat of an active interstate exit ramp. "PCS, three ten and three oh three are ten six this location. Ten fifty-five, ten sixty-three. Multiple. Start the call-in list. And the S.P.s."

"Ten four, three ten." Off in the distance, I heard more sirens. My number code mumbo-jumbo would expedite the whole crew—off-duty deputies, ambulance, village officer, a state trooper or two if they were in the neighborhood, and the county coroner. The spectators would arrive without being called.

I knelt again by the body, this time turned so that I was facing up the interstate exit ramp. Brains, bone, and blood mixed with gravel. The massive head, neck, and upper-torso injuries were not survivable. I guessed that he'd been flung out on the Suburban's first catapulting rollover, to be crushed into the asphalt by the heavy vehicle. There was enough remaining of the right side of his face that I recognized sixteen-year-old Orlando Torrez, the rookie deputy's little brother.

Unless he could tear apart steel with his fingers, there would be little that Sergeant Payson could do for whoever was crushed inside the mangled Suburban. And the condition of the occupants must have been gruesomely obvious, because in a moment I saw Sergeant Payson clamp a hand on the deputy's shoulder and point back toward me. Payson kept his husky, urgent voice low, and Torrez nodded, the nod turning to a despairing headshake.

As he approached me, Torrez kept looking back over his shoulder at the wreckage. He couldn't walk a straight line, and if I hadn't known better I'd have pegged him as a drunk. I stood up, and Torrez' eyes locked on the body of his younger brother. Of the seven Torrez siblings, Orlando was six years younger than Robert. The awful cloud of disbelief settled on big brother's shoulders as he hustled toward me.

Behind us, the interstate's unguarded exit ramp couldn't be ignored. We couldn't just stand there exchanging sympathies, offering a likely target for someone speeding off the interstate. I reached out a supportive hand toward Torrez, at the same time keeping an eye on the long exit ramp. He ignored my gesture.

His swarthy, handsome face ashen, Torrez said nothing as he knelt beside his brother. I swept the area with my flashlight.

The intersection's huge arc light cast hard shadows, and I turned toward the ramp behind me. Even in the artificial light, the Suburban's tire scrubs were clear, marking a plunging course down the exit slope. Sure enough, the youngster had been catapulted out on the first violent roll-over.

"He was with Elli," Torrez said behind me. I half-turned as he pushed himself to his feet and looked at me. "He was with Elli. She's inside the truck." Elli. Elli Torrez, one year younger than Orlando.

"Three oh three, three ten."

"Three oh three." Payson was behind the wreck, where the metal was twisted and pummeled by the interstate's support column.

"How many?"

"I count two. Passenger compartment is compromised, but from what I can see, two. You got one more?"

"Affirmative with one. But I'm looking."

The rookie deputy already knew the status of the Suburban's two remaining passengers, if that's all there were. He'd seen his little sister and knew she was gone. But maybe…maybe if he could rip the bloodied steel cocoon from around her, there might be a chance. If he could somehow push the pieces back together…I knew the illogical desperation he felt just then.

Deputy Torrez turned back toward the Suburban, but I caught him by the elbow, hoping I could distract him with practical matters.

"Right now we need to close this ramp, Robert. Right now, before some tired tourist drives through the middle of this." If Payson had found one of the passengers still alive—if I had been mistaken in my initial, quick assessment based on seeing altogether too many of these collisions, and we could have done something to render aid—the sergeant would have shouted for help.

I clamped a hand hard on the young man's elbow. He was a head taller than me at six-foot-four, and powerfully built. But as I snapped, "Take my unit," I shook him hard. "Take my car up this ramp and block the interstate exit lane, diagonally, facing traffic. Use lots of flares. We'll get all the help we can. Everyone is rolling on this." Torrez stood immobile. "Right now, Deputy. Take my unit."

Payson's flashlight darted this way and that, and I hoped that he hadn't pinpointed yet another victim.

"Elli was with him," Torrez said again, voice a whisper.

"I hear you, and I'm sorry." I took him by the elbow again and tried to turn him—like trying to turn a planted oak tree. Putting my hand in the center of his chest, I eased him away. "The EMTs will be here in a minute. There's nothing you can do for the victims. But listen—" and I raised my voice "—we need this ramp blocked before some half-wit slams right in the middle of us." It seemed logical to give the young man something to do, something to help him work around the numbness.

"All right."

Even as he turned toward 310, I heard another vehicle up on the interstate, tires hissing on the change of pavement as he slowed for the exit. I started to jog up the ramp, staying right in the middle of the lane, the beam from my flashlight cutting quick arcs. Sure enough, a white pickup with white Texas plates appeared, and the driver had just hit the downslope when he saw me huffing up the center of the ramp, my portly figure framed by the bloom of emergency lights. He stabbed the brakes. No one was following behind, and he rolled down the window as he reached me.

"Park it right here. It's going to be a spell." The driver surprised the hell out of me. No lame "What happened?" or "Is anyone hurt?" comments.

Instead, he glanced in his rearview mirror and then at me as he said abruptly, "What can I do to help?"

I looked hard at him, saw a middle-aged, burly guy with a buzz-cut shorter than mine, a guy whose eyes were locked on the dark form of Orlando Torrez' corpse on down the ramp. From our vantage point, we could look past the victim and see the remains of the Suburban tangled around the pillar. He held up an identification wallet. I hit it with my light and saw that Carl Beason carried a lieutenant's shield with the El Paso PD.

"Lieutenant, we need to make sure that *no one* comes down this ramp." As I spoke, I flattened myself against the lieutenant's pickup as Deputy Torrez started to skin past us, keeping my Crown Vic on the pavement, every light ablaze. I held up a hand to stop him.

"Pop the trunk." When Torrez did so, I found one of the small yellow tarps, folded tightly in its baggie. I retrieved it, slipped a flare out of the box, and slammed the trunk lid down. I slapped the door. "Everything you need is in the back," I said to Torrez, but the car was already rolling.

Beason pulled his Chevy into reverse, the well-concealed wiggle-waggles blossoming in the truck's grill. "We'll take care of it," he said, and backed up the ramp after Torrez. The young deputy would angle the sedan across the exit ramp where it first split away from the eastbound lanes. A tractor-trailer thundered by in the far lane, not bothering to slow down.

I took the tarp and headed back down the ramp, pausing long enough to cover Orlando Torrez' body. Five feet away, clear of the tarp and the first bloom of grass on the shoulder, I shoved the flare's base nail into the ground and snapped the striker against the top.

By the time I reached the Suburban, Sergeant Payson was walking north, away from the wreckage, to intercept the first rescue vehicle and one of the village patrol units. That confirmed for me that there was nothing we could do for the other two victims, both of whom were trapped either in or under the truck. If one or both had been alive and pumping blood, Payson would never have left their sides. The mere fact that the sergeant was *walking* to meet the crews told me all I needed to know.

Payson sent the first arriving village unit up the westbound exit ramp on the far side of the interstate, and as other officers arrived, we would disperse them as we could. I saw Tony Abeyta, one of the village part-timers whom I thought the county should head-hunt away from the village. He'd parked his personal vehicle north of the overpass, helping to block lanes. I winked my flashlight at him, and he jogged over.

"Stay with the victim." I nodded back at the tarp. "We're covered topside, but watch the ramp behind you and don't turn your back on 56 and 61. No one comes through." I didn't wait for questions, but strode back toward the Suburban.

This wasn't one of those thirty-miles-an-hour jobs where bumpers, fenders, and a chrome strip or two were dinged and dented. The destruction was catastrophic, with the engine block lying fifty feet north in a puddle of oil, the big Suburban's frame sheered, the passenger compartment twisted and gaping.

Elli Torrez had been crushed between the buckled roof and door, sandwiched against the concrete bridge support. I couldn't reach her to check for a pulse, but the blank, staring eye and cleaved skull told the whole story. Deputy Robert Torrez would carry that as a final memory of his sister.

The other passenger was somehow locked under the truck. One leg up to mid-calf projected out from the tangle of steel. I couldn't find a pulse, couldn't tell if the leg was even attached to a body.

A small gaggle of rubber-neckers gathered at the north entrance to the overpass, and I suppose that, the budget being as tight as it was, we could have sold tickets.

I took a deep breath. "PCS, three ten."

"Go ahead, three ten."

"Make sure the rescue team is headed this way. We're going to need the jaws."

"Ten four. Sergeant Payson already called it."

"Good man."

The painstaking accident reconstruction to follow would shed some light, but the results of the crash looked typical. Careening much too fast, the heavy Suburban had left broad, sweeping skid marks on the exit ramp, rolled once, and then careened across the intersection where the change in vector had collapsed tires and then forced a triple somersault. Its flight had been abruptly smashed to a halt against the concrete bridge support. The driver and Orlando and Elli Torrez would have been flailed about like rag dolls, the crash would not have been survivable, even with seat belts snugged tight.

"What do you have on the ramp?" Sergeant Payson's voice was soft over my handheld, using the car-to-car channel that hopefully was a little bit private. He was in the process of directing another village car into position, blocking southbound on Grande, then he turned and walked my way.

"One ejected." I kept my voice down. "It's one of the deputy's younger brothers. His little sister is in the wreck, pinned against the column."

"Well, shit."

"Just the two in the Suburban as far as you could determine?"

"Affirmative. They're both gone. No doubt at all this time."

"So most likely three occupants. The tire marks make me think that the Torrez kid was the first one ejected. Maybe yes, maybe no. As soon as you have someone to break free, make sure the whole area is surveyed. All of the triangle, every inch. It'd be hell come first light to find a fourth youngster dead in the weeds a little farther up the ramp." I took a long, ragged breath. "I put Deputy Torrez up on the interstate, blocking the exit ramp. He doesn't need to be part of this. The first passerby was a lieutenant from El Paso PD. He's assisting Torrez now."

"Good thing."

I stepped aside to allow the fire rescue truck to pull in closer, staying out of the mad scramble of rescue workers who would bring the metal-forcing jaws into play. Payson, satisfied that the streets were blocked, jogged back to join the effort, but paused when he was within earshot without using the radio.

"I couldn't see the one jammed under the truck. I tried to find an ankle pulse, but…" He shrugged helplessly. "It'll be hell gettin' him out of there."

I didn't need to check the Suburban's tag. "The vehicle belongs to Willis Browning."

"Yep," Payson said again. And that just about covered it.

Chapter Two

The two-year-old Chevy Suburban hadn't glided out of its eastbound interstate lane onto the exit ramp. The last seconds of its passengers' lives had been far more violent. The heavy truck had swerved at the last moment, a maneuver so abrupt that the tires had charted their squalling course on the interstate's asphalt. The driver had overcorrected as he managed to hit the ramp entrance, the big Chevy cutting tire ruts in the right-hand shoulder gravel, two hundred and one feet down the ramp. That started the final tussle between gravity and momentum.

Essentially, the two-and-a-half-ton truck plunged wildly out of control as the driver ran out of options and skill.

Four hundred and thirty-six feet down the ramp, the Suburban careened to the left so hard that wheel rims cut grooves in the pavement, rolling the right front tire off the rim. That added enough resistance that the truck essentially tripped over its own feet. It vaulted over, pitching Orlando Torrez out and then crushing him on the roll. At one point, the vehicle went airborne, pirouetting around its right front quarter, then completed two and a half additional rolls before bashing into the concrete bridge support.

By the time rescue crews pulled the twisted hulk away from the concrete pillar, our audience had grown to a dozen folks, most of them from the Posadas Inn, just beyond the interchange. Two or three of them kept trying to edge closer under the overpass, but they quickly learned that none of us had any patience for them. They should have stayed in bed, but the draw to see some gore was powerful.

The county coroner, Sherwin Wilkes, pronounced each of the three victims. Their seat belts were still neatly retracted, unused. That would be noted, of course, but I doubted that seat belts would have accomplished much in a crash as violent as this one. Part of Chris Browning was pinned against the transmission hump by the collapsed steering wheel, and because most of him was more or less in the area that would be occupied by the driver, we decided odds were good that he had been behind the wheel before the crash.

I'd had the dubious pleasure of issuing a ticket or two to Chris in the past month or so as he delighted in his new driver's license. By the time the Suburban shot out of control on the Posadas exit ramp, sixteen-year-old Chris Browning had been driving solo for two months.

As the last body was loaded into the ambulance for transport, I turned to see Deputy Torrez trudging down the exit ramp. He stopped for a couple of seconds at the spot where his brother had died. I saw officer Abeyta say something to him, and Torrez just shook his head. After a moment, he continued on toward me. By now, we had three officers up top to keep him company— Lieutenant Beason had stayed through the whole mess, now joined by K.C. Woodard, a young New Mexico State trooper, and our own Deputy Tom Mears. Ideally, they would have sent eastbound traffic across to the other side, making both east and west single-lane traffic. The center median had its own hazards, though, and they'd settled on closing down the right-hand eastbound lane of the interstate a quarter of a mile before the exit ramp, eliminating any possibility of someone darting through.

"I'm sorry you had to ride right into the middle of this," I said to Torrez. "In a few minutes, the sheriff and I will want to go on over and talk with your folks. You need to be with them. They'll probably want to go to the hospital. Do you want to ride to the hospital first, with the ambulance?"

He shook his head, just a quick little jerk as if I'd struck him. He started to say something, and had to try twice. "We got a witness up…" He left the rest of the sentence go. "Mears wants to know if you're ready to talk to 'em."

"A witness? Absolutely." Deputy Mears could have used his own handheld to contact me, but rightly decided that giving young Torrez something physical to do was the better strategy…even if it meant walking by the chalked outline of his little brother one more time. As well, Mears clearly understood the importance of not blabbing details over the airwaves, to be monitored by anyone with a scanner.

Among the various investigators clustered around the wreck, I saw the burly figure of the boss, Sheriff Eduardo Salcido. The sheriff was a close friend of the Torrez family, and I knew he'd want to deliver the devastating news himself. He'd link up with Father Bertrand Anselmo, and the two of them made a formidable pair.

"Check in with the sheriff, and then go with the ambulance." Torrez stood as if planted there. He shook his head again, and his voice was a whisper. "I need to know what happened."

"I understand that. So do we all." The sickening aroma of blood, body wastes, and alcohol clearly told me what had happened—those and the evidence of the Suburban's out-of-control, tumbling plunge down the ramp. "Right now, your family needs you more, Robert." He lived in a modest single-wide mobile home on the lot adjoining his family's, off of MacArthur, just blocks away. Had the elder Torrezes been sitting out on their porch, they might have heard the wreck that killed their children. "Do you know where the kids were coming from?"

"They said Lordsburg."

"Lordsburg?"

"Some 4-H deal."

I glanced at my watch as I saw one of the EMTs make a move to close the first ambulance's rear doors. "The sheriff will want to talk with you."

"Yep." He wiped at his left eye, but made no move to join the crowd at the ambulance. "Both gone," he whispered and shook his head. "Look, sir, I need to know. Before I go home to talk with the folks."

The young man was right. Despite so much obvious evidence of a classic roll-over/ejection as a result of excess speed, there was so much that we *didn't* know. "Let's see what your witness topside has to say, then," I agreed.

My car was still on duty up on the interstate, and in silence Robert Torrez and I trudged up the incline, past the flares and cones and signs and flashing lights and then on west along the interstate's shoulder for a hundred yards to a silver-colored Cadillac with Ohio plates. An elderly man was outside the car, leaning against the driver's door, arms folded across his chest, watching the officers direct the sporadic traffic.

"This is Mr. Riley Holmes." Torrez' voice was little more than a husky whisper…and he didn't have to check his notebook to recall the name.

Holmes wanted to look twenty years younger than he probably was, the skin pulled so tight around his angular tanned face that it looked as if someone was holding him up by his hair… except his hair was clearly manufactured by someone else. Gravity was working on his belly, and he made an effort to suck in the gut. I extended a hand. His grip was moist and soft.

"Mr. Holmes," I said. "Undersheriff Bill Gastner." I ducked my head, looking in at the woman in the passenger seat, blond and attractive in the soft dome light. Perhaps a trophy wife, perhaps a daughter. Perhaps a secretary. "I understand you folks may have some information for us."

Holmes let the door close all the way and reached forward to touch the driver's side rearview mirror. It was hanging limp, the stem broken and the glass shattered. A shallow swipe about three feet long gored the elegant body paint near the mirror, with traces of blue paint showing up nicely.

"To my way of thinking, this is about as close as you can come," he said. "Damn idiots."

I stepped back and surveyed the car's slab flanks. No other damage was apparent. "Just the mirror and the scrape?"

He nodded.

"Where did this happen?"

"Just back a few miles. Maybe ten." Holmes said. "I saw this truck comin' up on us real fast, and for a minute I didn't think he was going to pull out into the passing lane at all. Well, then he did, like a crazy man. And he sheers on by and *whack*, there goes my mirror." His hands did a dramatic dance to illustrate. "I feel the lurch of the sideswipe. The he swerves left again and kicks dust from the left-hand shoulder, and I thought he was going to dump it right there in the median." He waved on down the road. "This is as far as he got?"

I didn't respond to that, and instead asked, "Can you describe the vehicle for me?"

"'Course I can. Chevy Suburban, two-tone blue. Nice clean truck, looked spanking new. New Mexico license, but I'll be damned if I could catch the number. He was rippin' by just too fast."

"When he swiped you, how fast were you going?"

Holmes hesitated. "Cruise was set right on eighty, Sheriff. Yeah, I was goin' a little bit fast, but a nice quiet night like this?"

"And he blew right by you?"

"I'd estimate he was cookin' close to a hundred. Maybe a little more. Didn't know those trucks could even go that fast. And I think it was kids. The one was turning around, kneeling on the passenger seat like he was trying to reach something in the back. I just caught a glimpse…that's all I saw. I *think* they had the dome light on, but I'm not sure. And then they were gone." He slapped his hands together, the one grazing the other.

"You stopped?"

"Well, sure. I pulled off at that little rest stop just west of here? Nothing but two garbage cans and a wide spot on the shoulder. I checked out the damage, and the wife, she suggested I take a photo of it, for the insurance, you know. So right away I dug the camera out and did that. I needed the time to let my nerves settle. Hell of a thing. All the while, I was hoping that one of you highway patrol boys would happen by so I could report it all, but my God, this stretch of country is empty. I didn't have anything to clip the wires on the mirror, so I thought, what the hell, I'll just let 'er hang. And about the time we were pulling back onto the highway, here comes a state trooper, flyin' low. That's when we figured, you know? That's why we stopped when we saw all the lights."

"We're glad you did, Mr. Holmes. I'm going to have one of the officers take a statement from you and your wife, along with all your information." I bent down and looked at the woman.

"I'm Eloise." Her lower lip trembled.

"Eloise, if there's anything *you* can remember, we'll want to hear it." I straightened up and said to Mr. Holmes, "If you'd round up your license, registration, and insurance, I'd appreciate it. And the deputy will want photos of your car's damage as well. We'll make arrangements to have your film processed. You may have information in the background of the photos that we'll need."

"You bet. Anything to help. It was a fresh roll, so there's nothing on it that we need. You're welcome to it." His face wrinkled a little. "They went off the edge down there or something? It's a bad one?"

"As bad as it gets," I replied. "Can you guestimate where you were when you were sideswiped?"

"Oh, yeah."

"I mean you could pinpoint the spot?"

"Oh, yeah. He hit us, and then I saw the blue rest stop sign. I mean, just right together. I just had time to slow down and turn off."

"That's good. One of the officers will want to document that location with you. There will be some debris there…bits of the mirror rim and so forth…they'll pinpoint the point of the original collision for us."

"Not exactly a needle in a haystack, but gettin' close," Mr. Holmes said. "We'll give it a try. You want me to drive on back there?"

"No. Until we're finished, I want you parked right here. And I want you to try and relax. When the time comes, you'll be riding with one of the officers. In the meantime, we'll take a statement from your wife as well." I heard the whoop of sirens as first one and then the second ambulance departed.

I beckoned to Torrez, who stood by the back fender of the Cadillac, expression impassive. During my conversation with Riley Holmes, he hadn't said a word.

"Walk back with me." I gestured toward the east, toward the closed ramp. We had reached the crest of the ramp when one of the diesel fire trucks down below cut loose with a long blast of its air horn. A white Oldsmobile drove south, the wrong way on the northbound lanes under the bridge. The car cleared the immediate accident site, then executed a lurching, awkward U-turn.

What we didn't need was a frantic parent on the scene. Our dispatcher hadn't telephoned him, but Assistant District Attorney Willis Browning had his own police scanner.

Chapter Three

Sheriff Eduardo Salcido intended to meet with Browning, but the distraught man didn't give the sheriff the chance. Salcido stretched out a hand toward him and said something that I couldn't hear, but Browning had already put the scene together. The second ambulance had just screamed away. The DA turned on his heel and dashed back to his car. He moved quickly for a heavy guy—even heavier than me. And then, with a chirp of rubber, the Oldsmobile shot up the one semi-clear lane, under the bridge through the remains of the yellow tape that he'd already ignored.

Sheriff Salcido turned and saw me. "Oh, boy," he said, his head shaking. That's about all the profanity the sheriff ever allowed himself. "This is a bad one, Bill." He pronounced my name *Bee-il,* his accent heavy and tired. "I guess Browning is going on over to the hospital."

He turned and nodded at Deputy Torrez' approach. "How's this one doing?"

"Holding up," I said, then added, "I think." Robert Torrez didn't exactly drape his emotions or innermost thoughts on his sleeve. "He should be with his folks now, Eduardo."

"Let me tell you what," the sheriff mused. He smoothed his luxurious mustache. "I'll take him with me, and we'll go get Modesto and Ariana. I'll accompany them to the hospital."

"That would be good. He wants to stay here and help, but I don't think that's a good idea."

Salcido shook his head vehemently. "He's got enough bad memories now to last the rest of his life." He exhaled a long, heartfelt sigh. "You're going to stay here and make sure we cover every inch, okay?" During his twenty-year stint with the New Mexico State Police decades before, Salcido had earned a reputation as one of the best accident reconstruction specialists. This time, he wasn't just avoiding work. To him, the most important job was dealing with relatives—and both Browning and the Torrezes would be at the hospital. When he was finished there, no matter how long it took, I expected he would return to the scene to make sure we didn't miss a single paint chip.

"Yes. And we have a witness." I nodded up the ramp. "It looks like the Suburban sideswiped another vehicle a ways back on the interstate…before losing it on the ramp. They're a snowbird couple from Ohio. Mears is taking a statement from the driver and passenger now, and then they're going to go back down the highway and search for fragments. The collision ripped off their driver's side mirror. We'll find the pieces, and that'll pinpoint the first impact for us."

"*Por Dios,*" the sheriff murmured. "To do this, let me tell you, they came down that ramp way, way too fast."

"Chris Browning lost it long before the ramp, Eduardo. My guess right now is that he just panicked. Maybe he felt or heard it when he touched the other car, maybe not. But no experience, speeding, and I'm guessing drunk…every card was stacked against him."

"I smelled the beer in the truck."

"Yep. I don't know about you…" I reached out a hand and clamped it on Deputy Torrez' shoulder as he reached us, holding him in place as I said to the sheriff, "…but I'm real interested in finding out where they got the booze."

"I want to work on that," Torrez said.

"What you want to do is take a few days off to be with your family," the sheriff said.

"What good will that do?" The question wasn't insolent or insubordinate—just a flat, quiet question that begged an answer.

The sheriff regarded Torrez for a long moment. The ghost of a smile touched his broad face. Eduardo was a true gentle man. In all the years I'd know him, in all the years I'd served under him as deputy, chief deputy, and now undersheriff, I'd never heard him unnecessarily pull rank with one of his officers.

"Someday you will know," he said softly. "When parents lose a child, they will take some comfort in drawing the other members of the family in close." He made an inclusive gesture, like a mother hen gathering the chicks. "So you be there with them now, Roberto. The rest of this," and he turned to nod at the carnage, "anybody can take care of. Your folks? *You* take care of them." He studied Torrez long enough that the young man shifted uncomfortably.

"That little thing in the paperwork...*notification of next of kin*...you'll find out that's the hardest part, Roberto." He held out a hand, and when Torrez took it, Sheriff Salcido clamped his other hand on top. "Let's go now and tend to business." He didn't release his grip, but turned to me and said, "Don't miss a thing."

Chapter Four

I suppose that under normal circumstances when a vehicle shoots by on the interstate, there is little trace left of its passing. Maybe some microscopic, unidentifiable rubber particles, a trace of exhaust gas mixing instantly with the atmosphere. It's here, and then gone.

On the other hand, Chris Browning's Suburban had left graphic evidence of its violent journey, and Deputy Tom Mears, assisted by Trooper K.C. Woodward, created an impressive diagram without too many assumptions. Nine point one miles west on the interstate and one tenth of a mile west of the rest stop, the truck had kissed the Caddy. The officers collected twelve fragments of glass and metal, including a mirror rim piece carrying a swipe of the Suburban's blue paint. The truck would have towered over the low-slung sedan. The impact would have been between the Suburban's slab side riding high on the Cadillac's door.

Between the initial collision and the exit ramp, we guessed that Chris Browning had controlled the heavy Suburban with difficulty, allowing it to wander from lane to lane. As drunk as he likely was, maybe he thought he had it made…all he needed was a little more speed to make it a really wild, memorable ride, and more important, to leave those witnesses from Ohio in the dust.

Sergeant Avelino Garcia, a longtime patrol deputy, now semi-retired yet working as the sheriff's department's skilled photographer, documented each fragment, scuff, and gouge. He would assemble the photos into a beginning-to-end montage that told the graphic story. And because this was a multiple fatal, the odds were good that the whole sorry mess somehow would end up in litigation. Families would look to lay blame, no matter what had happened.

The photos hinted at the one action that might have saved three lives. There was no evidence that Browning had ever lifted his foot off the accelerator, had ever backed off. The adrenaline rush had pushed that big truck well over the kid's ability to control it. At more than a hundred miles an hour, those seven minutes from Cadillac kiss to abutment finale must have been exhilarating and then, in a blink, terrifying.

"Tox is going to be interesting," Mears observed as I pondered his artwork. A dapper young fellow, Tom Mears was meticulous. His twin brother, Tim, was a rising star at Posadas State Bank, and Tom's uniform was about the only way I could tell them apart.

"It looks to me like he didn't recognize the exit ramp until the last second," Mears said. "He had to swerve real hard to make it into the exit lane, and careened on down the ramp, each swerve getting worse. There's a real classic gouge in the pavement where the right front tire rolled off the rim." He made a tumbling motion with his hands. "Even before the tire rolled under, it had gotten to a point really quickly where there was nothing he could do to catch it...even if he'd been cold sober."

Each "event" on the map was marked with a small circled *p,* followed by an index number, indicating that Sergeant Garcia had captured a photo of the evidence.

Garcia continued to shoot photos as Les Attawene tried to arrange bits of the smashed Suburban for transport. This was no job for a tow truck. Instead, Attawene used the flatbed car carrier, pulling the wreckage on board in bundles and clumps of tangled steel and plastic.

As they tumbled loose during this lengthy process, personal effects were bagged and labeled—a pathetic little collection: a sock whose mate was still on Elli's right foot, a partial bag of Cheetos that had sprayed all around the interior of the truck, a tire jack that had somehow slipped its moorings and flown about before ending up bloodied in Chris Browning's lap, a ball cap with a grease-stained logo for Giardelli Trucking, a second cap carrying the Posadas High School Jaguars' logo and the name "Chris" markered on the inside sweat band.

Two items in particular drew my attention. A lightweight robin's egg blue windbreaker carried both the Jaguar logo embroidered in script across the back and the name "Darlene" over the left breast. The only place I'd ever seen those fashion statements was on the back of Jaguar cheerleaders. I knew most of the cheerleaders, and Darlene Spencer came to mind. She might have ridden in the Suburban at some point, but not this final trip.

Despite allegedly headed to or from a 4-H gig, none of the three victims had been wearing a 4-H jacket, or had thought to toss one in the truck, anticipating a chilly evening.

The second item of puzzlement was a short, hardshell rifle case that contained no rifle, but did include an unbroken box of Winchester-Western .30 carbine ammunition.

That jarred my memory cells as well. I knew that Willis Browning owned an aging military M-1 carbine, one that always piqued my interest from a collector's standpoint with its Winchester legend stamped behind the back sight on the receiver when it left the factory in 1943. Willis had been in love with the optional thirty-round banana magazine that hung from the gun's belly. I'd even seen him trying to qualify with the little gun during one of our department shoots, frustrated by its habit of jamming every dozen rounds or so.

I knew that Willis routinely carried the stubby carbine in his Suburban, protected in the hardshell case. At one time he'd even leafed through some of our police gear catalogs, looking for a vertical dashboard mount like the ones that held our shotguns in the Crown Vics.

An empty gun case with no gun posed some questions.

Two beer cans, unopened by teen fingers but one of them burst with the violence of the crash, joined a few other odds and ends.

By four a.m. Thursday, the last of the glass and slivered steel was swept clear, a bag of oil-absorbent sand dumped on the oil slick, and the yellow tapes spooled up to reopen the highways. Sergeant Garcia headed for the office to process his black-and-white film so we'd have fresh prints for the day shift. Lieutenant Beason, with enough work in his own jurisdiction without lingering any longer in our patch of desert, headed home to El Paso. Mr. and Mrs. Holmes accompanied one of the officers to our office to finish a detailed statement, then decided the night had been long enough. They holed up in the Posadas Inn, trying to get some sleep before pounding the pavement again toward their home in Sandusky, Ohio, the remains of their mirror snipped free and stowed in the Caddy's trunk. One of the deputies took the Holmeses' roll of film and headed for Deming and the nearest one-hour print processor. I held little hope of any great revelation in the Holmeses' photos—lots of nice pictures of darkness, maybe.

The eastern sky was beginning to lighten, and with everyone else gone, I stood at the intersection, ruminating for a long moment. I hadn't been to the hospital—a nice word to avoid referring to the morgue—but Sheriff Salcido had lots of practice, and a deft touch with the bereaved. He might even find a tactful way to work in an uncomfortable question or two before Mr. and Mrs. Torrez headed home.

A heavy sedan whispered south on Grande. I recognized the white Olds as it crept through the highway underpass, staying well to the right, away from the point of collision.

The assistant district attorney had no one at home to commiserate with. Chris Browning had been an only child, and Willis' wife, Carolyn, had been savaged by malignant lymphoma five years before. I knew that the years since had been hard on the widower. His weight had ballooned until he waddled, the compression driving his knees inward until they knocked.

Browning swung the Olds in a wide turn, then parked with exaggerated care behind my cruiser. He sat for a moment as I approached, and then pushed himself up and out. One hand lingered unsteadily on the top of the door. Sweat glistened on his round face, on the heavy jowls.

"Willis, I'm sorry," I said. He slumped against the side of the Olds then, one hand still stretched out for support, a man on the edge of collapse. "You need to go home."

"To what?" He pushed himself upright and gazed up the exit ramp, his breath coming in choppy little gasps. "We had one of these last year, didn't we?"

"Yes." He'd seen the crushed *descanso* commemorating the crash the year before that had killed Freddy Sandoval. "Seems like every year, one place or another."

He waved a hand in helpless apology as he staggered around the front of the car. Spasms of violent retches shook him. When there was nothing left but dry heaves, he dropped awkwardly to one knee, one hand on the ground, the other on the front bumper. I popped the trunk on 310, found a clean roll of paper towels and stripped off a handful. He took them gratefully and managed to stand up, using the car for support. He panted heavily.

"I'm sorry," he mumbled. "I feel like shit."

"No need to apologize. This sort of thing turns a man's world upside down."

"I'm sorry that Chris…" he stopped and tried again. "I don't know." He looked up at me pathetically. "I need to know what happened here tonight. I talked to the sheriff, but I knew you'd give me the straight story."

"We all need to know, Willis, and we'll sort it out," I said. "The deputies will sift through it bit by bit until we know every detail."

He shook his head slowly. "Christ, this must have been hard on that new deputy. The Torrez kid? Walking right into the middle of something like this? His brother and sister, both…"

"Yes." I was impressed that, at that moment, Willis Browning managed to find a little compassion for the plight of others.

He shot a glance at me after my cryptic response, and reached for the door of his car, leaning hard against it. His gaze kept drifting back to the scarred highway support pillar. "Have you talked with the Spencer girl yet?"

"The Spencer girl…"

"Darlene? She's good friends with Elli Torrez, for one thing. And she and my son…well, they were pretty steady."

"I haven't talked with her. We found what looks to be her jacket in the truck, though. She was with them earlier? Do you know about that?"

"She was supposed to go with the kids. That's what…" His face crumpled and he turned to the car, forehead resting against the vinyl roof. "Christ, I don't believe this." He pushed himself upright and wiped his face. "Chris said that Darlene was going with them to Lordsburg. She and Chris, Orlando and Elli. All four of them."

I looked back up the exit ramp. Other officers and I had tramped along the ramp enough times to leave paths through the mowed weeds on each side of the road. Come light, we'd check again, but I was reasonably sure that we hadn't missed something so obvious as a fourth battered corpse. Until the Suburban swerved hard enough to trip over its own feet near the bottom of the ramp, none of the passengers would have been thrown out.

"If she did go, she didn't come back with them."

Browning heaved a gigantic, shuddering sigh. He patted his eyes with the remains of one of the paper towels. "So what now?"

"You know the procedure, Willis," I said. "There's a whole world of things we need to know. If they'd careened across the center median into oncoming traffic instead of down here…"

Browning grimaced and wiped his mouth. "Well, they didn't, for whatever consolation that's worth."

"I understand that. But you've been in this business long enough that you can invent scenarios as well as I can. I *think* what we have right now is a youngster who made a serious mistake. We have a credible witness telling us that excess speed was involved. The marks on the pavement corroborate that."

He sagged against the front fender of the Olds, his weight sinking the springs. "A credible witness?" The light wasn't good, but the misery on his huge face was clear.

"It appears that the Suburban sideswiped a car back down the interstate a ways. About ten miles back west. The witness says his own cruise control was set at eighty. Husband and wife both claim the truck swiped them while passing at high speed, without ever slowing down or stopping. The elderly couple stopped and took their own photos of the damage. Paint residue on both vehicles leaves little doubt that's what happened."

Browning stared at the ground for a long minute. "Tell me what else you think, Bill."

"I'm guessing right now, but I wouldn't be surprised if the blood-alcohol stats will offer some answers. That's where we'll head. We need to know where they were, and talk to folks there as well."

"I could smell the booze," he said. "You think Chris was into it?"

"I'll wait for the tests. We found two beer cans, one ruptured. That could account for the smell."

"And then?"

"If alcohol was involved, we'll want to know the source."

"What did they find in the truck?"

"Sergeant Payson has the inventory. I'll be meeting with him later today."

"But as preliminary…"

"I don't want to do 'preliminary' without knowing exactly, Willis." The little carbine was missing from its case, but perhaps it was in the closet at Browning's home. There would be time to sort all that out. I didn't want eight different people, some of them so bereaved they couldn't think straight, trying to play detective.

Browning made a strangled sound and convulsed into coughing spasms as he sucked tears and snot down the wrong way. "This is my son we're talking about," he managed finally.

"And I'm sorry. Believe me, I am."

"They took the wreck to the county yard. Les just had time to drop it off before he had to go out on another call." Willis leaned so much weight on his Oldsmobile's fender that the chassis groaned. "I need to drive over there and see for myself."

"You can look through the fence, Willis, but we both know that's as far as you go, the circumstances being what they are."

"I guess…" he started to say, and racked another coughing spell. "I guess I need to call Schroeder."

"Yes, you should," I said. "I would be surprised if the sheriff hadn't done that already." Dan Schroeder, the district attorney and Willis Browning's boss, worked out of Deming.

As if he had to think it through as each nerve synapse fired, Browning shuffled around the driver's door of the Olds, then collapsed in a weary heap in the seat, both feet still outside on the pavement, the bottom arc of the steering wheel creasing his belly.

"I don't much want to go home," he murmured, and looked up at me. "You ever feel that way?"

"Sure." I tried to offer a sympathetic smile. "That's probably why I'm still standing around out here right now. One of these things hits a little community like ours, and the shock waves go on and on."

"Chris was accepted to the pre-law program at Stanford for the fall term. Did I tell you that?"

"You must have been proud."

"And that doesn't count for shit, does it? Not now." He grunted loudly as he hauled his feet into the Olds and slammed the door. "I guess I'll see you when I see you." The car whispered into life. "And thank God that Darlene Spencer wasn't with them all." He looked up at me. "I'd better call Francine and tell her. She'll have heard about the crash. She'll think…"

"Darlene is probably home by now, Willis. But if she's not, you can reassure Francine. That's a good thing to do, Willis. And why Lordsburg, do you know? Did Darlene know?"

"Planning and working on the Fourth of July float. That's what…" and he choked and coughed again, violent heaves twisting his gut. "Christ, I can't even say his name." He tried again. "That's what my son said they were doing."

"In Lordsburg? Why there?"

He nodded, looking off into the distance, his head ticking a bit side to side like a fat metronome. "Doesn't make a lot of sense, does it? I didn't even think about it at the time. I know that Giradelli Trucking is lending them a lo-boy to use. Maybe that's where it's parked. I don't know." He thumped the padded steering wheel. "One favor?"

"Name it."

"When you find out the tox or blood alcohol, will you call me?"

"Of course." His request made it sound as if it were a huge favor. Such numbers went to the DA's office routinely. But the agony in his tone made it clear he was talking as a dad, not an assistant district attorney.

He nodded and pulled the car into gear. "Thanks." He let his head fall back against the head rest for a moment, then sighed mightily and straightened up as he let the car drift forward.

Chapter Five

By eight the next morning, Sergeant Lars Payson's desk overflowed with enough paperwork to have killed a forest. He'd been at it deep into the night, then gone home to catch a couple hours' rest before returning to the Sheriff's Department at seven a.m. Thursday. As the coordinating officer for this particular nightmare, there were myriad details for him to pursue and record. Lars was good at the job. Most cops abhorred paperwork. Payson might have, but he tackled each scrap with careful diligence, his precise use of language coupled with error-free typing.

He glanced up from a potpourri of eight-by-ten glossies as I walked in.

"You know," he said, tapping the set of photos into a neat packet, "the instinctive thing to do when you hit an exit ramp is to lift your foot. I mean, there's a friggin' stop sign at the bottom, for Christ's sakes. Everybody knows that, no matter how much of a newbie he is."

"Good morning, Sarge." I picked up a coffee cup and eyed the cannister.

"I just made it." Payson retrieved the preliminary police report. "It's interesting that in this case, the driver didn't appear to do that. There's no evidence that he ever tapped the brakes."

"Inexperienced kid. He froze at the wheel," I offered.

"Maybe so. Panic time. Maybe so."

I turned when I felt someone in the doorway behind me. JJ "Miracle" Murton, one of our part-time dispatchers, looked at us, hesitant to interrupt. As always, he ducked his head before trying the first word. Unless the world was ending and I had no one else to choose, I refused to allow JJ on the dispatch desk during swing or graveyard, when most of the actual emergencies happened. On rare occasions, he worked dispatch for the village as well. I suppose to their credit, County Sheriff Eduardo Salcido and Posadas Police Chief Eduardo Martinez—aka "the Two Eduardos"—were more tolerant of the man's shortcomings than I was. Maybe he was related to them somehow.

"Uh, Francine Spencer asked that you call her, Sheriff."

"She asked for me? Not Sheriff Salcido?" *Undersheriff* must head the list of most awkward titles, and almost no one acknowledged it. Even Sheriff Salcido, the one legitimately elected to the office, called me "Sheriff."

"She asked if you'd call her just the moment you came in."

"All right. Thanks." I turned back to Payson. "You sent Torrez home?"

"He went with his folks and the sheriff when they left the hospital. The sheriff went with them. The good Father Anselmo was headed that way as well," he added, referring to Bertrand Anselmo, the local Catholic priest. "They both talked with Browning. The sheriff's concerned about him."

"A rough deal."

"Yep. But Torrez will be all right. He's tough for a Mexican." He managed to say the nationality as if it were somehow an insult. Payson was fond of ethnic jokes, even targeting his own Swedish heritage just to keep things in balance. "The kid wanted to work today. I told him to give it a break, take some time off, be with his family. I told him that a week or two off would be even better, but he didn't seem interested in that."

"Maybe in a case like this, it's better if he keeps busy," I suggested. "Before somebody corners me, let me give Francine a call. Put her mind at ease. Browning told me last night that the Spencer girl was supposed to be riding with Chris. Obviously she wasn't."

"Uh, oh. She was out all night, though?"

"Apparently so. Francine heard about the crash and because the daughter hadn't come home, I suppose that tripped mom's worry switch."

"Lucky little Darlene, then. She sure as hell wasn't at the crash scene." He shrugged with his version of sympathy. "That doesn't mean she isn't shacked up with somebody else, gettin' into all kinds of trouble."

He grinned up at me and changed the subject. "Are you going to the meeting? The sheriff said he wasn't, and if I saw you first, I was supposed to remind you about it. Consider yourself reminded, sir."

"I suppose I'll make an appearance, if I can't find a good excuse."

"The sheriff says that you'll know what to say."

"He does, does he?" The second Thursday of each month was an opportunity to practice sleeping with my eyes open. On this day, without even a try at sleep all night, I'd be lucky if the eyes didn't just slam shut with my snores filling the Commission chambers.

The Posadas County Commission met during a marathon, all-day session that addressed all the monumental issues affecting one of the smallest and least-populated counties in New Mexico: how many weed-whackers to purchase for the cemetery; whether or not to change garbage collection days at the transfer stations; how much monetary support, if any, to give to the public library. In short, all the issues that keep the wheels of county government squeaking.

This time, they'd want the latest word from us about the horrific crash that would be the talk of the town. People in Hell asked for ice water, too.

"You could take this pack of morgue photos for show and tell," Payson said helpfully.

"You're a sick man," I replied. Someone was expected to represent the Sheriff's Department at the county meeting, no matter what catastrophes were making the news. During the past year, as Sheriff Eduardo Salcido lost interest in politics as he moved ever closer to retirement, I'd often had the short straw selected for me. Even Lars Payson had shared the experience a time or two.

Dispatcher Miracle Murton reappeared, clinging to the doorjamb as if someone had stolen his knees. "She's on the line now, sir. Mrs. Spencer, I mean."

And indeed Francine was, voice quavery, not sounding like the efficient bookkeeper that Posadas Electric Cooperative paid her to be.

"Oh, Sheriff, this has been just awful."

I couldn't argue with that, and could guess this wasn't a conversation to launch by saying, "Francine, how are you?" So I jumped right in. "Have you talked with Darlene this morning?"

"Sheriff, she hasn't come home yet." A loud snuffle interrupted, and after she gathered herself together, she added, "I heard about the accident with Scotty and the others and just…"

"Francine, Chris Browning's father tells me that Darlene intended to accompany the Torrez children and his son to Lordsburg. Is that correct, do you know?"

"She told me she wanted to do that, and I said absolutely not. We argued back and forth, and she said that she was on some 4-H committee, and just had to go. I finally caved, Sheriff, and I'm not…"

I waited a moment, heard the tissue box rattle and the nose honk. "I mean," she continued, "why would they have to drive all the way over there to work on a parade float? I told her that she should just drive herself, but she and Chris… they've gotten pretty close, and I think it was more that than working on some float thing."

"We're looking into all of that," I said. "Right now, we don't have any answers for you, other than that it appears certain that Darlene was *not* riding in the Brownings' Suburban at the time of the crash. That's the extent of what we know."

"But where *is* she, then? It's not like her to just stay out all night, without a say-so. Although…" She hesitated, and her voice dropped. "She turns eighteen next month, and that's been hard on her. She wants to be an adult, and she wants to be a kid. I'm not on her 'first to know' list. You know what I mean?"

"I do." My four, all grown and flown now, had made life interesting for me from time to time. One of them still made it a point not to speak to me.

"Sheriff, I just don't know what to do."

"She'll show up," I said with far more confidence than I felt.

"If you hear anything that I should know, will you call me? I'll be at home all day. I just couldn't face work after hearing about last night. And now, worrying about Darlene."

"Of course."

"All of this is *so* sad. And I can't help but worry. Darlene and Chris were so close, you know. He's a year younger, but they graduated together, and they've been just about in lockstep their entire senior year. But now…and poor Willis…"

"Yes, ma'am." Then, with more optimism than I felt, I added, "When you hear from your daughter, and I'm sure you will before long, give me a buzz, all right? If I'm not in, just leave a message with dispatch."

When I hung up, I sat silently for a moment, mulling. The simplest answer was that Darlene Spencer had been with her boyfriend earlier in the evening, maybe even riding to Lordsburg with the three kids. But not on the return trip. Riding home with another friend after a spat with Chris? Spending the night with a friend in Lordsburg…or elsewhere? Feeling "almost eighteen"?

I glanced up at the clock. Down the hall in the commission annex, a room that was as grand as a school's portable classroom, the supervisors would gather in a few minutes. I wasn't going to talk about the accident under investigation, so I had nothing out of the ordinary to present. They could read about the crash on Friday in the *Posadas Register*. That wouldn't stop them from asking. I attended because the commission room was nicely air conditioned, and on the remote chance that one of the county commissioners had a valid question for us.

A cat nap that resulted only in a crick in my neck didn't help much, and by the time I cleaned myself up, shaved, and changed clothes, I was resigned to my fate. Deputies all knew that we would have questions for Darlene when she turned up. Sergeant Payson knew where I was—there wasn't much else we could do at that point. At nine-fifteen, I entered the County Commission chambers as they finished the prayer and pledge, just late enough to miss the gaggle of gossips who waited by the doorway until the gavel rapped.

Our two-page sheriff's report had been included in the commissioners' packet, and no surprise, Randy Murray leaned into the microphone about half an hour into the meeting, after the bills had been efficiently approved and paid, and it was the Sheriff's Department's turn to report.

Murray questioned everything we did, I think because he enjoyed hearing his own voice. This time, it was a bid item for a new patrol unit that drew his attention. Maybe he hadn't heard about the crash the night before, because he didn't ask a question about that.

"I've said this before, and I'll say it again." Murray's brow furrowed in concentration. Of course he'd "say it again." And again. And again. "The county would save a basketful of money if Sheriff's Department cars didn't go home with the deputies after their shift is over." He rested his left hand over his heart. "*I* drive to work. My *wife* drives to work. I don't see the point of a county car retiring for the day, sitting in some private driveway until the deputy returns to work."

He fell silent, and I assumed that his gaze locked on me meant that some response was expected.

"And your question is?" I didn't bother to rise from my seat to use the microphone. I knew I probably sounded insolent, but what the hell. I was too tired to worry about it. The recorder would pick up our conversation just fine. Randy was half my age, and fond of asking the same question month after month until he received an answer he agreed with. A short, sleek man who always reminded me of a harbor seal, the commissioner hiked himself well forward in his chair, careful not to rumple his polished black suit.

"Well, my question is, Sheriff, why do we still do that?"

"And *we* will continue to do it," I said, keeping my tone reasonable, "as much as we're able." This wasn't County Commission policy, after all. Randy Murray could whine all he wanted, but it was Sheriff Eduardo Salcido who made the decisions for the Sheriff's Department, including budget matters. "It's far more efficient," I continued, "for the law enforcement officer who's on call twenty-four/seven to have his mobile 'office' near at hand."

"Oh, come on. How long does it take to duck over to the department's parking lot and pick up a car?"

I smiled slightly and didn't answer.

"I'm serious," Murray persisted. "What's the deal here?"

"Now, I…" Commission Chairman Roland Esquibel started to say, then stopped as if someone had pulled his plug.

"The best thing would be for you to come to the department and do a ride-along for a few nights," I said. "Then you'd see for yourself what the deal is, Randy. The simplest answer is that there are times when seconds *do* count." I shifted to let the hard seat wear another spot. "The sorry truth is that each officer does *not* take a car home. We like to keep the vehicles strategically placed, though."

Murray held up a pencil as if my attention had been wandering. Maybe it was. "Somebody told me that most of the time, we only have one deputy on the road in our county."

"That's an exaggeration," I said. "Some of the time, that's correct. Not *most*. It's common during the graveyard shift to have just the one officer to cover both the county and the village." I took a deep breath, thought about more explanation, and decided against it. Nothing I said would convince Murray, once he had an idea in his little pinhead. But he persisted, switching his train of thought effortlessly.

"I heard sirens all over the place last night."

"Yes, I'm sure you did."

"So what happened?"

"An MVA down by the interstate."

"That's the one with the three kids?"

"Correct." The community grapevine was a marvel. The dozen or so folks in the commission chambers fell deathly silent, all the usual private whispered conversations jerked to a halt. Murray was bright enough to understand the intent of my clipped reply, and shifted gears yet again. He read my disinterested expression accurately.

"Back to my point. In that instance last night, would there have been a delay while someone drove down to the Sheriff's Department to pick up a car?"

Number one in the stupid question department. "That didn't happen." *And a delay wouldn't have mattered*, I almost said. "We had two deputies on the road when that call came in, both riding in the same car. And I responded from home. In my unit. Had we had *another* emergency call at the same time, we would have had some logistical problems."

"It just seems to me that *most* of the time…"

I cut him off with an impatient wave of the hand. "There is no *most of the time* in this business, Randy. If we could schedule or calendar emergency calls for convenience, we would, believe me."

Murray grimaced with irritation, thumping his forefinger on the commission desk. "Did you not purchase a new patrol car last year?"

"Yes." I smiled at his tone, a holdover from his former career as a metro attorney litigating settlements against drunk drivers… until he himself made the same mistake that his targets did. Then he decided to start a new life in Posadas. He elected to hide his face, some folks would say. He specialized in settling estates, writing wills, and handling divorces. Only recently had he come back into the daylight to take a seat on the County Commission.

"And the year before that?"

"Yes."

"How many units are currently operational?"

I looked at the ceiling and did a quick count. "We have six that are not rolling junk, and two that spend their declining years doing things like county fair or parade duty. As undersheriff, I'm on call twenty-four/seven, so one of those six lives full-time with me. Ditto for Sheriff Salcido. We try to reserve a vehicle for each shift sergeant. That makes a total of five, leaving one to be shared around the clock."

Murray frowned. "I don't see how that works."

I smiled indulgently. "Neither do I. Sometimes it's a scramble. Often, a road deputy takes his sergeant's vehicle, or the sheriff's, or mine."

"Six cars, and that's not enough?" Murray said in wonder. "For a county this size?"

"That's the nature of the business. Like I said, we're a twenty-four/seven outfit, Randy. And when one of the units is in the shop, which happens too often, well…" I spread my hands in surrender. "But see, the thing is, regardless of the condition of our fleet, when Auntie Minnie is having a coronary because someone is trying to break into her house, she expects someone from our office to respond. And not next week."

"So…"and he shuffled papers. "If this expenditure is approved by the sheriff, that puts you at seven units?"

"No. One of the units is scheduled to be retired. It's showing a hundred and ninety-six thousand miles, and has all kinds of issues."

"Who currently uses that one?"

"I do."

"And so you get the new one." He could be so righteously smug, even when dead wrong.

"Nope. We'll do some shifting around. Our road deputies always drive the newest and best units."

Dr. Arnie Gray, a chiropractor in his first year with the commission, leaned forward. "If you could—I mean if the department budget would allow it—how many units would you bid out?" Gray had done his research when he won the election, and he'd talked to both me and Salcido. He *knew* what we wanted, and what we needed.

"Three this year, three next year."

"Jeez," Murray yelped, and leaned far back in his chair as if struck. He swiveled from one side to another, surveying the small audience to make sure they appreciated his performance.

At the same time, a strong aroma of perfume cascaded around me, and I turned just as Hilda Gallegos knelt down in the aisle beside my seat. She held out a small note.

"Okay, thanks," I whispered. I rose and nodded at the commission. "Just a bank robbery in progress," I said. "I'm going to see if my car will start." I held up a hand. "Just kidding. But if you'll excuse me for a bit?"

"Bill, thanks," Roland Esquivel, the commission chair, said, obviously relieved. "Any more questions, and we'll save 'em for the next meeting." He scanned the agenda while I made a quick exit, following Hilda's broad beam.

"JJ said it was important, or I wouldn't have interrupted," she stage-whispered over her shoulder.

"That's fine. You saved me."

I started to draw my handheld radio off my belt, thought better of it, and ducked into Hilda's office to use her phone. Murton answered on the fourth ring. I guess he liked to make absolutely *sure* that the damn thing was ringing before committing himself.

"This is the Posadas…"

"JJ, it's Gastner. What's up?" I interrupted.

"Oh, good. Sheriff, you got a minute or two?"

So much information, so concisely worded. I took a deep breath. Hilda had returned to her desk and was trying not to listen.

"Who, what, where, when," I prompted, and for a moment the flood of questions challenged our dispatcher.

Then he gushed, "No, I mean up the hill on 43? Just this side of Consolidated, at the boneyard there. Derwood Taylor? He's one of the foremen up there, and he wants to talk to somebody. I guess a burglary or something. I got Bishop way the hell and gone down to Regál on a domestic. Sergeant Payson is still in his office, and Mears is thinkin' of doing some checking out west, but they're both on O.T. Sarge said you might need rescuing." Miracle chuckled uneasily. "He said to give you a shout. I mean, Sarge did."

"I'm on my way." I hung up and nodded my thanks to Hilda.

"You have a better day, Bill," she said. The deeply sympathetic look she offered told me *she'd* heard all about the crash the night before.

The aging 310 started with an ominous clanking noise from somewhere down under, and I waited a moment for things to settle down. In the rearview mirror, I watched the light cloud of blue exhaust smoke drift away. My first inclination was to head for Lordsburg and some answers, but Deputy Tom Mears was already on the road in that direction, and he didn't need me breathing over his shoulder.

Consolidated Mining's Derwood Taylor had claimed to have an emergency, and had asked specifically for me. Visiting the mine site would give me a few minutes to clear out the cobwebs.

County Road 43 wound out of the village to the northeast, past the drive-in theater and various scruffy little trailer parks. I'd heard that before long, the Consolidated copper mine would close. If that rumor was true, most of the trailer park residents would move on, leaving the neighborhood desolate and weed-strewn. The outer boundaries of Posadas would shrink inward, the blight extending into the inner village, where marginal businesses would close their doors.

I drove with the windows down, watching for the herds of youngsters who lived and played along this section of the macadam highway.

The wrinkly prairie started its slope up the skirt of Cat Mesa and then, beyond the intersection with old State 78, started to climb in earnest. On the flank of the mesa, Consolidated Mining spread out to the eastern plain like a vast, ugly sore. The copper that the company had first pursued had run thin, but apparently scrounging for rarer trace minerals had kept them in business long enough for the operation to be a valuable write-off. Although the bigwigs denied it, I gave the mine until the end of the year, with just a modest reclamation crew left behind.

Just downhill, and outside the chain-link and razor-wire fence of the boneyard, Consolidated had stored a huge inventory of used railroad ties, a stinky mountain of creosote-soaked oak too vast to clutter the boneyard itself. Who knows what they were thinking? Why they needed the timbers was a good question, since as an open pit, they had no tunnels to shore up. Maybe it was just one of those "good deals" that someone couldn't pass up. The railroad ties were the only items worth stealing, but usually thieves don't have that sort of ambition.

I let 310 drift to a stop on the shoulder of the county road, and could smell the rich odor of the sunbaked ties fifty feet away. Derwood Taylor's white Chevy pickup, sporting the fancy company logos on the doors, was parked at the far end of the pile. He dismounted, carrying a clipboard as I guess all good supervisors are required to do.

"PCS, three ten is ten six Consolidated." I waited until Miracle acknowledged. I could picture his chicken neck craning as he looked at the ten-code chart to confirm that I'd used the "don't bother me" code. I hung up the mike and got out.

"Mornin', Sheriff!" Taylor called. He skirted along the bottom edge of the ties, waiting for me to climb the shallow bank from the roadway. Off to my right, several sets of tire tracks marked the shoulder of the road and scuffed dirt on the bank. With a little running start, someone had backed right up to the pile.

"Derwood, how's your day going?"

"Well, not so bad. You've had a bad one, though. Last night?"

I nodded. "Yes, we did."

He waited a moment for me to add graphic details, but when I didn't, turned back to his railroad ties. He ran a hand along the side of his head just under his cap, making sure his well-oiled hair was still neatly tied back in the short ponytail. "We got somebody helping themselves," he explained. "See these?" He walked to the nearest set of tire tracks through the crushed grass, then stopped and stomped a boot up on the first railroad tie. No dust covered its surface. "Looks to me like he backs right up to the pile here and helps himself."

"Well, that's easy to do, with no right-of-way fence," I said. "Why does Consolidated store these outside the yard?"

He shrugged. "You'd have to ask the boss man. That's what he wanted."

"They make an attractive nuisance like this."

"You know, sometime they're planning to haul them all to a wholesaler somewhere, and maybe they thought it'd be easier to load flatbed semis here on the road. I don't know why they bought them in the first place, to tell the truth. Anyways, they're not free for the taking."

"How'd you come to notice a few were missing?"

"I didn't. One of the drivers saw two Mexicans loadin'. He said they had five ties in the bed of their truck already. Some little beat-up foreign job."

"When was this?"

"He saw 'em last week sometime."

"Last *week*?"

He shrugged helplessly. "Yeah, I know. Kinda slow on the uptake."

"Your man didn't talk to them at that time?"

"Nope."

"And they just come back to help themselves, a few at a time."

"I guess they do. They're takin' the eight-footers, leaving the tens." He shrugged. "Small truck."

"Your guys didn't happen to catch the license, I suppose?"

"Nope."

"Make and color?"

"Dull yellow, one of the guys said. Off-color right-front fender. He thinks an older YoteTote. All banged up."

I pulled the small notebook out of my pocket, and flipped to an open page. "So an older yellow Toyota." I smiled and didn't bother to write anything other than the date and Derwood Taylor's name. I knew who owned the truck. I'd seen it on the two-tracks of Posadas County or in the village regularly, even deep in Mexico where its owner worked more often than not… and no doubt where the railroad ties were starting a new life.

"We got some *No Trespassing* signs that are goin' up today, too."

"Well, that'll help, maybe. What's your guestimate at the total number of ties taken?"

Taylor frowned at the pile, lips moving as he counted to himself. "Right at twenty, twenty-four. I mean, you can see the fresh marks." He shook his head. "Look, I know this is penny ante stuff, especially after last night, but the boss wanted something done."

"Glad you called," I said. From awful to the ridiculous. That's the way life went. "Your call saved me from the rest of a boring County Commission meeting." I smiled and extended my hand. "Ten bucks a piece? Is that about what eight-foot ties are bringing now?"

He nodded. "Don't be wastin' a lot of time on this," he said. "You find 'em, just tell the builder or whoever it is not to take any more. Or stop in the office first for an invoice. That's all. We got to inventory everything, you know."

"Done. That and two hundred and forty bucks for the ones already taken. And maybe the signs will help."

My radio belched out some static before Taylor had the chance to reply. "Three ten, PCS."

I twisted around and worked the radio off my belt "Three ten, ten eight."

"Three ten, ah, what's your ten twenty location?" I looked heavenward, and even Derwood Taylor grinned at the redundancy.

"Three ten is ten eight, Consolidated." *As I already told you,* I didn't bother to add.

"Ah, ten four. Can you…?" and there was a pause. There he went again, consulting the wall chart. "Can you ten sixteen back here for a bit? No, I mean ten nineteen. Ten *nineteen.*"

I sighed. "Ten four. ETA eight minutes."

"Yeah, roger that. Mears needs to talk with you." I had explained to Miracle Murton on several occasions that all the eager ears in Posadas County didn't need to hear his explanatory asides, but to no avail.

"Thanks for comin' by, Sheriff. I'll tell the boss," Taylor said. His face brightened. "And if whoever done it can come up with two hundred and forty bucks, why, that's the end of it right there. We'd sure appreciate it."

As I turned around, I examined the tracks where Rueben Fuentes had backed his Toyota off the road, putting his tailgate right at the first pile of tempting ties. The bald back tires had lost grip here and there, spinning down through the bunch grass. Knowing the old bandit as well as I did, I knew that Rueben wouldn't deny taking the heavy ties, pilfering from an unprotected stash immediately beside a public highway—as if they were being offered for public use. On occasion, I was sure that some of the state Highway Department's gravel went missing in the same way.

One thing I was sure of—Consolidated wouldn't be getting the ties back any time soon. Once they were on the jobsite in Mexico, there they'd stay.

Chapter Six

"Point zero eight for young Browning, sir," Deputy Tom Mears said by way of greeting.

I stopped to digest and translate the blood-alcohol information. "Right at the legal limit…if he were an adult."

"That's right. As a kid, point zero two would earn him a DUI. Bye, bye license."

I accepted the paperwork that Mears offered and read the fine print. "At zero eight, he might have been able to drive under normal circumstances. Might. But not at more than a hundred miles an hour. And not when he met a tricky exit ramp."

"No, sir." Mears waited patiently while I scanned the rest of the document.

"Elli was sober," I said. "That's interesting. Not even a taste, then. Fifteen years old, and she's saying no?" Her brother was a different story. Orlando's blood would have made effective antifreeze. "Point two one?" I read incredulously.

"Really, really snoggered, sir."

"Damn near toxic." Unlike Robert, his towering oldest brother, little Orlando Torrez might have weighed ninety-five pounds dripping wet. Like his mother, he had been slight of build, not much more than five feet tall.

"There's evidence that he was vomiting, maybe thrashing around not long before the crash. Traces in the Suburban itself, but plenty on the boy's clothes. The preliminary post shows that there was so much liquid from his asthma inhaler that it had been running out the kid's nose." He handed me a page of notes. "Dr. Perrone is going to investigate this further, but he thinks that Orlando Torrez was dead before the crash." He pointed at one entry as he read it.

"'Preliminary examination indicates acute system failure that appears to have been brought about in part by the combination of high blood-alcohol levels and possible corticosteroid overdose coupled with a major asthma attack. Evidence suggests cardiac arrest several minutes *before* the fatal crash.'" Mears sat back. "Like he said, that's all preliminary, but Perrone said he was willing to bet on it at this point."

He accepted the paperwork back. "We won't know for sure until the complete toxicology profile is complete, but I talked with Deputy Torrez, sir. He says that his brother had serious asthma. The kid used two different kinds of inhalers, including an empty one that we found on the floor of the Suburban. Another one went out the same window his sister did."

I sat on the corner of the deputy's desk, arms folded across my chest, lost in thought.

"Our witness remembers seeing someone trying to crawl over the seat, from front to back," I said. "I find it hard to believe that Mr. Holmes would be able to see much, unless the Suburban's interior light was turned on. Even then, with the speed and the collision? We need to find out about that. And if there was some sort of medical episode going on—if the kid is in the middle seat convulsing or something like that, then maybe his sister was trying to clamber back there to help him. Mr. Holmes says that he remembers seeing the front seat passenger up and leaning over the back. Could have been a lot going on in that Suburban just before the crash."

"And the driver is trying his best to get them to medical help as fast as he can," Mears said. "I can see that."

"That's possible. The sister sees that Orlando has stopped breathing and does what she can, all the while yelling at the driver to flog the horses. If he understood what the hell was happening. That might have been playing out when they took a chunk out of Mr. Holmes' Cadillac."

Mears nodded. "I think that at this point, all we can do is back-track 'em. I shot on over to Lordsburg, and found out nothing. The County Extension agent hadn't heard of any 4-H gatherings, and Giradelli Trucking said they haven't delivered the lo-boy for the float. So *that* hasn't started. The agent said she hadn't seen the kids since a club meeting two weeks ago." Mears shrugged.

"They said that they were attending a 4-H confab of some sort," I persisted. "That's what Bobby said his brother told him. Wednesday night is an odd time for a 4-H meeting, seems to me, but Browning says they were working on a float for the Fourth. Darlene Spencer's mother says the same thing." I grimaced. "Whatever they did, whatever they were up to, they got their stories coordinated from the beginning."

"Party time somewhere, maybe. Have you had a chance to talk with Darlene?"

"She hasn't shown her face yet." I sighed. "She wasn't riding with them at the time of the crash, and that's kinda funny when her boyfriend is driving. Maybe they had a tiff of some kind, and she hooked a ride with somebody else."

"Nothing unusual about that," Mears said.

"Except she didn't make it home. As of this morning, when mom called me, Darlene *still* hadn't shown up. What we do know is that the Suburban hit the abutment at seventeen minutes after nine p.m. *I* heard it, for Christ's sakes. If they were flyin' low on their way home from Lordsburg, they could have left there well after eight, unless they had some stops to make. This asthma thing with Orlando gets me, though. Maybe that explains the speed. The driver's got one passenger dying or dead, another one going nuts climbing over seats trying to reach him…Hell, no wonder Chris made mistakes in judgment. You've had the chance to work up the liquor inventory?"

Mears nodded and flipped open a file folder. "Among other things, two unopened cans of Coors, one of them ruptured by the crash. No liquor bottles, empty, full or otherwise. No empty beer cans. One half-empty two-liter bottle of generic lemon-lime soda that *didn't* rupture. A bag of Cheetos that did." He looked up at me. "Not much there. They didn't do their drinking in the car. Or if they did, the containers went out the window."

"And that's likely. Nothing that might be construed as 4-H materials?"

"No, sir."

I walked over to the large map on the west wall. "Thirty-six miles from Lordsburg to Posadas. All we know for sure is that when they hit the Posadas exit, they were *on* the interstate. We don't know about before that." My index finger traced the heavy, straight line of the interstate, tapping each of the infrequent interchanges. "They could have accessed the interstate in any of four places." I looked at Mears. "And it's just as likely that the little squirrels didn't even *go* to Lordsburg. And if they did, it sure as hell wasn't for 4-H…unless one of the H's is hooch."

"Lots of party spots."

"Indeed." I gazed at the map. If the kids had slipped out of town to take part in some high jinks, and Posadas County hosted plenty of parties in plenty of secluded spots, why would they bother with the interstate?

"Fastest way home," Mears said, as if reading my mind. "Mr. and Mrs. Holmes are still in town, by the way. I'll go through it again with them."

"See if they can conjure up a better recollection of what the front seat passenger was actually doing when the two vehicles touched." I shrugged. "And if the dome light was on in the truck. Although nobody told them beforehand that they'd have to remember details, so 'conjure' might be the name of the game in this case."

Three passengers, three fatalities. What was left that we needed to know? Like a nagging sore, it was just that…a *need*. An optimist might claim that revealing every detail in the chain of events might help us prevent a repeat. Not likely, unless a fourth party had somehow been involved—a supplier of booze to underage kids, or someone who had frightened the trio of kids so badly that Chris Browning had felt compelled to put the hammer down, flailing that big Suburban beyond common sense. A kid gasping and turning blue in the backseat certainly qualified as frightful.

I looked past Mears to the assignment board out in the hallway. The little magnetic chip showed that Robert Torrez had returned to the office, on duty after all. I sympathized. He wasn't going to sit home through any of this.

In dispatch, Miracle Murton was sitting with his chin propped in his hands, staring down at the new computer keyboard.

"Torrez' twenty?"

Murton startled at my question and pushed the keyboard a little farther away, as if he'd been caught watching something prurient dancing among the keys.

"He's, ah…"

"I thought he might be." That confused Murton even more.

"No, Sheriff, he's out west. Herb Torrance? Herb called in a complaint about somebody shooting the hell out of one of his cattle tanks. Bishop is still busy down in Regál. That new kid was just mooning around here, so I sent him on out to see what the deal was. If he wants to work, seems like west is the quiet side, and well, you know old Herb."

"Yes, I do. What does Bishop have going?"

Murton tapped the desk with his pencil, looking officious. "Neighbor water troubles." He pulled the blotter closer and pushed his glasses up. "The Clevelands called. Well, Luciano Cleveland did. He thinks…"

I held up a hand in gentle protest. Luciano Cleveland, who had lived the first fifty years of his life in Mexico City before moving to the tiny hamlet of Regál to start the peach orchard of his retirement dreams, guarded his spring tenaciously. Actually, the rolls of cheap black polypropylene piping were his. The spring itself, a hundred yards inside the national forest boundary, wasn't.

The water burbled out of a vein from the vast bulk of the San Cristóbal Mountains behind the village. The pipe carrying the water ran out of the forest, across property owned by Miriam Hidalgo, who probably neither knew nor cared about the waterline, and eventually found its way to Cleveland's peach orchard. The eighty-year-old Luciano kept a wary eye peeled for water thieves. Unfortunately, several of his other neighbors were in that category. Of course, the U.S. Forest Service might argue that Luciano was the biggest thief of all.

Deputy Howard Bishop, who knew maybe ten words of Spanish, was steady and patient to a fault. Luciano Cleveland would keep him busy for hours if allowed to do so. "Maybe I'll swing down that way after a bit," I said. I liked Luciano, and his coffee was always hot and rich.

"And Sergeant Payson is still pushin' paper." Murton relaxed a bit. "Hell of a lot of overtime this week."

"Always is. Come to think about it, I haven't talked to Herb in a couple of weeks, so I think I'm going to cruise out that way first and make sure our young deputy stays out of trouble. If Bishop needs anything, remember I'm just up on 14."

The Torrance ranch spread out across the western side of Posadas County, edging up against Bureau of Land Management acreage and, on the west side of County Road 14, a little patch of heaven owned by Rueben Fuentes, my current suspect in the case of the purloined railroad ties. If I could lock Rueben and Luciano Cleveland in the same room, in company with a jumbo bottle of good tequila, the majority of petty nuisance calls that we fielded would be eliminated.

Herb Torrance, on the other hand, went about his business quietly, minding his growing family and his angus cattle. He had complained that one of his stock tanks had been vandalized, but I knew that Rueben had had no hand in that. But who knows what he had seen as he bounced and jounced his old truck through the country, hauling railroad ties to Mexico?

Reuben would be across the border now, working up a sweat on some gorgeous project or other. I wasn't going to chase after him down there, but after an endless night, I'd favor one of the shady spots on the western side of the county for a quick cat-nap when my eyes drooped. Especially since Alice Torrance made some of the best pastries in the civilized world.

Chapter Seven

Wild West trick shot specialists like Bill Cody or gun factory reps like Ad Topperwein used to wow crowds by drawing pictures with their amazing shooting. I've seen historic photos of those Indian heads, or cowboy profiles, or liberty bells, rendered by bullet holes through thin metal plate…half an inch or less between neatly punched bullet holes, spaced with precision and, even, one might say, artistry.

I tried it once years ago, but I was working with my .357 magnum revolver, and the recoil made it a challenge to stay on line. That's my excuse, anyway. My Indian head, blown into the white lid of a washing machine dumped in the county landfill, came out looking like the Elephant Man after a bad night.

"Bill, do you know how much one of these tanks costs now?" Herb Torrance said. "I just put it in last year, too." A real honest-to-God working cowboy in his faded denims, white shirt with pearl buttons, and scuffed boots with heels run down, Herb worked his tongue around a generous pinch of Copenhagen. As if that wasn't enough nicotine to meet the need, he fished an Old Gold out of the pack without removing the pack from his shirt pocket. "Goddamn, Sheriff, they did it, didn't they?"

"Yep, they did."

Herb was lanky, just under six feet with bad knees and a spine that was starting to take on an artful bend. Half a hundred bullet holes pierced or scarred the galvanized metal sides of his newest stock tank, and most of them weren't the modest little holes from a twenty-two caliber prankster. The metal was pretty tough, strong enough to hold up when the cattle leaned against it. Unless they hit just right, most twenty-two slugs would have just glanced off anyway. On top of that, the vandalism was done without much regard for artistry. No pictures here. Just a riddled tank.

On the far side, fragments of glass dotted the tank's rim where the pistoleers had set bottles and cans. At least they'd started that way, maybe, with no intent to damage the tank. A litter of torn cans and glass shards lay in the tall grass beyond, and one or two had spun back into the tank. I could picture the hilarity as one drunken, errant shot missed the target and punched through the tank. I imagine that that started the bullet fest.

I measured one hole with the tip of my little finger. Nice fit, but inside the tank, the explosive exit rosettes erupted in jagged-edged tears. The water had drained down to the level of the lowest holes, streaking the metal. Wasps and butterflies were going nuts sopping up this rare bonanza. It made me wonder how the word went out around the insect world.

The walls of the tank where the sun struck the metal had dried, but in the shade, some driblets of water still clung to the metal.

I leaned on the tank edge and looked down. "Not too long ago," I said. A few rounds, fired after the water had drained down, had punched through both sides of the tank. Those rounds striking below the waterline must have sent up satisfying geysers.

"Wish't I'd a caught them at it," Herb said, then tilted his head. "But maybe not. They'd probably just as soon shoot at *me*, anyways." He turned and pointed. "But that bothers me more, Sheriff." Herb nodded at the windmill. Dozens of holes let sunshine through the idled blades in fascinating patterns. "Tore up every damn one of 'em."

"Maybe there was a breeze, and they were enticing targets," I mused. "Did you call dispatch this morning, or was it Alice?"

Torrance shrugged, the thin muscle and bone of his shoulders hard against the worn cotton. "I was in town this mornin', so I didn't hear the shooting, if that's when they done it. Now, Alice thinks it was yesterday, though. She thinks that she heard 'em shooting yesterday, late. Maybe so, I don't know. She thinks lots of things, sometimes." He chuckled dryly, then shrugged. "I was out in the shop 'til way after dark. Didn't hear a damn thing over the welder. I came out to check on things today and found this."

I leaned over the edge and watched the half dozen koi assembled down below, waiting for treats. The little fish, four or five inches long, had less than six inches of water in which to navigate, but seemed content enough. The watercress and other weeds fanned out now on the surface, dragging their stems in a tangle. Little black beetles with oar-like legs rowed through the aquatic jungle.

"It's not damp around the holes, even on the shady side, so it's been a few hours, anyway."

"That's what the new guy was sayin'. He stopped by for a few minutes. He collected some spent bullets and some brass, but I don't know as there's much any of you can do about it unless you catch 'em in the act." He pointed with a jerk of the chin. "He picked up a bunch of the cans, too. And some bigger pieces of busted bottles. Don't know what for."

"Fingerprints, I suppose," I said. "A fingerprint on the can doesn't mean much, though. Doesn't prove who put it there, or who shot it."

I gazed off to the south. What was a well-marked two-track leading in to the windmill site—what I'd followed in with the aging Crown Vic—became just a trace through the bunch grass beyond, angling down through an old lava flow to Bender's Canyon—a grand name for a little wrinkle in the blanket of the prairie. If I imagined hard enough, I could follow a track or two off through the bunch grass. The tracks would take me down into Bender's Canyon, and then loop back out to County Road 14.

The canyon palisades were an eroded remnant of some prehistoric sea bottom, all the soil washed away, then carved and smoothed by once-a-hundred-year floods. Kids loved the cliffs because they were accessible, treacherous, overhanging and water-streaked in spots, a grand place to practice freestyle rock-climbing or rappelling. There were enough rock ledges and overhangs to provide camping shelter. The BLM, which owned the land in the canyon, had even considered designating the site as a rock-climber's recreation area, signing the place in from the highway.

I had heard that, and immediately had visions of a dozen kids being swept away when a cloudburst upstream rampaged down through the canyon. Maybe the BLM thought about that, too, since no progress for development had been made.

Herb lit another cigarette as he regarded his punctured tank, offering the pack toward me. "I'm trying to quit," I said. "Again."

"Good luck with that." Torrance thumped the side of the tank with heel of his hand. "I guess I can try weldin' this up. What I got don't work for shit on galvanized steel, though. And I got a few of them screw-in tank plugs with the rubber gaskets? They might hold for a time."

"File a report with us, Herb. You can claim this on your homeowner's."

"Hadn't thought of that."

I stepped back and examined the tank. "This must have a drain plug?"

"Sure." He skirted the tank and stopped opposite the windmill's feed pipe. "Lemme fetch a wrench. The plug's in there pretty good."

The midday June sun was warm, and the entertainment was pleasant. The day was so different from the night before that I was loath to cut short my visit to the Torrance ranch. I watched the water striders scoot across the water's surface and the agile water beetles dive through the vegetation like little glossy submarines, spooked when my shadow loomed over them.

In a moment Herb had the plug out, and the draining water cut a dribbling, lazy arc.

"Your man didn't bother to drain the rest of it," Herb observed. "He's a long-legged son-of-a-gun. He just did one of them sort of kips over the rim like it was nothing. I told him,

'You know, there's a stile right behind the mill.' He just said, 'Thanks,' and over he went. By then the water was down to a few inches, so it wasn't so bad. Soaked his boots, though."

I grinned, trying to picture myself "kipping" over the side of a four-foot steel tank. The lead in the *Posadas Register* would scream, "Two-ton Undersheriff Drowns in Stock Tank after Breaking Neck During Mystery Fall."

"I'm not that eager," I laughed. The draining water had started to cut a mini-arroyo in the dirt. I ambled around the circumference and found the stile with bunch grass and a riot of little yellow composites growing up through it. I kicked the wood gently to wake up dozing reptiles, but nobody was home.

"Lemme give you a hand." Herb offered, and we tussled the stile upright, then heaved it up to straddle the tank's side. "I guess I could leave it in the tank all the time, but it gets so damn slippery."

"I don't need slippery," I agreed. "You said Torrez recovered some slugs?" Now that I was contemplating actually climbing inside, I looked down at the slimy tank innards without much enthusiasm.

"He fished out a whole handful. I guess that's what he was after. And he took some pictures of the tire tracks. Don't know what they're going to tell him, but he don't talk much, that one." He waved a hand over toward my car. "And then he picked up some brass. Wasn't much, but a few pieces, over there in the grass. I was surprised there wasn't more, all the holes there are."

I glanced across at the faint marks through the grass. "The tracks. I wish him luck." I leaned on the tank again, gazing out across the twelve feet of water surface, low enough now that most of the aquatic plants held their heads above the retreating surface. Herb and I stood there in companionable silence. He'd spat out the chaw and substituted another of his Old Golds.

Across the tank, a cow-killer walked along the tank rim, pausing at each glass fragment. A full two inches long with a stinger like a sharp tack, the red and black wasp was as fearsome looking as he was a gentle giant…at least to humans. Tarantulas didn't think much of him lingering in the neighborhood. If we stood there long enough, the wasp's curiosity would prompt him to hike the tank circumference to visit.

"I never did catch his name."

I glanced at Herb. "The deputy?" *No...the wasp*, Herb was polite enough not to say. But I wouldn't put it past Herb Torrance to have pet names for his livestock. "That would be Robert Torrez, one of our new hires." I grinned. "He's one of Sheriff Salcido's distant cousins. I'm sure you know his dad...Modesto?"

Herb nodded in recognition. "One of my sons was a classmate of his, then. The boy is big for a Mexican."

"He is that. I think he'll work out all right for us. He just got back from the academy a couple of weeks ago. He did well." I shrugged. "We give him a gun, badge, and a car and tell him to stay out of trouble until he's earned some experience." None of that had worked so well the night before, I thought, but Herb hadn't asked about the accident—maybe he hadn't heard about it—and I saw no cause to bring it up. "Did Alice happen to mark the time when she heard all the shooting? You said yesterday, sometime?"

"Hell, I don't know. I mean, folks shoot out this way all the time. That ain't nothin' new. This time was a little different. I mean, so many, and all." He turned in place. "What are we, about seven-, eight-tenths of a mile from the house? Maybe a little more. And she claims she heard 'em. Enough racket that she knew it wasn't hunters. But, say, you know better'n me." He sucked on the cigarette and then talked around the plume of smoke. "The border isn't what it used to be. Lots of traffic comin' in that way, and some of 'em aren't up to much good, if you know what I mean. So she gets nervous. And she figured it wouldn't hurt to call and have it checked, just in case."

It didn't make a hell of a lot of difference. The shooters were long gone, most likely headed back to Albuquerque, or El Paso, or wherever the hell they came from. Maybe it was just a gang of frustrated, soon-to-be-out-of-work miners. Whoever it was, it had been a group effort.

I didn't need to pester Alice Torrance about when she made the call. Dispatch would have logged it to the second. The only downside was that if it had been a daytime call, Miracle Murton would have been sitting dispatch, and there was no telling what he might have written down. In any event, he hadn't passed the complaint on to the deputies.

Just enough water remained inside the tank that it was a sloppy mess of fragrant vegetation and a handful of now frantic koi. I kept both hands on the stile and paid attention to my footing. Slimy with algae, the steel tank bottom was slick as wet ice. I could tell that my boots wanted to skip out from under me, depositing my avoirdupois on top of the nervous koi. Once standing on the tank's bottom, I kept my feet still, bending at the waist—which in itself was a trick. The water was still a bit turbid from the young deputy's efforts, but the sun was just right for prospecting.

The first slug I found shown bright. I took two steps toward it without shuffling, raising as little silt as possible. The bullet's nose was deformed, its trip through the thin galvanized metal of the tank side enough to start the mushroom. A silver-tip, and I guessed it at thirty-caliber—just about the most generic bullet on the planet, the sort of thing that would come out of a .30-30.

I spent fifteen minutes stooped and harvesting until I'd stirred up so much mud even the koi were invisible. Herb watched impassively, elbows resting on the tank rim. He enjoyed one cigarette after another, kibitzing when he thought he saw the wink of bright metal.

Some of the evidence was just fragmentary, and a few were big old pumpkin rollers, the sort of slugs fired from a .45 automatic. Several large dents showed where rounds hadn't broken through the tank's galvanized hide…a humbling experience for some yahoo who thought his hand cannon was a power house. Too bad a ricochet hadn't bounced back and hit him between the eyes.

What interested me most was a set of enormous holes, fully forty-four or forty-five-caliber, that had punched through the tank wall as if it had been waxed paper. The group included five shots, the holes tight enough to be covered by the palm of my hand. I made a patient search, but found none of the slugs. Maybe the deputy had already fished those out.

I took pity on the koi. "You better screw the plug back in and run the mill." I headed toward the stile. "You've got some unhappy goldfish." Herb fitted the plug, but the wind wasn't cooperating. The eight-foot Aermotor had been still when I arrived, and remained so. Herb reached in and worked the brake, making sure. The mill groaned a quarter-turn against an errant heat wave and then stopped.

"It was running yesterday?" I asked.

"Yep, part of the time, anyways. Well," and he gazed up at the stationary blades, "maybe later this afternoon. That's the way the wind is, you know. Just the time you want it to blow, everything goes still as hell. If the wind don't pick up some this afternoon, I'll bring a tank out. The kids tell me I ought to go for a gas engine." He shrugged. "Maybe I should. 'Course, then the yahoos would just shoot *that*." He scrutinized the handful of bullet fragments that I held out. "Huh?" A stubby index finger moved the collection this way and that in my palm. "Some of those are clean enough you could almost load 'em up again."

"I count at least four different guns here." An obvious little pure lead fragment from a .22 or .22 magnum, the .30-caliber jacketed rifle slug, a .38-caliber pistol bullet, and the big, round pumpkin roller .45. "A regular shooting gallery they had." I turned and surveyed the grass around the tank and the hard surface cut by the two-track in from the county road. "At least they didn't leave their brass littered all over the place. Tidy little sons-a-bitches, weren't they?"

"What's in season now, anyway? I didn't think anything was."

"Well, nothing other than water tanks, windmills, and old cars and dumped refrigerators. It's all pre-season warm-up."

"Three ten, PCS."

I turned and regarded my aging sedan as if it had spoken out of turn.

"You can run, but you can't hide," Herb observed laconically as I strode over and pulled open the door. I dumped the collection of rifle slugs in one of the center console's cup holder, and pulled the mike off its clip.

"PCS, three ten. Go ahead." A long pause followed, so I repeated myself.

Nona Salcido, the sheriff's wife, department matron, and now fill-in dispatcher while Miracle took a break, sounded harried. "Uh, Bill, hang on just a second."

I looked over at Herb and took a deep breath to shore up my patience.

"PCS, three ten," I prompted. I liked Nona, but she was about as useless in dispatch as Miracle Murton.

"Ah, three ten, Deputy Torrez needs to talk with you. Are you still out at Herb's?"

"Three ten is ten eight at Torrance's Number Two."

"Three oh eight is trying to reach you, but I think he's out in a dead zone for both the unit and his handheld. He says he can't read you."

"Probably because I wasn't on the radio," I said aloud without pressing the transmit bar.

"Just a second, Sheriff." Of all her jobs, Nona was the most uncomfortable behind the microphone. On top of that, the ten-code continued to be more of a mystery to her than it was to Miracle. On top of *that,* she had never accepted that the police radio wasn't a telephone gossip channel.

"I *think* he's saying that he's down in Bender's Canyon."

"Ten four." I looked off in that direction. Three hundred yards would take me through the runty trees and brush to the rim of the canyon. Maybe I could just shout at Torrez. With the characteristic vagaries of our radio system, he could talk to dispatch thirty miles away, but not to me.

"Three oh eight, three ten."

I waited for the radio signals to wrap their way around the landscape, maybe sending a pulse or two down into the canyon. Nothing. I saw movement, and the deputy's Stetson appeared as he trudged up the incline. He was in no hurry. His hands swung loose at his sides, and every now and then, he'd stop and gaze off at something in the brush. As he approached through the scrub, finally reaching the old two-track, I could see that he was chewing on a stem of grass, Old Farmer Brown himself.

The possibilities were endless, but the image that came to mind first was of the department Blazer, one of our older vehicles, stuck up to its hubs in the sands of the canyon bottom, a perfect target for the next summer cloudburst.

He nodded at Herb Torrance and removed the grass on which he'd been chewing. With the energy reserves of a fit twenty-two-year-old, he was breathing as hard as if he'd been sitting and reading a book.

"Sir," he said, "there's a spot you need to look at."

How generic was that? "A spot?"

"Yes, sir."

"Is your unit stuck down in there, or what?"

"No, sir. I didn't want to drive in the area any more than necessary." He spoke as if he were reading his lines from an index card, and his voice was just one notch above a whisper.

Herb lit another cigarette, and Torrez took a step sideways to move out of the smoke. "You're welcome to take my truck on down there if you want," Herb offered. He'd driven one of the ranch trucks, a brute Ford 350 with a cattle-feeder on the flatbed.

"No, that's fine, thanks just the same. A walk will do me good." I lifted a hand in salute. "Lead on, Macduff."

Once clear of the cattle-stamped flat around the windmill's tank, the trail eased down a gentle slope through the scrub. With their feet near the canyon floor, an errant elm or two thrived, providing nice pockets of shade. The trail was not a thoroughfare. Every now and then, I saw a partial bootprint, but there hadn't been enough foot traffic to carve a dusty trail, even from Herb's cattle, which would enjoy the shade as much as humans would. After a hundred yards, I saw the walls of smooth sandstone ahead of us, yellow in the morning sunshine.

Our trail switched to the right to avoid a jumble of boulders, and Torrez stopped. He'd evidently driven back out to the county road from the windmill site, then up the passable trail into the canyon proper. We didn't walk that far, but I could see the white top of his parked Blazer down below.

I hadn't been prepared to see a yellow crime scene tape, but there it was, strung across the trail and circling an area about half the size of a tennis court.

Without comment, Torrez ducked under the tape, and immediately stopped, one hand holding the tape up a little. "Just over there by that mesquite."

I turned and surveyed the hillside. The target of his interest wasn't hard to find. He'd pushed an evidence flag into a soft patch of earth, the red of the flag bright against the tawny rocks. The muted brown of the gunstock was clearly visible.

Torrez didn't move, and neither did I. If you find something as interesting as a firearm abandoned in the boonies, odds are good that there'll be other items of interest along with it, forcing the list of questions to grow. Sometimes, the answer is painfully simple. Posadas County had hosted its share of suicides over the years, and usually the victim was found clutching the gun of choice—or at least lying beside it.

The last thing we wanted to do was walk through an area of question with careless size twelves, destroying critical evidence.

"Did you take photos yet?" I asked.

"Some."

From where I stood, it appeared that the gun had most likely been leaning against the unruly growth of a creosote bush, then fell over. I could see no immediate reason why anyone would drop the gun in that particular spot. I looked down at my feet and then let my eyes follow the faint track up the grade. "You walked over to it?"

"Right along there." Torrez indicated the trace of a path that ended with the evidence red flag.

"You didn't pick it up." That would have been most people's reaction, I was sure.

"No, sir."

"You still have your camera?"

"Yes, sir."

"I'm going to walk over to the evidence flag. I want a photo when I'm about halfway there that shows both me and the flag. To show the route we took."

He nodded.

I didn't walk…I ambled, taking care to keep my boots on rocks when I could, my hands in my pockets. I counted the steps, and after only ten, I could see the outlines of the gun clearly. I stopped and turned back to Torrez. "You know, I don't like coincidences one little bit."

I shook my head and continued on until I was looking down at the M-1 carbine, its thirty-round banana magazine securely in place.

The night before, we'd found an empty rifle case in Willis Browning's wrecked Suburban, the rifle case that usually contained his personal military relic. My first thought, when I'd seen the empty case, was that Willis had changed his mind about letting his son go solo in the truck with the gun along for the ride. Teenagers were a curious bunch.

But why not just take the case out of the truck? That didn't make sense, either.

The rifle hadn't been in the wrecked truck because, I was already willing to bet, it was lying out here under the stars. Which meant that the kids had been here. I was jumping to conclusions, though. Coincidences *do* happen.

I beckoned the young deputy. "Scrunch yourself down there and tell me who manufactured that thing."

"Winchester, sir." His answer was immediate, without the need to scrunch.

"But you didn't pick it up?"

"No, sir."

I sighed. "How many of these can there be in one small, rural county?"

"It's Browning's, sir."

I looked at him. "It looks like it, but tell me why you're so certain."

"Before he bought it from George Payson last spring, I looked at it a few times at the gun shop."

"You were thinking of buying it?"

"Yep."

"But…"

"The back sight ain't original, and somebody buggered up the front barrel band screw. Easy to fix, but Payson had the price jacked way up."

I bent down with my elbow on my knees, moving my head to bring the right tri-focal zone into play. Sure enough, Joe Hobby had tightened the barrel band screw more than a few times with an ill-fitting screwdriver, making marks as individual as fingerprints. The after-market rear sight had been tapped into place with something only slightly less weighty than a sledge hammer. "The sight still isn't right, and the screw's still buggered." I straightened up. "Now just suppose."

Torrez regarded me silently. I was delighted that he hadn't just charged in and snatched up the gun. He'd seen it, and instantly took the time and effort to treat the area that included the rifle as a potential crime scene. The lad had paid attention during evidence classes at the academy.

"It won't take long to confirm it, but suppose you're right… suppose that it *is* Willis Browning's rifle. I find it hard to believe that *he* would have carried it here. I mean, with his weight, he can hardly maneuver on level, smooth ground. I talked to him briefly out at the wreck site, and I didn't ask him about the gun. I mean, I knew about the empty gun case found in the Suburban and all, but…" I heaved an irritated sigh. "I was more concerned with other things."

I straightened up and surveyed the terrain. "It's easy to understand why kids come out here. It's a gorgeous place. Nice spot to go picnicking, nice spot to go do whatever it is that kids do nowadays." I looked back down at the little carbine. "And a nice spot to go shooting." I glanced sideways at the deputy. "Windmills and water tanks and such. So why leave the M-1 here?" Torrez had no answer for that, and didn't attempt to venture something profound. "You scouted around the area a little bit?"

"Not yet. As soon as I saw the carbine, I taped off the immediate area, then tried to call in."

"So much for hi-tech radio technology." I glanced down at his feet. His leather boots were still damp. "Herb doesn't have a clue who might have shot up his property. Did you find anything interesting? He says you went wading."

"I picked up sixteen pieces of .30 carbine brass from a spot about thirty paces north of the tank. New issue, Winchester-Western." He pointed at the carbine on the ground with his chin, Indian style. "Didn't find no .30 carbine slugs in the tank itself."

"But lots of other stuff," I said. "I have a few pieces to add to the collection. Interesting that there are no other empties. I mean, *somebody* shot the hell out of that tank and did a little work on the windmill itself, and not just with an M-1 carbine. I saw the work of three or four separate guns."

It wasn't a comment that demanded a reply, and Torrez didn't make one. "I'm guessing the obvious possibility…the kids *were* here. That's the only thing that makes sense to me."

"This ain't Lordsburg," the deputy observed. "I never thought that they went there anyways."

"The canyon is a popular spot. The carbine here ties them to it." The water-polished rocks were perfect for free climbing, and grottos, caves, and shelves had been cut over the eons to make attractive party rooms. The lack of casual passersby and the limited access to the canyon itself meant that no one was going to walk into the middle of ongoing recreation.

"The Prescott kids are out here all the time. Them and the Torrances and their buddies." Torrez nodded to the northeast. "Just follow the canyon for a couple miles and it about runs right into Prescott's front yard."

"And you can come in on the two-track from the county road, just like you did. You don't have to go through Torrance's ranch. And…" I turned at the waist, looking down slope, "they could have driven out that way, then taken the county road north and jumped onto the interstate at the interchange. A straight shot into Posadas that way."

"Fastest way," Torrez said.

"The other alternative is take the county road south, and take State 56 into town. Either way." I shrugged. "So what spooked 'em? Assuming they were here. What spooked 'em enough to drop the carbine and hightail it back toward town?" The obvious answer was going to be an uncomfortable one for Bob Torrez, so I voiced it for him. "If Orlando suddenly had an asthma attack, and the kids didn't know what to do, that would account for the panic."

"Elli would know what to do." His voice was scarcely more than a whisper.

When Torrez fell silent, I added, "The kids would want to get him out of here, get him to medical help. It's a frightening thing. Elli might have known *what* to do, but she might not have had the wherewithal to do it."

"Maybe, could be."

"Had Orlando been ill recently?"

"Not no more than usual. Last week, he had some trouble."

"Huh." I nodded at the yellow tape. "And why right here? Why this particular spot? It's not down in the canyon, which is the usual party site. It's not in the pasture up by the windmill, where the shooting recreation took place." I turned a circle, trying to imagine what might have happened. "You've been outside the perimeter?" He shook his head.

"See," I said, "you and I walked down the little trail that follows the old two-track from the windmill. The kids might have done the same thing. It's no big hike. I mean, as the crow flies, we're, what, a hundred yards from the windmill? Fifty yards down into the canyon? It's a small area. But that trail downslope? We're off that beaten track by a dozen yards." I gestured at the carbine. "Why did whoever it was walk up here to lay down the M-1?"

"Don't know. Takin' a leak, maybe."

"Maybe so, Roberto. Maybe so."

I motioned with both hands. "Let's just concentric out a ways." From the faint trail to the carbine was roughly north, and my plan was to survey all the way to the top of the low ridge. I walked counterclockwise around the perimeter marked off by the tape, with Torrez going clockwise. Aging bottle caps, fading aluminum zip-tops, a crumpled cigarette pack—all the usual "humans were here" junk marked their territory. The number of cigarette filters that remained long after the tobacco and paper had faded away always amazed me. No wonder Smokey Bear was always trying to beat tourists over the head with his shovel.

I happened to glance up when, about thirty yards northwest of the carbine site, where a gray juniper stump and a swarm of prickly little seedlings attempted to cling to the rocks, Robert Torrez stopped short.

"Hey?" He waited motionless while I made my way up to him. He never looked at me as I approached, didn't point, didn't move a muscle.

"Oh, shit," I whispered and stopped short, shoulder-to-shoulder with the deputy. The girl lay crumpled on her back in a small alcove formed by Volkswagen-sized boulders, head turned away from us, black hair fallen over her face. She wore no jacket, and blood soaked the left shoulder of her t-shirt. Her blue jeans were unbelted and unzipped, bunched along with light blue panties below her knees.

Her shoes and socks were in place, but her left leg was flexed at the knee, her foot cocked as if she had been trying to kick. The ground around her left shoe was lightly scarred by her dying efforts.

Watching where I put my feet, I knelt down and touched the right side of her neck. My own pulse was slamming in my ears, and I closed my eyes, concentrating on my search for her right carotid artery. The skin was silky and almost warm. Almost. I shifted my fingers several times to find the pulse, but felt nothing.

Chapter Eight

Posadas County Coroner Sherwin Wilkes kept a brave face. In his other life, he enjoyed a strong chiropractic practice, now in partnership with freshman County Legislator Arnie Gray. The connections with the legislature didn't end there, since Dr. Wilkes was the legislative chairman's brother-in-law. Still spry from spending so many hours on the rugged Posadas golf course, he ducked under the yellow tape that now included about an acre of hillside. For the second time in as many days, his face was pale, with sweat standing out on his forehead.

"My God, how did you find this place?" he said.

"Luck," I said. "The assistant medical examiner is on his way. He was in Deming, so it's going to take a little while."

Wilkes edged closer to the thin space-blanket that reflected sun so bright it hurt the eyes. I nodded at Deputy Torrez, and he and Sergeant Avelino Garcia, who had chauffeured Dr. Wilkes to this forlorn spot, carefully secured two corners of the silver blanket and drew it back. Wilkes knelt, and I heard the repetitive *crick* of Garcia's camera.

Wilkes said nothing for a few seconds, his tongue sucking little clicks against his palette. He reached out and drew the fall of hair back from the victim's face. "Darlene Spencer," he said. "Oh, my." Shifting position a little, he placed a hand on each side of the girl's neck and closed his eyes. "Oh, my," he said again. I hadn't been able to think of anything more profound, either.

Ever so gently, he turned the victim's head a bit to the right and left. Looping his stethoscope free from the collar of his jacket, he took his time, seating the earbuds just right. He roamed the bell around the corpse's chest without disturbing the t-shirt.

After a long moment, he straightened back and then pushed himself to his feet. "All right," he said. "Dr. Perrone's on his way, you said?"

"Yes." Alan Perrone, commuting each day from Posadas to Deming to run the small medical examiner's office there, would take Wilkes' preliminary report without question, but in cases like this one, Wilkes knew his own limitations. Cause of death was not clear, and the circumstances leading to that death were anything but obvious.

He shook his head. "I can't tell you much, but I can tell you this, Sheriff. The girl hasn't been dead long. No rigor, and I would doubt that her core body temp has dropped even ten degrees." He glanced over at me. "And that's the limit of what I'm willing to give you. I can pronounce, but," and he turned wearily back to regard the corpse, "you're going to need a hell of a lot more than that. Looks like a head injury of some sort. As for the rest…"

The "rest" was our concern, and the mind does a good job of leaping to conclusions. Find a dead girl with her jeans and underwear pulled low, and we start looking for the bastard who raped her before smacking her fatally in the head. Clearly, there were problems with that easy scenario. For one thing, rapists generally forced the whole view, top half as well as bottom. The victim's white t-shirt, and the bra underneath it, appeared undisturbed.

Wilkes stopped at the sound of voices and vehicles down in the canyon. The EMTs would have had a challenge bringing the ambulance up Bender's Canyon two-track…not because of the footing, which in this weather was firm and packed, but because of the "gates," a series of house-sized boulders that loomed on either side of the southwest entrance to the canyon. They were scuffed in more than a few places, showing automotive paint left behind.

I guessed that Deputy Scott Baker, an EMT during his spare moments, was driving the rig. He would eschew the long way around, through Torrance's ranch and then down the trail to the windmill. Instead, he'd come directly in the mile and a half from County Road 14. Once in the canyon itself, and facing the boulder gates, he'd fold in the ambulance's big wing mirrors and go for it, trying his best not to leave another offering of paint on the rocks.

"Deputy, you need to make sure everyone respects the yellow tape," I said. "Things stay untouched until the ME gets here. And I mean *untouched.* If there's a speck of fiber left on a tree limb somehow, or a boot-heel print in the soft dirt between a couple of rocks, that could make or break the case. "

Torrez nodded and backed away.

Dr. Wilkes watched Torrez. "I remember when that deputy was a skinny little twerp."

"That's hard to imagine, Doc." I bent down and pulled the space-blanket up to cover the victim. I remembered Darlene, with her unfailing good humor, cavorting about in the cold, cheering the Posadas Jaguars to once-in-a-while victories. As she did that, Chris Browning had been on the field, doing his best. How did it all end up like this I thought, and then shook that sorry image away. I was glad that Willis Browning was not here to see this.

"You haven't had a moment to contact Francine, I imagine," Wilkes said.

"No. She called me earlier, concerned when Darlene hadn't come home last night. Mom was afraid the girl had been involved in the crash."

Wilkes frowned, pondering that for a long moment. "The other kids were out *here,* you think? They were headed home from *here?*"

"It looks that way."

"Then how did this happen…?" He shook his head. The conundrum was obvious to him, just as it was obvious to me. He'd pronounced the three teens killed in the crash of the

Suburban around ten o'clock the night before. Earlier in the evening, they could have been out here—all four of them. If Darlene had been killed then…if her death had been what caused the panic that maybe set off Orlando's asthma attack…then rigor would have been fully advanced by now. But she had died not many minutes before we found her body—maybe as much as an hour—about the time that Deputy Torrez was wading around in the stock tank. Maybe even while I was standing in the pleasant sunshine, yakking with Herb Torrance.

Typically, my mind tried to jump ahead to conclusions—but none of them made any sense to me. I didn't know what had killed Darlene Spencer. I couldn't comprehend why, if they had been witnesses to the event, the other three kids hadn't brought the injured Darlene back to Posadas. If they'd found her injured and bleeding, hell—stuff her in the big Suburban and get her to the ER. That wasn't complicated. But kids—hell, even otherwise rational adults—did bizarre things under pressure.

Dr. Alan Perrone's autopsy would solve a portion of that mystery for us. Some of the blood on the girl's t-shirt had dried to a brown crust, but not all. Some of it was still the consistency of warm molasses. And that meant that either she had been hurt recently, or had lain out under the stars all night, struggling against her injuries, alone and without comfort. She had made it to a new day, but not by much.

I caught sight of Deputy Baker, spiffy in his EMT duds, as he stopped to talk with Torrez. Behind him, a second EMT, Wendy Ritter, waited with the featherweight gurney. Everyone was going to be in suspended animation until the medical examiner arrived, so I caught Torrez' eye and beckoned him back.

"Stay with her for a few minutes." I nodded toward the waiting EMTs. "They know to wait for Perrone?"

"Yep."

"I'm going to see if the sheriff wants to contact Francine. I want to stay off the radio, so I'll go back up to the ranch and use Herb's phone. In the meantime, I want a photo panorama of this whole area." I made a circular motion. "All the way around, outside your tape. When Perrone gets here, we'll go from there. I should be back by then."

I started to turn away and stopped. "Someone has to drive Dr. Wilkes back to his car out on the highway. I don't care who does that, but I want *you,*" and I pointed at Torrez, "to stay here and make sure the scene is secured. Sergeant Garcia can work the photos, and Perrone gets in the circle as soon as he shows up. But that's it. No other clodhoppers stomping the scene."

Torrez nodded, a pained expression on his face as he tried not to look at the victim. And this time, I didn't even earn a "yep."

Herb Torrance had left the windmill and tank, and I followed his tracks back to the ranch house…a sprawling, older model double-wide tucked into the side of a hill within a quarter-mile of the county road. A blue heeler, belly sagging from the excited mouths of four pups, led the barking, tumbling mass to greet me. By the time both my boots had hit the ground, I'd been licked and peed on. The only one who stayed on her feet was Beulah, the long-suffering bitch. The pups squirmed and danced and ground their new fur into the dust.

Herb still sat in his truck, writing something on a most executive-appearing clipboard. In a moment, he dismounted. "Beulah, get 'em out of here." His tone was entirely conversational, but sure enough, the heeler did exactly as she was told, leading the squirming, yipping mass of puppies toward one of the barns.

"Herb, I need to use your phone."

He nodded at the house. "You know where it is. Just help yourself."

Alice and Herb Torrance were busy raising nearly as many kids as Ariana and Modesto Torrez, but on a calm, clear day like this, all the older ones were either off with chores or visiting neighbors—there was one other family, the Prescotts, within five miles. The two youngest Torrance kids, Desi and Melinda, greeted me at the door, reminding me of the wide-eyed kids captured in those black-and-white Depression-era photos.

Melinda, maybe five years old and a hundred years wise, looked me up and down gravely. "Beulah had puppies," she said. At that announcement, three year-old Desi's head snapped around, and he pointed a crooked finger after the flow of dogs.

"I see that."

"There were six of them, but two came out dead." She pronounced it "day-yed."

"Ah, I'm sorry to hear that." I looked around for Herb, who was headed toward the house.

"What'd Torrez find?" He ushered Melinda away with a gentle hand on the back. "Scoot, now," he said to the two children.

"We've got a real situation," I replied. Alice appeared in the hallway that led back to the labyrinth of bedrooms in the spacious home. "Bill," she greeted. As stout as her husband was skinny, I knew that she kept a close watch on her brood, and that despite those tight reins, her oldest boys, Patrick and Dale, still managed to spike her blood pressure from time to time.

"It's going to get a little busy around here," I said. "I need to use your phone. Our radios aren't worth much down in the canyon."

"You just help yourself. I'll put coffee on."

"No, thanks just the same. I'll only be here a minute."

"Then you can take some with you."

I knew better than to try and sidetrack Alice's determined hospitality. I headed for the phone on the little end table near the sofa. Miracle had returned to dispatch from his overlong, meditative trip to the can, and he answered promptly.

"JJ, I need you to find Sheriff Salcido ASAP," I said.

"Oh, now, he just headed out your way, Sheriff. Just a few minutes ago. He caught the call for the coroner, and figured he'd save some time. You know who the vic is yet?"

The vic? After success eliminating three whole letters from a tough word, maybe JJ Miracle would tackle something really challenging, like "perp."

"I need to meet with him at the Torrance ranch headquarters. Find out his ETA for me."

"Just a sec, sir." He didn't bother to cover the phone, and I could hear the background radio conversation clearly. The sheriff was just crossing Salinas Arroyo, highballing south on State 56. That put him just about halfway to the Broken Spur Saloon, about where County Road 14 intersected the state highway. Even the way the sheriff drove, that put him twenty minutes out. Murton wrapped up his radio call and came back on line.

"I heard," I said. "I'll be able to get him on car-to-car in a few minutes, then."

"Got that. Say, ah, the mom called again. She's hopin' to talk to you when you come in."

"The mom?"

"Oh. Francine Spencer? She was camped out here for half an hour earlier. She had someplace to go, I guess. She ain't here just now, but she's sure enough worried about her daughter. I think she wants the whole darn department out searching for her. Shacked up with a boyfriend, is my guess."

I hesitated, and glanced at Herb. His wife had left the room, and he nodded toward the front porch, tactfully moving out of earshot.

Witless Miracle might not, but Francine knew. If she'd been sitting on one of the old wooden church pews out in the Sheriff's Department lobby, she would have been within earshot of the radio traffic, especially with the blabby Miracle feeling the need to amplify and explain. "If she comes back," I said, "tell her to wait in the sheriff's office...or mine. We're going to need to talk with her."

"Ten four. I'll do that. You're going to need the whole crew again?"

"For what?"

That flustered Miracle. "I mean, the call for the coroner and the ME and all."

"We'll get back to you." I had no intention of telling Miracle that Darlene Spencer's body was cooling down in Bender's Canyon. I started to hang up, then had second thoughts. Much as I hated to inflict Miracle Murton on anyone, this wasn't going to wait until everything was convenient for everybody. "Give Willis Browning a call for me. I'm going to need to talk with him before the day is out. Don't set an appointment, and don't send him out here. Just give him a heads-up that I need to speak with him, and tell him to mind his radio. And then let me know."

"Will do, Sheriff."

"And give Ernie Wheeler a call. Have him come in as early as he can. When he does, make sure he's up to speed on everything that we have going on." Wheeler was sitting swing dispatch, and he was competent enough that he could have stepped right into one of the road patrol slots, were it not for a knee ruined playing soccer. I'd never heard him flustered, or overly dramatic. His radio delivery was smooth and unhurried. There had been times when that unflappable delivery had helped a shaken deputy regain control of his nerves. If I hurt Miracle Murton's feelings by booting him out of the dispatch chair, too damn bad.

I didn't make it to the front porch before Alice Torrance intercepted me with a large chrome beverage container, one of those quart-capacity things that truckers use. "No cream, no sugar, as I recall. I know you won't stand still for a piece of lemon cake, but at least take this."

"Lemon cake?" She started to look hopeful when I said that, but I backpedaled. "No…we've got a mess right now. But thanks for this." I hefted the container. "I'll get this back to you."

"Not to worry about it," she said. "The bank gives 'em away. I think we have a dozen."

"You're a jewel. Thanks."

Out on the front porch, Herb waited, one boot hooked on the railing. He straightened up as I walked past. "We're going to get busy out here, Herb. Are you going to be home most of the day?"

"You betcha. Anything I can do?"

"Not yet. Perrone's on his way out."

An eyebrow escalated a quarter of an inch. Ever discreet, Herb didn't immediately blurt into cascade of questions. He hissed out a plume of smoke and said only, "Got one, huh?"

"Yep. We got one." I looked out across the prairie, the playground for his kids. "And I'll want to talk with Dale and

Patrick sometime today. They might have heard something, seen something, or someone…"

"I'll make sure they're handy," Herb said.

On the way back, I slowed as I passed the windmill. A breeze touched the vanes, and the mill groaned. The expended cartridge casings that Torrez had collected indicated that the kids had been here…with Chris perhaps eager to touch off a few rounds through his father's carbine. A ballistics check to compare empty shell casings to the bolt face, firing pin, and chamber marks was easy enough.

Then the kids had gone into Bender's Canyon. And then what?

Chapter Nine

Francine and Darlene Spencer fit a tight mother-daughter mold. Before this day, at least, both of them had been pretty but not breathtakingly beautiful, both with the same black hair with copper highlights. Both had had striking hazel eyes, flawless skin, and rich, full mouths that could drive men and boys crazy. Both had trim figures with curves in all the right places, although Francine's had softened with a few pounds over the years.

Now Francine sat, knees hugged tight, head down, outside the yellow crime scene ribbon, but facing the spot thirty yards away where her daughter had been found. Standing just behind her, leaning against one of the fractured boulders, Deputy Howard Bishop, bulky with a large, doughy face, looked as if he wanted to be somewhere else.

I nodded at him and approached Francine. She didn't look up. And I felt a twinge of irritation, once again, at JJ "Miracle" Murton, who evidently had blabbed enough during his various radio transmissions that Francine had been able to overhear, and put two and two together...even if JJ hadn't.

"Mrs. Spencer?" I hoped the formality would help her stay tuned, since I certainly knew her well enough to go with "Francine," or even an occasional "Franny," her nickname of choice.

She lifted her head as if she were slowly counting to one hundred, or many a thousand, and didn't want to lose her place. I bent down, one hand on my right knee.

"Bill, Bill, Bill," she murmured, her "Bills" dying away like little echoes in a box canyon. "They won't let me see her. I need to be with her." She looked up at me, eyes black-rimmed from lack of sleep, wet with tears. "I don't even know for sure that it *is* her. I have to know."

"Francine, you're going to have to trust me for a little bit."

"Tell me there's a chance it might be someone else?"

"I wish I could say that."

She shook her head violently as if to fling the tears away. The sigh that escaped was one of those quavery things that told me how close she was to a full blubber. "How can he even *be* here?"

"How can who be here, Francine?"

"The Torrez boy. Bobby. After…after what happened last night." She struggled with the last two words, her voice climbing into a pathetic peep. "How awful this must be for him."

"Yes, it is. But he's working to help us discover what happened, Francine. We all are."

She drew another long, shuddering sigh and spent a little time raking the mussed hair out of her face. "Were they all here? All four of the kids? Is that what you think?"

"It seems probable."

"They did this and *ran?*"

"Francine, first things first. We don't know yet what the *this* is. That's why we're waiting on Dr. Perrone. He was in Deming when he got the call, so it's going to be a few minutes."

"That's what Bobby said." Her voice took on a little edge. "He wouldn't let me through that damn tape. Bill, I *need* to see my daughter."

"Of course you do."

"He won't tell me what happened."

"That's because Deputy Torrez doesn't know, Francine. He's been ordered to protect the crime scene, and that's what he'll do. Whatever it takes."

"Crime scene," she murmured. For a long moment, Francine Spencer sat silently, staring across the little clearing, across the trail. She was ninety feet away from her daughter, and it might as well have been ninety miles.

"Was she molested?" Francine's voice was small and hesitant.

"We don't know, Francine."

"Is there any reason to think so?" Agonizing experience tells the same tale as the criminology textbooks: find a dead young woman in a lonely spot out in the boonies with her pants and underwear pulled down, and there's every reason to think ugly things. At this early stage, I already had a couple of reasons to question the textbooks, but that wasn't something to discuss with the distraught mother of the victim.

"We'll know more after Dr. Perrone finishes."

She snuffled. "In other words, yes."

"I'll say it again, Francine, we don't know. I wish we did. We don't. Give us some time and I'll have some answers for you. For now, no one disturbs the site. Because there are so many questions, the next step is the state medical examiner. All right? And when Dr. Perrone gets here, you're going to stay outside the tape with everyone else while he works."

She closed her eyes, resting her forehead in her hand as if she had a monumental migraine building…as indeed she might. "Was she out here all night?"

"I don't know, Francine." Her tortured face said that I might as well have just said "yes" and got it over with.

I stood up straight, smoothing out the kinks. Deputy Bishop watched impassively, ready to chaperone Francine, should I decide our conversation was over.

"You have two daughters," Francine said.

"Yes, I do." And I didn't add that during their adolescent years, they had both given me plenty of cause to worry. As had my two sons. Grown and gone now, three of the four had families of their own to fret about…the fretting was one of the costs of parenthood, I suppose. I wasn't much of a grandparent, since I didn't spend my time commuting around the country visiting the urchins. I didn't remember all their birthdays, but I had the names and dates written down somewhere. Sometimes I remembered Christmas. Sometimes.

"I don't know how I'm going to tell Casey." I knew Casey Spencer, a delightful gal four years older than Darlene. I knew Casey had earned an associate's degree in criminal justice from one of the community colleges up in Albuquerque, and had landed herself a job with one of the counties up in the northeastern part of the state.

"I'm no help there," I said, "but sooner rather than later is better. Same with Sam. When Dr. Perrone is finished, I'm going to ask you to make a positive ID for us. You can notify the rest of the family any time after that."

That earned a grimace. "You make it sound so easy." She and Sam Spencer had been divorced for a decade. Sam had found true happiness driving a transcontinental Greyhound bus, and I hadn't seen him in years.

I heard vehicular traffic, then the powerful, deep bleat of an air horn. Someone didn't like the way traffic was stacking up in the canyon. It would get worse. In a moment, I saw Alan Perrone's trim figure making his way up the hill out of the canyon, escorted by a trio of cops—rookie Game and Fish Officer Doug Posey, Deputy Tom Mears, and Sergeant Lars Payson.

"Excuse me for a few minutes, Francine," I said, and beckoned to Deputy Bishop, who had already read the situation and was moving toward her. I whistled sharply, and when Torrez looked my way, I held up a single finger and pointed at Perrone.

Cops don't like being told by other cops that they can't enter a crime scene, but I wasn't concerned about hurt feelings or turf stomping. Until we had some fundamental answers from the medical examiner, I didn't want a single superfluous bootprint in that little glade, and my deputies all knew that.

I met Dr. Alan Perrone at the tape. He shook hands, his grip gentle but firm, and did the same with Robert Torrez. "I'm sorry about last night," he said to the young deputy. "That's got to be horrible." He glanced across at Francine Spencer and lowered his voice to a hoarse whisper. "Dr. Wilkes gave me a heads-up. Is that the mother?"

"Yes. Francine Spencer. She overheard our dispatcher and took it upon herself to come out."

"Can't say as I blame her."

I reached out and held Sergeant Payson by the elbow as he started to duck under the tape. "I need you here to make sure no one steps into the crime scene, Sergeant. If you want to organize an area sweep, go ahead. Give all these clowns something to do. But nobody else comes inside the tape."

"What do you want the kid to do?" Payson nodded toward Torrez, who had stationed himself about a dozen feet away from the corpse, hands clasped behind his back in a pretty good version of "parade rest." The usual rookie task would be to sign everyone in, making a complete record of who had visited the crime scene, and when. But I was curious. I had wanted an early opportunity to watch Robert Torrez at work, and this was clearly it.

"Dr. Perrone, Torrez, and myself will be the only ones inside the perimeter—at least until Dr. Perrone is finished." Payton nodded as if he understood.

I turned back to Perrone, who stood idly fingering the yellow plastic tape as if waiting for someone to say, "On your mark, get set, go!"

"Alan, we're going to have to be very careful with this one."

Perrone didn't ask what was bothering me, but just nodded assent. Torrez had approached, silent and watchful.

"Robert, lead the way. Take the same route you took when you found her."

I followed them, taking care to place my feet exactly where Perrone's spiffy Wellingtons touched down.

The deputy started to lift the space-blanket, but I held up a hand. "Give me a moment," I said, and retraced my steps back to Sergeant Payson, who sure enough had found himself a clipboard to start the check-in process. I reached across, borrowed his pencil, and added my name.

"Lars, have Bishop escort Mrs. Spencer back down the hill to her car. This is going to get ugly, and she just doesn't need to see any of it. She'll do a formal ID after a bit, but not now… not while Perrone is working."

"Wondered about that," Payson replied.

It took Francine Spencer a few moments to decide whether she was going to accept Deputy Bishop's escort, but finally she yielded, allowing his big hand to guide her.

When they were out of sight, Torrez lifted the space-blanket and gently folded it down below the victim's feet.

Perrone gazed down at the victim for a long moment, eyes roaming over the body. "Sergeant Garcia took plenty of photos, I imagine," he said at last.

"And Deputy Torrez, as well." I realized that Garcia wasn't in the area. "Where is Garcia, by the way?"

Payson heard me and shook his head in disgust. "I think he's down in the canyon. Mears and a couple of the others are tossing that area."

"Ask him to come up," I said to Torrez.

Perrone frowned as he took his time snapping on the blue gloves. "Okay, then. Bill, is there any *other* reason to believe that she might have been assaulted?"

I kept my voice so low that the physician had to look directly at me. "Nothing beyond the obvious. What we see at first glance."

"Huh," Perrone grunted. He hitched up his slacks at the knee and knelt close to Darlene's head. With a single finger he lifted the thatch of hair out of her face. Bending so low that his forehead was nearly on the ground, he first examined the injury that had produced so much blood. Darlene's body was half-sitting, half-supine, as if she'd been sitting but then collapsed back against the rocks. The blood flow had cascaded down the girl's left cheek, down her neck, and then split, some dripping off onto the ground, some soaking the white t-shirt down as far as her left breast before running off under her left armpit.

"Massive hemorrhage," Perrone mused. "Did you fellows check the back?"

"She hasn't been touched."

"Let's do that and get a core temp at the same time."

There are no secrets kept from a medical examiner, but nothing about dealing with a corpse is pretty. Francine might have been angry with us for escorting her from the scene, but she didn't need to watch any of Perrone's matter-of-fact machinations. Robert Torrez stoically provided support of the corpse while the young physician worked, and the deputy never looked away. I saw him chew on the inside of his lip once in a while, especially when Perrone did his swab work before putting the long-stemmed rectal thermometer in place.

"Right at thirty-four degrees Centigrade." He didn't look up, didn't make the calculation for us, but my middle school memories of rule-of-thumb conversion said that ninety degrees Fahrenheit was close enough—and far warmer than it had been, even in June, when the sun sank low.

Perrone shook his head. "All kinds of things tell us that she didn't die right away. Give us just a few more degrees on that body temp, and some resuscitation attempts might have been called for." He made a face. "But probably not. Not with the sort of brain hemorrhage we have going on here."

He brushed up the t-shirt carefully. "No significant scrapes on the back, no other injuries, so if she fell, or collapsed, she didn't go down hard. No cacti stuck through the t-shirt, no juniper needles, no piñon pitch. And the t-shirt was not all scrunched up..." His eyes roamed down the body. "There's no sign that she was defending herself from some kind of assault. Quite a bit of foot activity—push, pull, kick out..." Leaving Torrez the job of supporting the body on its right side, Perrone examined the back of the skull methodically, running his gloved fingers through the hair.

"No exit. So." He nodded at Torrez. "Let her back." Once more, he leaned close. "This wound is really interesting." He touched a probe just below the ridge of bone forming the left orbit, but without touching the eyeball itself. "A bullet would just punch through—maybe through, and then through the skull, maybe not. But here we have something that looks as if it were inflicted with a sharp object of some kind. It's almost a slit, really. Some bruising around the wound, and the amount of blood leads me to believe that a deep artery was lacerated. Again, I'm just guessing right now, but I'd go with general incapacitation from the head wound, then exsanguination. But it took a while." He touched the victim's neck, looking carefully down to the t-shirt collar. "No compression bruising, no bite marks."

"She struggled through the night?" I asked.

The young physician took his time answering. "Struggled? I'm not sure. Unconscious, maybe. And the marks around her feet would indicate some small amount of struggle, maybe." He sat back on his haunches. "I would guess so, but you know, there's nothing that really tells us when she was injured. Just the time line of coincidence." He looked sharply at me. "If the kids were out here, we have some reason to believe that this girl was in their company, but she *wasn't* in the truck when it crashed in Posadas shortly after nine…" He shrugged deeply. "I've read all the paperwork on that, and your officers did a thorough job. See, there's *lots* of coincidence to think about, lots of possibilities." He pushed himself to his feet and stripped off the gloves. "If the kids in the Suburban were running scared…not just racing for the adolescent hell of it…this," and he nodded at Darlene Spencer's corpse, "…this is plenty of reason for them to be frightened out of their wits. But right now, the operative word is guess. *Guess.* Just like I'm *guessing* that the dried fluid on her right thigh is urine."

"Rape?"

"We'll see. If I were a betting man, I'd say not, and be thankful for that. There are just no signs of force, Bill. A young, healthy, athletic girl like Darlene could have put up a hell of a fight. We'd expect to see signs of that. Unless the assault occurred after an incapacitating injury."

Perrone looked pointedly over at Torrez. "Who's the hunter here?" The only reaction that prompted from the deputy was a raised eyebrow. "You'd do well to *really* scour this immediate area, Deputy. The old fine-toothed comb bit." He frowned. "Luminol first, with really thorough photo documentation of what you find."

"That's why I want Garcia to hear this," I said. I liked Avelino Garcia, and knew that he was a master photographer—a real problem-solver with a camera. One unfortunate character trait at times lit my fuse, though. There were moments when Garcia seemed to believe that our job was to be satisfied with whatever photos he chose to take. He'd wander around a crime scene, following his own agenda.

"I don't see any sign that this girl moved far after being injured. On the contrary, it appears to me that maybe she dropped like a sack of rocks. So this immediate area?" Perrone turned at the waist without shifting his feet, drawing an encompassing circle in the air. "Anything at all that might tell us what she was doing, which way was she facing, anything that might indicate where the second person was at the time of injury. I mean, she didn't stab herself, although stranger things have happened. A scuff on the ground from a boot heel. Out-of-place rocks or pebbles. Broken sticks." He held up both hands in frustration. "I'm no tracker, but I *do* know that we leave signs of our passing, even when we think that we don't." He looked hard at Torrez, and then at me. "Clear?"

"Yes, sir," Torrez whispered.

"Good." Perrone heaved a sigh. "Let's get her covered up and transported. Let Mrs. Spencer do the formal ID at the ambulance. And I'll let you know what I find out the minute I can."

The two heavy Nikons hanging from his neck, Avelino Garcia made his way up from the canyon, and we met him at the tape. It wasn't much of a climb, but he was breathing hard, sweat bagging the armpits of his Army surplus shirt.

"Sarge, before they move the body, we're going to need one series of photos showing north-south-east-west, including this whole area. Maybe you've already done that, but if not…then when we come back tonight for the Luminol, we'll have something to compare."

He pulled out a small notebook and thumbed the pages. "I still need east-west, then," he said.

Deputy Torrez had moved a few yards to the north, bent down, and stuck a pencil point-first in the ground. "Include this area?" he said, but he made it sound more of a suggestion than a command. The spot he'd chosen was near the end of a massive alligator-bark juniper stump, its roots and horizontal trunk like old polished steel. At one time, for centuries, perhaps, the old juniper had twisted its way into the rocks to gain footing, near the crest of the rise. Traces of black char still touched the inside folds and crevices of the trunk where a fire a century ago had swept the area. Then one of New Mexico's famous winds probably had shrieked through, laying the old giant flat.

I took my time as I made my way over to where Torrez stood.

"I can see the windmill from here," he said.

"We're not all that far, as the crow flies."

"Nope."

"So what's this?" I pointed with the toe of my boot at the pencil, but even as I said that, I saw what the deputy had marked. The bulk of the liquid had long since sunken into the ground between pebbles, rocks, and thousand-year-old lichen dried to a crisp, but there was enough shade to protect traces that even I could see…not much more than little clean spots on the rocks.

"Bag some of it," I said. "Even just a few crystals on a slide might tell a story. The Luminol will show us the outline of the original deposit." Garcia had been watching us impassively, and he nodded agreement, then snapped photos that featured the pencil marker, the stump, and even Bob Torrez' boots.

"What time tonight?" Garcia asked.

"Let's shoot for nine o'clock," I replied, and then to Torrez, "I'll find someone to relieve you early on."

"I'm okay."

"I know you are. But some sleep sometimes makes the brain work a little clearer." I looked at my watch. Torrez' evening ride-along with Payson had turned sour, and if the young deputy had managed any sleep at all, it had been just a few minutes.

"I'll have someone assigned by four this afternoon. They'll relieve you, and then you can plan to be back here by eight-thirty."

I didn't give him the chance to debate, but added, "Keep your radio on. A good share of the time, somebody who commits a crime will return to the site. In a remote spot like this, they might have gotten curious about what we've found. Gotta come see, you know?"

I walked out of the taped area that now included the tagged carbine, picked up the paper-wrapped gun and held it up to attract Torrez' attention. "I'm going to put this in your unit," I said. He nodded, and I trudged down into the canyon. Deputy Tom Mears had had the common sense to tape off even more area, keeping the parking lot removed down-canyon from the site. I glanced downstream and saw that the EMTs had managed to find a spot wide enough to turn their rig around, and it now awaited with its rear doors open, backed up right against the tape. Sheriff Salcido's Buick had added to the mix, and he had trudged up to join Mears and Game and Fish Officer Doug Posey. Their trucks boxed in Francine's black Honda.

Torrez' K-5 Blazer was open, and I placed the bagged carbine on the floor behind the front seats. The keys were not in the ignition—hopefully they were in his pocket. I locked the truck and joined Mears.

Beyond the yellow tape, they had thrust a dozen or more evidence markers into the sand and gravel of the arroyo bottom. Mears was crouched under one of the sculpted overhangs, the sandstone marked with streaks from rare water flows down the face.

"They were thinking of having a fire." He nodded at the collection of kindling, dropped beside a neat circle of basketball-sized stones. I nodded, watching where I put my feet. A box that had once held half a dozen Little Debbie snack cakes was crumpled up in the firepit, ready for the kindling. Near the rock sidewall, a paper bag was crumpled shut over the unmistakable shape of a six-pack, and a naked, empty tequila bottle lay in the sand.

"So…ready for a fire, but on a warm summer evening. But they didn't. And they left early. If we're to judge by what happened later, they left in a hurry. Because of Darlene, or something else? That's our problem." Mears looked up at me thoughtfully. "Did the kids come here to party, then heard shooting up at the windmill, and trotted on up there to see who it was?"

I caught the eye of Darby Ashford, one of the EMTs. "We're ready for you," I called. She was busy tending to Francine Spencer, who sat on the ground, her back against the left front wheel of her Honda.

I heard his breathing and turned to find that Sheriff Eduardo Salcido had been standing behind me, silently listening.

"What do you think?" His voice was little more than a whisper, his back to Francine. "I heard what you said, but…"

"Number one, I think that the kids *were* out here, Eduardo. That's the first step. The first grand assumption. Other than say-so, we have nothing that connects Darlene Spencer with the others. No witnesses have come forward to say that all four were seen together. But it makes sense that they were all here. Number two, Torrez collected spent thirty-caliber carbine shell casings from up by Herb Torrance's water tank, and it won't be hard for ballistics to show whether or not there's a match with Willis Browning's carbine. Number three, the deputy is certain that the carbine we found up there on the trail *is* Browning's. He recognized it."

I shrugged. "Personally, I think that Darlene was with the other three kids out here, ready to partake in a little party time." I intertwined the fingers of both hands. "I *don't* know what happened after that. It appears that Darlene has a single, significant penetrating injury," and I touched my left eye. "Although we don't know the extent, or what caused it. Is that what spooked the kids, made them run? We don't know, but it's a logical assumption."

Salcido gazed at me for a long moment. "If they were here and needed help, why didn't they just go up to the Torrance ranch? It's not far. They knew the Torrance kids…maybe they were all partying together, you know."

"I don't think so. I know Patrick and Dale pretty well, Eduardo. If someone had been hurt, they would have run for help. Likely they would have told their parents. No way they would have just left her here."

The gurney and the EMTs had gone up the slope, and now were making their way back down on the unsure footing. Francine rose, her hands clasped together and pressing into her mouth.

Salcido shook his head wearily as he watched Francine. "I need to be with her now." His brow furrowed. "But someone else was here, you think? Someone besides the four kids? And maybe besides the Torrance kids?"

"Almost certainly," I said. "Somebody used Herb's stock tank as a shooting gallery, and that wasn't the kids…certainly none of Herb's brood. They helped put that tank in, and they routinely climb that windmill to maintain it. No way they'd vandalize their own equipment. The damage looks as if at least four different guns were used. The kids had only Willis Browning's old military carbine."

I stopped and heaved a couple deep breaths. "But I'm willing to speculate some, Eduardo. The damage to the tank was fresh. When I checked it mid-morning today, the water hadn't all drained. The windmill wasn't pumping, but there were wet spots where the bullet holes leaked."

"What have you told momma?" He nodded at Francine Spencer.

"Nothing. She saw only her daughter's covered body. She'll make the formal ID now."

He nodded. "Okay." He cleared his throat. "By the way, they took Browning to the hospital a little earlier. His heart, they think."

That shouldn't have come as a surprise, but it still took me a moment to absorb it. "He looked bad last night," I said. "Most of us looked bad."

"Bad all the way around," Salcido agreed. "I'll talk with Francine for a little bit, see what she can tell me about her daughter's activities last night." He ducked his head as if apologizing. "Then

I'll go to the hospital and see if Browning is going to be able to tell us anything." The crow's-feet around his dark eyes crinkled, the creases running deep. "You look like you need to curl up under a tree for a while yourself."

"I probably will."

He started to step away, then hesitated. "How's *mihijo* doing?" I had stopped thinking of Robert Torrez as a kid, but Eduardo had me by a dozen years. To the sheriff, no doubt, anyone under thirty was damn near an infant.

"I couldn't ask for more. He's going to take a break for a few hours, and we're meeting again here after dark to take some exposures with Luminol. We'll see."

Salcido grimaced at that. I don't know what bothered him— probably the fact that Luminol illuminated ugly things. "I'll try to be here," he said.

The EMTs paused with the gurney long enough for Francine to gasp and stagger backward when Sheriff Salcido eased the body blanket back. The victim's head was turned to the left slightly, almost hiding the wound. Some folks like to use the soothing word "peaceful" to describe the dead, but that's something from the undertaker's sales pitch to make customers feel better. Darlene didn't look peaceful to me. Francine would go through her own brand of hell for several days, and then Darlene would be a painful memory.

One by one, the various vehicles cleared the canyon, and with Robert Torrez tending the site up the hill, I was left to myself. I made arrangements for Deputy Paul Encinos to cover the site starting at four, but Torrez was still rooting around, taking notes and burning more film. He had no questions for me, and it seemed prudent—and instructive for me—to leave the young man alone with his thoughts.

I moseyed up-canyon, hands thrust deep in my pockets. Not far to the northeast, a deep swale in the prairie erased most of the canyon, and with a short detour up-grade, I found myself on a dome of prairie overlooking the windmill site and the hillside dotted with runty acacia, rabbitbrush, creosote, and an occasional tough juniper. I loved the prairie, with its tawny canvas, its potpourri of wonderful aromas, the murmur of grama seed heads nodding in the lightest breezes. To Darlene, desperately hurt and abandoned, the peace and solitude of this country must have been terrifying.

The sheriff's suggestion about finding forty winks under a welcoming tree was a good one, but not many likely candidates grew on this section of moisture-starved prairie. The ravens followed me, engaged in a constant guttural chatter of raven talk, sometimes sending one of their flock for a low pass over my head.

I found a convenient rock and sat, facing west. The kids' voices would have carried to this spot last night, sharp and clear, punctuated by bursts of shrill, alcohol-filled laughter. It appeared from preliminary lab tests that at least one of the youngsters—little Elli Torrez—had not touched any of the beer or spirits. Maybe she was already worried about her brother, who had touched far too many.

And Darlene Spencer? Clearly, she had ridden out to Bender's Canyon in the Suburban with the other three. I couldn't see any other way it might have happened. The autopsy would reveal how much she had imbibed, if any. Regardless, it would have been a raucous bunch, enough to give the ravens something to be cranky about.

Who had heard them? The ravens drifted overhead, this time five of them, now and then uttering those almost musical little gargles. They knew, but they weren't telling.

Chapter Ten

Down below to my right, just a few yards from the windmill, my county car sat in the sun, the insides no doubt a furnace. Movement caught my eye, and in a moment Deputy Torrez appeared through the brush several yards west of the rugged trail we had used previously. This time, he was pushing the little walking wheel, the measuring gadget we routinely used at motor vehicle accidents. He walked easily, in no hurry, planning his route so that the measurement would be as accurate as possible.

"Well, that's not going home and getting some rest," I said to myself. Once more at the water tank, he leaned the measuring wheel against the warm metal, and then turned to the windmill. For a time, he just stood there, looking up at the Aermotor. He could certainly see me easily enough, but he never turned or acknowledged my presence. Once, he backed up several paces, changing the perspective. The sails were facing southwest, where our breezes most commonly originated. Not a hint of wind stirred them to motion.

Apparently satisfied, Torrez walked to the array of braces at the windmill's base, and in a moment, he shrugged out of his Sam Brown belt and all its hardware. He draped the wide, heavy utility belt over one of the horizontal braces, drew the revolver from its holster and tucked it behind his back, secured by his trouser belt. He walked around to the narrow metal ladder that accessed the maintenance platform thirty feet over his head.

By that time, I was on my feet and walking down-slope toward the mill. If Torrez saw or heard me, he didn't react. Instead, he climbed methodically, testing each skinny metal rung before putting his weight on it. I was delighted that Robert Torrez hadn't bother to ask permission for whatever it was that he was doing. He didn't show much inclination to "play well with others," but what the hell. I had plenty of deputies who were social gadflies—who'd travel in packs if they could.

By the time I reached the water tank, the deputy was standing on the maintenance platform high overhead, sidling in close behind the sails, his right hand on top of the transmission housing as if he were standing beside a good friend, one hand on the shoulder.

"Good view from up there," I greeted.

"Better up where you were sittin'," he replied. "I need a panorama from up there." His compact Olympus camera was tiny in his big hands, the strap tight around his wrist. In the next couple minutes, he took both his panorama scenery shots as well as several photos of the two windmill sails nearest him.

"Just punched right on through," I said, then realized that wasn't a rocket science observation, since the individual windmill sails that made up the mill's wind-catching disk were thin metal not much more resistant than one side of a tin can. Torrez didn't reply, but eased forward and reached out to the inner steel band, one of two that connected the sails and kept them oriented. He paused.

"Herb has the brake set," he said.

"You want it off?"

"Yep."

"Watch your footing, now. We can't afford a workman's comp claim." I stepped to the tower and pulled the iron brake lever down. In the forty years since I'd pulled the brake handle on my grand-uncle's windmill at his farm in North Carolina, the Aermotor mechanics hadn't changed much. In a moment the windmill sail drifted around one blade's worth, uttered a little groan, and rested in place. With no breeze to assist, Torrez took his time, working the sails by hand around a full revolution. He stopped now and then for photos, and seemed fascinated by one particular area of damage. He held on to the transmission housing with one hand, one boot blocked against framework that enclosed the sucker rod down through the center of the tower, and leaned out farther than I would have liked. The little camera clicked and clicked again.

"We can call the cherry picker out here if you need a photo from the front of the sail," I said.

"Might need to," and he shot a final exposure with his arm outstretched, the view angling in from the side. With an impatient shake of the head, he turned away and faced the northeast, gazing out over the windmill's tail vane. Looking back toward the sail, he pushed the whole assembly around to give himself room, then folded his six-foot, four-inch frame as only the young and fit can. He sat down on the edge of the platform, legs dangling. He fished another roll of film out of his pocket, rewound and emptied the one from the camera, and replaced it.

"There isn't enough damage to prevent Herb's using it, I wouldn't think."

"Don't think so." He looked back over his shoulder at the sails. "Peppered it pretty good, though. Like sixteen times."

"Straight-on shots? Through the front of the sail?"

"Mostly."

"So the shooter was standing facing the sail, probably." It wasn't a question, and I didn't expect a reply. Young Torrez didn't disappoint. "But you found the empty casings over there," and I waved a hand back along the two-track leading into the site. "The breezes are fitful. Last evening the sails could have been facing any old way." Again, Torrez didn't respond to the obvious.

"We don't know for sure that Chris Browning was doing the shooting at the sail," I said. "I'm not sure you can gauge much by holes punched in tin."

Torrez sat silently for a moment, taking his time organizing an answer. Watching him mull things over, I had the errant thought that in coming months and years, lawyers were going to learn quickly that Robert Torrez on the witness stand would force patience on *them*, rather than the young deputy being rattled by the pressure.

"I'm goin' by that there ain't .30-carbine bullets recovered from the tank, so I don't think he was shootin' that way. I mean, we found less than a box of empties, so he wasn't shootin' much."

"So you think he let fly a few times at the windmill? How many cases do you have?"

"Sixteen."

"So you have sixteen holes in that mill. Then someone else tore after the tank."

"Yup."

"Three ten, three hundred." My handheld, and Torrez' hanging from his belt at the bottom of the mill, squawked in unison.

"Three hundred, three ten." The radio remained silent for a heartbeat or two, and then the sheriff's soft voice, made metallic by the electronics of the radio and broken by the distance and terrain, reached out to us.

"Willis Browning passed away early this afternoon."

"Shit," I muttered, then keyed the radio. "Ten four."

"Perrone's really going after it. He'll have some results on the girl by late this afternoon."

"Ten four."

"Everything okay out there?"

"Affirmative. We're going to need the county's cherry picker for a bit. If they could get that out to us this afternoon, it'd help. Have them come right to Herb's windmill."

"You're sure you'll need that?"

"I'm sure."

"Then I'll call over there right now."

"Give 'em an hour to get here," I called up to Torrez. I watched him climb down, as graceful as a big man can be on such a thin structure, unhurried and mindful of what metal he grasped.

With both feet on the ground, he gazed upward, and by the set of his jaw I knew he was thinking, thinking, thinking. To himself, which was fine with me.

After a moment, he shook his head and took a deep breath. "I need to measure from here," and he touched the southwestern leg of the tower, "over to where we found the body."

"Let me go stand on the stump," I said. "That'll give you something to shoot for. Maybe keep the line a little straighter." I paused. "You heard the sheriff?"

"Yes, sir."

The sudden formality of his answer startled me. "Willis worked well with us," I said. "We're going to miss him." Torrez nodded. It took me almost ten minutes to amble out of the windmill's glade, through the brush, and down the slope. I approached the old juniper carefully from the north, avoiding any of the tiny evidence flags that Torrez had planted around Darlene Spencer's final resting place.

Climbing up on the huge old snag, disturbing nothing but a little bit of lichen, I looked back and could just see Torrez' head. I waved, and he set off toward me.

"Two hundred and thirty-one feet," he announced when he reached me.

"From the base," I said. "Not much more than that from the top of the tower. Another foot or two." I waited while he made a notation in his pocket pad, and when he finished, I said, "So…" He didn't respond, but his thoughtful gaze had dropped to the victim outline, a light sifting of chalk dust.

"I'd like to know what you're thinking," I added.

He chewed on that for a while, then said, "I'm thinkin' that a little more than two hundred ain't too far for a ricochet." With his index finger, he traced an imaginary trajectory in the air… up from the shooter to the windmill sails, then angling down to where we stood.

Clever conjecture, and a bullet fragment would be consistent with the wound above Darlene's left eyeball—irregular, not quite knife-blade like, not the bruised hole we'd expect from an impacting bullet, and certainly not the explosive impact I'd expect from a high-powered rifle. I wanted the deputy to always think in terms of existing evidence, rather than grasping at straws, so I said, "It won't be long before Perrone has some news for us. If It's a bullet fragment, he'll find it, and then the fun begins."

"Yep."

The conjecture raised all sorts of questions. I could easily imagine a bullet glancing off the metal structure of the windmill, to go whining away. How Darlene Spencer happened to be in its path, more than two hundred feet away from the original target, might be as simply explained as her having to find a spot to take a piss. I liked that version since it explained the dropped drawers and the protection of the old juniper. I didn't much care for the possible alternatives—that someone had followed her to this private little spot, assaulted her, stabbing her with some sharp object like a tent stake or juniper spear...

"One thing I'm having a hard time wrapping my brain around," I said when Torrez finished with another round of his notebook jottings. "Chris Browning was sixteen or so. Darlene Spencer was going on eighteen. Your brother was what, seventeen?" He nodded. "And Elli was just fifteen."

"Yep." That came as little more than a whisper.

"Darlene had already graduated from high school. Chris was an early grad, a year ahead of his classmates, headed for college in the fall. Orlando was a junior, maybe?" The deputy nodded. "And Elli..."

"Just finished ninth grade," Torrez said.

"So what's the link? It seems unusual to me that Chris Browning would hang out with Orlando."

"Neighbors, sort of."

That flood of information didn't offer anything new. The Torrez clan owned three or four lots over on MacArthur, and the ill-fated Brownings owned both a ranch-style four-bedroom monstrosity on Belmont, a subdivision street across an arroyo from MacArthur, as well as an elm-shaded town house in Deming—a place Willis had purchased when it seemed likely that his wife would need extended medical care. She hadn't lasted long enough to make Deming home…and now, neither had he…or his son.

"They hung out together a lot? Chris and your brother?"

That earned a slow nod. "Wasn't much that little shit wouldn't do," he whispered. That, I knew. Sheriff Salcido had referred to Orlando Torrez more than once as a real *pistolo,* a perpetual motion teenager who could be counted on to make all the wrong decisions. Careening his motorbike around the county, there wasn't a stop sign he hadn't run, a speed limit he hadn't broken. I wondered if Orlando's older brother, now a member of the Sheriff's Department, had given any consideration to how he would deal with his wild-hare sibling.

On the other hand, Chris Browning was an athlete who had to work at being a star. I had the impression that between the two boys, there might have been a little hero worship going on. Little Orlando had the natural grace of a Pelé and his comic tendencies reminded me of Continflas, the Mexican actor. I could understand that Chris, even though a year older and cut from far different academic cloth, might have savored the little twerp's company. Even come close to idolizing him. Apparently so.

Less than an hour later, a cherry picker with county shields on the doors rumbled down the two-track from the Torrance ranch.

"Didn't know for sure if I had the right place or not," Skip Moreno said as he clambered down from the truck. A stumpy guy, he looked as if he'd just slid out from under some piece of county equipment in for repairs. I could smell the odd mix of oil, grease, and cigarette smoke from ten feet away.

"You do." I explained what we wanted, and in moments, with stabilizers planted and Robert shackled to the safety harness, the bucket rose quickly. The deputy oriented himself with the sun behind the camera, and after he hand-turned the sail to put the selected bullet damage within his reach, I set the windmill's brake.

Torrez photographed another half dozen bullet holes, but if there was a pattern there, I didn't see it. He finished and stood quietly in the bucket, surveying the terrain.

Doing his best to fill dead air, Skip Moreno turned a full circle to take his own reconnaissance of the country, and shook his head. "You had about everybody out here today, huh?"

"A fair crowd." I wondered what version Moreno had heard. The county maintenance offices had a scanner, of course. Maybe we had entertained a good audience. Maybe, if we were lucky, the listeners were content to think that we sure squandered a lot of resources on a shot-up windmill.

Finally satisfied with the scenery, Torrez looked down from his perch.

"Need a photo taken from here to there." He motioned back toward the juniper site. He turned the sail until the sample of damage he'd selected at first was about at the three o'clock position. "If you can set the brake right there…" I did, and he maneuvered the bucket outward, and then to the east, taking him around the sail. "That'll work," he said finally. After a change of film, he shot through another roll.

"Are you going to need Garcia to shoot this again?"

"Don't think so," Torrez said. "But it'd be good if Herb knows he don't touch this sail 'til we're done with it." Torrez lowered the bucket, letting it nestle smoothly on the truck's back.

"Comes in handy, don't it?" Skip's grin revealed maybe a dozen teeth, scattered top and bottom. "Old Bobby here worked for us one summer a couple years back. Nothin's wasted, is the way I see it."

"Yep." Torrez shed the safety belt and clambered down from the truck.

"You know, a few holes in them blades ain't going to make much difference," Skip observed, and I nodded agreement. He wanted more information, but I ignored the hints, and he didn't press. "I don't know why Herb would even bother with it."

"He probably won't," I said.

"Yeah, well, if that's all you need, I'm going to be gettin' back to town," Moreno said.

"Appreciate it," I said, and he earned a nod from Torrez as well.

The truck rumbled off, leaving plenty of dust in its wake. My watch said 4:02. Down below, I heard a vehicle, no doubt the relief deputy arriving. "I'll go talk to 'em," Torrez said.

"And I'll be back after I check on a few things," I said. "Find yourself some rest between now and eight-thirty. Go home and be with your family, Robert." Without indicating whether he thought my advice worthy or not, he trudged off toward the canyon, camera in one hand, walking wheel in the other.

Chapter Eleven

I heard Deputy Encinos call his location to dispatch, and I heard Torrez' Blazer leave the canyon. Reasonably confident that the crime scene would be in good hands, I bumped the Crown Vic back out the two-track, staying to the left when I reached the intersection with Herb Torrance's driveway.

He and his wife were sitting on the front porch as if their to-do list was blank. I gave them a salute with the roof lights, but didn't stop. I wasn't ready to give up more time to their enduring hospitality. If I sat on that porch just now, the eyelids would grow heavy, and after pie and coffee, away I'd go into dreamland.

A lingering question remained about the Torrance kids— there were a handful of them and Patrick, the oldest, would be fair game for some teenaged high jinks. The next in line, eleven-year-old Dale…I wondered about him. He was a BB-gun or maybe .22 risk, and I was sure there wasn't an unexplored inch of the Torrance ranch, or a critter living there that didn't hold him in mortal fear. But I couldn't see Dale poking holes in the ranch hardware. Chances were one hundred percent that Herb had already talked to the boys, and with his steely glare, the kids would spill any beans they might have tried to hide. But Herb didn't know about Darlene Spencer. At least, not yet.

I drove south on County Road 14 so slowly that my car scarcely kicked dust. Shortly, Bender's Canyon Trail angled in from the east, crossed the county road, and disappeared among the jumble of boulders that marked one end of San Patricio Mesa. I turned off the county road, passing by the sign that announced, "*CR14-b. This Road Unsuitable for Passenger Vehicles.*" Sure enough, it was unsuitable, and the old patrol car scraped bottom more than once. I jounced over two cattle guards before I reached a gate in the barbed-wire range fence.

Reuben Fuentes' homestead was a wonderful time machine. I don't think he ever sold anything, or made a run to the landfill. From a now-discarded garden colander that he'd fashioned in 1946 from a rusted wash basin to a 1919 Ford reduced by the years to nothing more than a firewall and front fenders, the yard around his home was what an archaeologist might optimistically call a "scatter."

Rueben and his wife, Rosa, had moved to this homestead in 1945, when he was looking for a safe haven from some troubles he'd had south of the border. He bought more than a hundred acres and the old stone cabin for twelve hundred dollars, without knowing that the land bordered a vast treasure of caves and lava tubes owned by the Bureau of Land Management. In 1945, the intriguing formations were just holes in the ground, before Carlsbad educated tourists became interested in such things. I can imagine that Rosa had been more than a little skeptical when Reuben toured her around the acreage that included the tiny two-room stone structure that he envisioned as their paradise.

Since then, Reuben had done his best to stay out of trouble, working various small construction jobs on both sides of the border. Rosa had always imagined her dotage to be spent home in Mexico with her extended family, but that wasn't in the cards. As lost in the boonies as this little rancho might be, a flu bug somehow managed to find her, and that was that. Reuben never remarried.

I reached one of the arroyos that crossed the fading county two-track and stopped. For sure, the crossing was unfit for the aging Crown Vic. Lots of tracks crossed, sure enough, sticking to the rocky places, but Reuben's little truck was much higher slung than the county barge. I dug out the binoculars from the center console and scanned the field in front of Reuben's little house. His four dogs had heard me, and now stood as tail wagging sentries just below the house. The little pickup was gone, and the dogs were clearly waiting.

For a moment, I sat quietly, engine switched off and all four windows lowered. One of the dogs felt the urge to announce himself, his barks in a steady one-two-three pattern with a second or two in between tunes.

My visit wasn't prompted by Reuben's theft of railroad ties. In a straight line, this particular spot wasn't far from Bender's Canyon, or even Torrance's windmill. Last night, Reuben would have been home, and could have heard a vehicle pass by on County Road 14. He could have heard the shooting, too, if the circumstances had been right.

He wouldn't have been alarmed, though. More than once during his colorful career, he'd survived being on the wrong end of a gun, and he still carried one with him. As long as the gunfire hadn't been on his property, he probably wouldn't have been concerned.

I started the car and backed around, leaving the dogs' curiosity unsatisfied. A few minutes later, down at the intersection of County Road 14 and the state highway, I looked northeast toward the Broken Spur Saloon. One or two cars graced the parking lot, early tourists searching out happy hour.

Instead of turning left, back toward town, I headed southwest on State 56, enjoying the long, curvaceous climb up the flank of the San Cristóbals, cresting Regál Pass with the Ford's temperature needle still in the green. From the pass, I had an unobstructed view of Old Mexico, a vast, arid land dotted with tiny enclaves of homes that followed the water. Tres Santos, a village of perhaps fifty people, nestled along a seasonal stream fed from the San Cristóbal runoff.

Just below me, the village of Regál graced a tiny sliver of land between the rising southern exposure of the Cristóbals and the five-strand barbed-wire border fence that extended out from the official-looking chain link at the crossing itself. I knew that the official border crossing facility, the portal from all things miserable and austere in Mexico to all things wonderful in the United States, was scheduled for replacement. A fancy little customs building would grace our side, and who knows what the Mexican authorities would design.

At the moment, the crossing was open twelve hours a day, six to six, from October through April, and six to eight during the remainder. Rumor had it that the crossing was going serious, to be open twenty-four/seven, if the Mexican authorities agreed to the change. For added security, the chain-link border fence at the crossing itself had been extended west up into the San Cristóbals before joining the barbed wire. Hikers could laugh at it and hunters could ventilate the support posts.

I glanced at my watch. Reuben Fuentes' habits would keep him on the job until near dark, and Tres Santos was but five miles south of the border. I could drive there in a handful of minutes, since the road to the village and beyond to larger communities like Janos was graveled and smooth. But I was in a marked county car, in what passed for a uniform for me, and between on my person and in the car I was toting a fair arsenal. Our relations with the Mexican authorities were smooth and cooperative. I wanted to keep them that way, and their border was not something to barge across as if I owned the place.

Before dropping down off the pass, I radioed dispatch, my mind set to hear Ernie Wheeler's clipped, efficient delivery. But JJ Miracle Murton, who loved working dispatch as much as any self-respecting road deputy hated it, had slipped back into the seat while Ernie ran an errand that couldn't wait.

"PCS, three ten will be ten ten, Regál." I predicted that all the tens were going to scramble Miracle's mind. Sure enough.

"Uh, three ten, say again ten nine."

"Three ten is ten ten, Regál."

"Uh, ten four, three ten." Whether or not Miracle understood the numbers magic, who knew? I'm not sure he had ever figured out why cops used arcane things like the ten code, but I was hoping he would see the uniformity of it, and understand that saying "ten ten" was faster and more precise than trying to explain that I was going out of service, but remained subject to call.

"Say, uh, three ten?" he continued. "There's a request here for you to return a call to Doc Perrone at your earliest convenience. As soon as you can."

"Ten four. What time was that request logged?"

"Uh, he called right at three oh five."

An hour ago. "What number did he leave?"

"He was over there to the hospital."

"Ten four."

I passed the first graveled street that wandered off west through the village. If the sun winked on it just right, I would be able to see Luciano Cleveland's water pipe where it snaked out of the brush and wound like a great black serpent down to his orchard. I didn't want to be cornered by the loquacious Luciano just then. I stuck to the pavement as I passed the Iglesia de Nuestra Señora on the left.

A gigantic, clumsy-looking RV was parked near the church, a family of five stretching their legs and gawking. I pulled into the graveled parking lot behind the Customs office and parked beside a dark blue three-quarter-ton Ford pickup that I recognized and another Crown Vic with government plates.

The pickup belonged to Todd Barnes, who had worked for us for ten years or so before joining the Feds. Life at the Regál border crossing had its moments—anywhere along the border could be a hornet's nest. A constant flow of illegals crossed the border daily, and some took pains to avoid spots convenient for the Border Patrol. Others, more hopeful, even camped out in the church, which was never locked.

As I got out of the car, one of the Mexican officers whistled loudly to gain my attention. I knew him, too. Pablo "Chucky" Montaño had never worked for us, but since he and his growing brood lived in the tiny village of Tres Santos, I saw them frequently when they drove north to Posadas on shopping excursions. From time to time, Officer Montaño stopped at the sheriff's office to sample our free coffee. I figured it was only a matter of time before the officer saw the paradise that Posadas could be, and applied for a job at our Sheriff's Department, his pathway to bigger and grander things.

I waved a greeting, and Todd Barnes met me at the door. The office air conditioner was on full blast and I cringed.

"Coffee, Sheriff?"

"You betcha," I said. "Thanks." Their coffee was as bad as ours, most of the time not quite hot enough, with an aging oil slick on top. "Has Reuben been through today?"

"Oh, yes." Barnes grinned from the eyes down, an expression that I was sure worked well with nervous tourists. "He's workin' down at the church in Tres Santos. I think they're building some sort of retaining wall to try and train that creek."

The Rio Plegado didn't accept training well. Most of the time a dry gravel bed that was a grand playground for neighborhood kids, the river could run bank to bank with a ferocious roar during one of the legendary cloudbursts. A favorite effort at erosion-control was the placement of old car and truck carcasses, and the Plegado seemed to take pleasure in rearranging those efforts, moving most manmade things downstream. On more than one occasion, it had moved people downstream, too— sometimes their bodies were found, sometimes not.

Built with more faith than common sense, the little chapel of the three saints perched on a graceful bend of the Plegado where the occasional raging waters eroded the bank. The line of collapse was creeping ever closer to the church foundation.

"He hasn't come back through yet, though?" I asked.

"No, sir."

"I think I'll just wait, then. He'll be along before long."

"You're welcome to wait in here."

I raised the cup in salute as I elbowed the door open. "Thanks, but your air conditioner will freeze my bones. You know, I was thinking of a nice spot over in the shade beside the church." The Iglesia de Nuestra Señora, white-washed until it hurt the eyes in bright sun, had adobe walls fortress-thick. Its interior would rival the climate of the air-conditioned Border Patrol office. The heavy shade on the north side of the church would be a nice compromise.

I nodded at the sheriff's radio beside their own console. "If you see him, give a shout to wake me up."

"I'll just throw a rock," Barnes said.

"Whatever works. You folks have been busy today?"

Barnes snorted in amusement. "You've got to be kidding. Middle of the week like this? It's to a point that we're inventing things to do. Hell of a night you folks had, though." He frowned over my shoulder and raised his voice. "You got ID, Bud?"

I turned and prepared to have my hand crushed by Officer Montaño's ebullient greeting.

"Look at this guy," Barnes scoffed. "He just walks across the border like he owns the place."

"Are you after somebody in particular, Señor Sheriff?" The Mexican agent carried himself fit and sharp in his uniform, with his close-cropped ginger hair and startling blue eyes looking more like those of a transplanted Irishman. The lilt of his speech gave him away, though.

I retrieved my hand and turned my Marine Corps ring a bit so it wouldn't gouge an even deeper divot in my finger. "When Reuben Fuentes comes through, if it's not too late. No big deal. I just need to chat with him for a minute."

"Ah. The man with the railroad ties," Montaño said. "He's building a retaining wall down at the church. I tell you what, he needs a bigger truck." He held his hand spread, angled sharply. "That old Toyota squats like a lowrider when he comes through. He can only carry six at a time." A billow of dust rising from the road to Janos drew his attention, and he thrust out his hand for another round of crush. "Let me get back to my side. I got a newbie workin' with me today, and he gets nervous being by himself."

I held out a hand for the crush. "Any interesting traffic through early this morning?"

"And you're looking for what?" Barnes asked.

"I wish we knew. We had an incident last night that most likely involved several shooters—at least with four different guns. Up on Herb Torrance's ranch. They blew hell out of a water tank and windmill." I don't know why I didn't mention Darlene Spencer's misfortune...maybe it was just as simple as "need to know."

Montaño laughed. "Not unless they were sticking arrows in it. We got three guys who talked a pig permit out of the lieutenant. But they're way over outside of Rio Mancos, over in that canyon area. They got a fancy collection of bows, Señor. No firearms."

"They were out of Albuquerque, or what?"

"All out-of-state. Like Kansas...I think it was from Nebraska. Snowbirds looking for something to do. If you need their truck's tag number, I have it in my log. And the names, too, if you like. You're welcome to it."

With a cheerful wave, Montaño walked back across the border just as the second Mexican officer, clipboard in hand, approached the driver's window of an aging Chevy pickup carrying Chihuahuan plates.

Remembering Miracle's message, I said to Barnes, "I would like to use your telephone for just a minute."

"You go right ahead. You know where it is."

I didn't bother to watch the transaction at the border gate, but in a moment the Chevy rumbled through, detained for nothing more than a wave of the hand from Barnes.

TC Trujillo, the second officer on duty, looked up from his small computer and flashed me a wide grin. I pointed at the phone, and Trujillo rose from his seat, a powerful, compact man who needed a mustache to put some age on his round, cherubic face.

"You need some privacy, Sheriff?"

"No. I'll just be a minute."

The first hurdle was reaching Dr. Perrone at all, but the operator at the hospital apparently knew exactly where he was. In a moment, his silky, quiet voice greeted me.

"There's both good news and bad news, Sheriff," he said. "First of all, Darlene Spencer wasn't assaulted. Not a mark on her body, except the one wound in her eye. No defense wounds, nothing under her fingernails…nothing. No sign of sexual activity, recent or otherwise. Traces we're finding on her legs are consistent with urine—and I'm willing to bet that it's her own."

"Is that the good or the bad?" I asked. The girl was still dead.

"Well, that's the good. Sure enough, she died, but she didn't go down fighting. She wasn't assaulted. What I really wanted you to know is that I did recover a single, large fragment of a projectile from the deep tissue behind her orbit, in the anterior of the cerebrum. The projectile's path was downward, and the fragment sliced open two of the major arteries in that area. Right where the ophthalmic artery branches off the interior carotid? The fragment sliced both of them wide open."

"So brain injury, and massive bleeding."

"It would appear so. The sad part is that the wound wouldn't have been immediately fatal. Had she had prompt medical care, there would have been a better than even chance."

"So she lay there all night."

"It would appear so," Perrone said again. "Tumbled around a little, maybe managed to crawl a few feet. That's all."

"So she would have been conscious? At least part of the time?"

"It's impossible for me to say. Maybe. In and out, maybe. There was some brain damage, but it's impossible for me to tell, right now, at least, what circuits might have been shut down."

"Huh." That was about as intelligent a comment as I could come up with. If Darlene had been with the other three youngsters when she was hurt, why hadn't they bundled her into the Suburban and sought help? At the very least there was a handy telephone up at the Torrances'. The simple answer was that nothing much rational happens in moments of panic.

"You recovered the fragment?"

"Yes. It's a pretty good chunk, and there are some rifling marks on it. A single track that's pretty clear. The FBI lab would be interested."

"Okay. Look, we're going to do some Luminol photos there in a little bit when it gets dark. That might tell us something."

"It might. If I had to conjure a scenario, I'd guess that the girl found herself a private spot to urinate, and was in the process when the fragment struck her. She took a tumble, but didn't go far. And there she lay."

"And there she lay," I muttered. "If she'd been conscious, she might have heard the Suburban drive off. She would have known she was alone."

"Maybe. The eye area is damn tender, though. The wound would have hurt like a son of a bitch when the initial shock wore off. No telling what she experienced."

I repeated my earlier thoughts to the physician, maybe in the silly hope that he would have an easy answer. "Why didn't they just scoot someone up to Torrances'...let them call for assistance? One of the others could have stayed with her."

"Who knows?" Perrone said with uncharacteristic frustration. "Remember that the Torrez youngster was getting ready to have himself a major asthma attack, if he wasn't in the throes already. Then pile this on top of it? I can understand their panic." He sighed. "You heard about Willis Browning?"

"Yep."

"Aortic aneurysm right at the cardiac juncture. Gone just like that."

Just like that. Except Willis Browning had spent a night in his own agony, trying to make sense of his crumbling world. He probably hadn't been able to distinguish between the heartache of losing his only son and the discomfort as his aorta ballooned.

Chapter Twelve

By the time I pulled in beside the church, the tourists in the RV had gone beyond the gawking stage. Some adventurous member of the traveling family had tried the door latch, found it unlocked, and the whole family had ushered themselves inside. Indirect afternoon light streamed through the five narrow, tall windows on the south side, while a hard bar of sunlight worked its way up the white wall at the front of the church.

The oldest son, maybe twelve, saw me when I appeared in the doorway. He had been leafing through the visitors' journal, reading names and places.

"*Hóla*," he said fearlessly. Their RV license said Pennsylvania. No doubt he'd had fun with his middle-school Spanish down south.

"Good afternoon, folks." I surveyed the five—Dad, looking like a pro football player just a season or two out of shape; Mom, with a build like a well-fed seal; a five- or six-year-old boy with an old-fashioned flat-top heavy with the grease on the front stalks; the guestbook-reading kid who hadn't started filling out his large-boned frame yet; and a teenaged girl trying her best to look oh, so bored. Compared to the world of her purple hair, I suppose we all were pretty boring.

"I hope it's all right to be in here," Dad said. He took three big strides and offered a hand. Even his grip was coach-like. "Pastor Wade Tomlinson." He swept a hand across his family. "Wife, Gladi; daughter, Trisha; son, Benny; and son, Tommy."

"Undersheriff Bill Gastner," I said. "And, yes, it's perfectly all right for you all to be in here."

"Pictures allowed?"

"As far as I know."

"You know, these are really charming places. We stopped by the Iglesia de Tres Santos, just a hop skip south of here? In Old Mexico? Another charmer. They're working on the riverbank near there, and we watched 'em for a little bit. Real artisans."

"Indeed, they are. You've been on the road for a while?"

He looked heavenward. "Oh, my. Can you believe all the way to Vera Cruz?" He flashed gorgeous teeth. "Now *that's* a haul, and we discovered that our faithful rig doesn't much care for Mexican gas."

"Yes, it is, and I'm not surprised."

"Way *too* far," Mom opined. She managed a warm smile anyway. The daughter looked heavenward.

"Got a brother working for one of the missions down there. I've been promising to visit before he finishes his tour, and we decided no time like the present. But now we're back home."

"Not quite," Mom added.

"Well, we're on the right side of the fence, anyway," Pastor Tomlinson said. "Another five days, and it'll be good to sleep in our own beds." He swept a hand to include the church's interior. "Just so simple," he said. "I was looking for a light switch, but I didn't find one."

"And you won't." I smiled affably. "An available light challenge."

He frowned. "You know, another thing. I noticed that there isn't any kind of lock, or even a provision for one, on the door, there."

"Nope. They're more interested in folks coming in than in keeping them out."

"Oh, I hear ya there. Any troubles with vandalism, that sort of thing?"

"Not yet. But the world will catch up with us eventually, I suppose."

"We can always hope not." He started to add something, but the sharp whoop of a siren—a single yelp impossible to ignore—interrupted us.

"Excuse me. You folks have a good remainder of your trip." Outside, the sun was bright enough to make me wince. Sure enough, Reuben Fuentes' battered Toyota was stopped on the Mexico side of the crossing, the gate arm still lowered just in front of the little truck's grill. Agent Montaño was laughing about something, and he patted the windowsill beside Reuben's elbow good naturedly, then pointed in my direction. He stepped back, the security barrier rose, and the Toyota rattled ahead.

The gate on the U.S. side was already up, and Reuben earned a two-fingered salute from Todd Barnes without being stopped.

Reuben pulled into the tight space between my car and the side of the church. I surveyed the back of the Toyota while the old man worked at getting out. A nice heavy-framed wheelbarrow almost filled the bed, along with a much-used collection of shovels and mattocks, and a wooden toolbox that might bring a fair price during an antiques auction. The remaining space carried an inch or so of sand leftover from a previous trip, and two unopened bags of Portland cement.

"Reuben, how's the river project going?"

He stood still for a moment, watching the border crossing, obviously deep in thought. "What's that old joke, Sheriff?" He pronounced the title as if it rhymed with Omar's last name. He turned to survey the big RV, and then grinned at me. "The *viejo* goes through the border gate *every* day, pushing a wheelbarrow of manure." He shook his head. "The guards, they can't figure out what he's smuggling, you know. Each day, they dig through the manure, trying to find the contraband." His accent caressed each syllable of the word, and then he laughed silently. "But they got to let him go, because they find nothing. Who wants to confiscate manure, you know?" Reuben made his way around the truck and extended his hand. He shook my hand warmly, without bruising either set of knuckles.

"And then what?" I prompted. I'd heard the joke many times before, most often from Reuben. But I liked to hear him end it.

Reuben shrugged and kept a straight face. "Years later, they find out that the man was stealing wheelbarrows." He shifted the position of his cap as his powerful little body shook with laughter. "Stealing wheelbarrows," he added reflectively, perhaps contemplating a new career. "It's going pretty good, you know. Anything works as long as there's no water in the Plegado. They should never have built the church there. I keep telling them that, and they keep not listening."

"I suppose not. How's Teresa doing?"

"She's Teresa, you know." A little expressive shrug left the rest to the imagination. I knew Teresa Reyes, Reuben's niece, well enough to imagine the now-retired teacher at the worksite, making useful suggestions.

"Did Estelle enjoy school in Posadas this year?" Seventeen years before, niece Teresa, recently widowed and without children of her own, had adopted a local orphaned child—no one seemed sure of the circumstances, but the hints were that one of the Plegado's rampages was to blame.

Now bright, gorgeous, and startlingly well-mannered, the youngster was spending her last two years of high school at Posadas High. During the school year, she left Tres Santos and lived with her great uncle across the border, and there was no quieter spot on Earth for concentrating on homework than Reuben Fuentes' little stone house. To accommodate her, Reuben had built a tidy addition to the stonework, including both bed and bath.

Reuben swept his hand in a sideways chopping motion. "Everything straight A's. The calculus, the chemistry, everything." He shook with another chuckle. "She even takes the Spanish, you know? I don't think she has to study too hard for that one." He shrugged and looked wistful. "You know the hardest part? It's when she goes home on weekends, and now for the summer."

I urged him over into the narrow slice of shade beside the back of his truck.

"You were home last night?"

"Where would I go?" Reuben enjoyed the ambience of the Broken Spur Saloon when he could afford It, and he was one of the few people the saloon owner, Victor Sanchez, would be civil with.

"Herb Torrance had some problems at his windmill and stock tank. The one close to the canyon? Somebody blew holes in both. Could have been as many as four guns involved."

Reuben's shaggy eyebrows shot up. "You don't say?"

"I *do* say," I was tempted to respond, but instead asked, "I was wondering if you heard any of the shooting. It's not far from your place, as the crow flies."

"You know," and closed his eyes, "a couple of times, maybe that's what I heard, just before dark, but I wasn't paying attention. The damn coyotes were bothering the dogs, and then *they* all went crazy. Those coyotes, they love to tease."

"But the gunshots?"

"Well, maybe." He shrugged noncommittally. "There was sure some traffic on the road, but there always is, you know. And then it sounded like somebody drove into the ditch, maybe up beyond Herb's place. That's what I thought probably happened, because I heard this loud bang, like someone ran into something. Those voices carry sometimes." He nodded as if that was the whole story.

"Nobody stopped by to use the phone?"

He shook his head quickly as if that were a silly question. "You ask Herb. Maybe somebody stopped there."

"I'll do that. But you say it sounded as if someone drove off the road...up above, you mean? Up north of the intersection of Bender's Canyon and the county road?"

"Some distance up there," but then Reuben shrugged. "That's not much help, no?"

"Every little bit." I knew that if he remembered something else helpful, he'd tell me, so I changed the subject. "Who's working on the flood control with you? You have some help horsing those railroad ties around?"

"Oh, we got more help than I need. They're eager, you know. They make me work harder than I want to."

"They're accepting donations for the materials?"

The crinkles at the corners of his eyes deepened, and he waited for the other shoe to drop.

"Consolidated Mines called," I said. "They're a little concerned about their stash of railroad ties going missing—just a few at a time, mind you, but still. One of the workers saw you and one of your volunteers loading your truck."

Reuben didn't try any excuses. He could have argued that the pile of ties, outside the fence and so temptingly close to the road, looked free for the taking. "How much do they want for them?"

"Ten bucks apiece is what they mentioned to me."

Reuben grimaced and ran the arithmetic through his head. "I don't know," he said slowly. "I can ask Father Anselmo, but you know…Tres Santos doesn't have much money."

"Consolidated might donate what you need." I paused. "If you ask them *before* you take them. Tell them what the project is."

He sighed eloquently, and I added, "Right now, they're looking for two hundred and forty bucks—for the twenty-four ties that have walked off so far."

Reuben gave that silent, shaking laugh of his once more, and looked resigned. "They got the number down already."

"They do," I said. "If you stop by and talk a donation out of them for the rest of what you need, I'll make sure the two-forty is covered."

Reuben looked a little vexed. "You don't need to do that."

"I know I don't. Will you take a few minutes tomorrow morning to go talk to them? I met with JC Powell earlier, and maybe he'll work with you. He's the yard foreman up there. Either that, or he'll know who to contact."

"I'll see what Father Anselmo says about this."

"That's a good idea. Maybe he'll go with you to chat with the mining folks. Nothing like an official Roman collar to help move things along."

The folks from Pennsylvania emerged from the church and nodded at us.

"Thank you, Sheriff," the pastor called. He detoured over to us and pumped my hand, then shook Reuben's as well.

"You folks have a safe trip home," I said.

"You bet. Thank you."

I watched the daughter, who stopped near the front of the huge RV and pensively rested a hand on one of its headlight rims. She gazed off toward the village of Regál, mouth just a little slack with wonder. No Golden Arches broke the skyline, no box stores, no 7-Elevens. Just the grand protective buttress of the San Cristóbals behind them, and the vast sweep of the Mexican plains to the south. Maybe I was judging her through stereotypes. Maybe she loved what she saw.

She favored us with a pretty good imitation of a Mona Lisa smile as she boarded her family bus. I wondered what she was thinking.

With a great belch of dense gray smoke, the RV clattered to life, its engine still complaining about Mexican gasoline.

"Pennsylvania," Reuben mused. "You know, I've never been there."

Chapter Thirteen

County Road 14 is a snaky byway that winds north-south through the western portion of Posadas County. I like to think of it as a limp piece of spaghetti draped over the tines of a fork. CR 14 crosses three state highways: NM 56 in the south, just a few miles removed from Bender's Canyon and carrying the bulk of border traffic; old NM 17, pretty much belting the center of the county and now little used after the interstate's addition of various entrance/exit ramps; and NM 78, giving quick access across the northern portion of the county, running by the municipal airport, and eventually ducking out of Posadas County near the tiny hamlet of Newton. In addition, the interstate splits the county across the middle.

Despite the twists and turns, CR 14 is smoothly graded by the county. Herb Torrance once served as a county commissioner, and maybe that helped encourage the regular maintenance. If the driver pays attention, the county road can be driven quickly—it can even be sort of fun with its roller-coaster twists and turns. I could see that Chris Browning, in a panic at the nasty turn of events, might choose to head north to the interstate entrance ramp. If there was a medical emergency, and it now appeared that there surely had been one, maybe two, why hadn't he just turned south, stopping for help at the Broken Spur Saloon? No matter how nasty owner Victor Sanchez might be, he wouldn't deny a phone call for an ambulance.

But Chris Browning could do the simple numbers. If he hustled to the saloon for help, sure enough, Victor or his helper would call an ambulance, after all kinds of questions. Our county Emergency Services were eager volunteers, but their response time was just fair. By the time the volunteers on duty got themselves together, called in the rest of the crew, and charged out with the ambulance, several minutes would have passed. If they'd been called to the saloon, that was twenty-eight miles. They'd drive out there, then drive back with a patient—or patients.

My hypothesis was that Chris had decided on a one-way trip, straight to the emergency room. He'd taken the gasping Orlando Torrez with him. But Darlene Spencer? Why was she left, lying there hemorrhaging, dying of a head wound? She wasn't that heavy. Easily enough, Chris could have dragged her to the Suburban and lifted her inside in an effort to rescue both Darlene and Orlando.

Monday morning quarterbacking was about as productive as gossip. Deputy Robert Torrez, a newbie investigator by any standards, had it right. Methodically chase the evidence. Measure, collect, mark, inventory. With no willing witnesses, that was all we could do.

I crossed Regál Pass northbound, shortly passed the Pennsylvania RV with a cheerful wink of the lights, and followed the twisting state highway the eight miles to CR 14. Northbound on that graded gravel surface, I slowed to a fast walk, sticking to the center of the road. The intersection with Bender's Canyon Road, offering access to Reuben's place off to the left and the canyon playground to the right, came and went. I slowed even more, all the windows down, the radio turned low.

Two miles north of that intersection lay the Torrance ranch, the house visible off to the right when travelers burst out of a dense tangle of water-starved mesquite, juniper, and cacti. The terrain was humpy-bumpy, and so was the county road, snaking this way and that. Why, in their infinite wisdom, the road planners hadn't just graded a nice straight line, filling in the dips and rills, remained a mystery. At one point, the road crossed a shallow arroyo and then snaked around the end of a small mesa, rock outcroppings acting as guard rails.

I spiked the brakes, slowing to a walk. And then I stopped. The fresh tracks scuffed gravel and dirt where the vehicle had slid off the narrow road, down into the bar ditch, and managed to find the only stump on that side of the road. Big, barkless, and probably good for another thousand years before wearing away, the stump was at least fifteen inches in diameter and two feet high, cut in the days when loggers or firewood-harvesters ignored the policy that asked them to cut 'em low and treat the slash to reduce the fire hazards.

It would have been a perfect seat for a weary hiker, until the ants living in it found his butt more edible than the drying hundred-year-old cellulose.

I backed up a little and turned the car onto the shoulder. By the time I got out, I could hear another vehicle approaching southbound. Torrance's pickup idled to a stop, and the rancher leaned on the windowsill, cap pushed to the back of his head.

"Still prowlin' around."

"Never stops." My gaze shifted to the stump. The tire track, gouged deep in the ditch, showed that the wheel had been cranked hard to the left as the vehicle skidded. Torn stump wood was mixed with bright flakes of what could be chrome, with grease and dirt driven into the scarred wood.

"Somebody hit that a good lick," Herb said. "We see that all the time."

"This is recent, though," I said. "Traffic hasn't obscured the skid tracks a bit."

He glanced in his rearview mirror. "There's lots of other places all along the road. County cuts down trees that are too close, like this one. And then they leave the damn stump." This one had been cut so long ago that the saw-cut was gray, the rings sandblasted with age.

Herb shook his head. "See," and he appeared to be settling into raconteur mode, "when they gravel and grade this, what with all the curves and hills and such, why, it's slippery as all hell.

Kinda like driving on marbles. There's enough straight stretches that you can get goin' way too fast." He grinned. "'Course, I don't know why I'm tellin' you all this. I guess you and the boys have scraped a few of 'em up from time to time." He climbed down from his truck to join me.

"Yes, we have." I knelt at the stump. The impact had been hard. I bent down, shifting my bifocals for a better view. "That's what that is." Herb put his hands on his knees and bent over. "That's a few flakes of chrome, driven right into the wood." I touched it gently, careful not to move it. "Maybe a paint smear." To the right of the stump, a piece of rubber lay in the dirt.

"That tore right off the tire," Herb observed.

"Could be." I straightened up. "Did you hear any of this?"

"Sure didn't."

"If it happened last night, yesterday evening sometime, I'd like to know about it."

"Hard to tell, ain't it? I mean about the time and all. Hell, little rain as we've had, it might have crashed last month."

"Maybe so. But I just visited with Reuben, and he remembers hearing something that could have been a vehicle crashing over here. He heard that, but no voices." I straightened up. "Did anyone stop by your place for help? To use the phone?"

"Not a soul. 'Course, the TV was on, so nobody hears a damn thing."

"I know how that goes. Let me get some pictures of all this and the skid tracks, just in case."

"Hard as they hit, they still managed to pull away."

I grinned. "With a pretty bad shimmy, I'm willing to bet."

I collected the small camera case that had been riding on the floor in front of the passenger seat, and took my time making sure I wasn't doing something photographically stupid. Cameras weren't my forte, but I couldn't see finding Sergeant Garcia for something this simple. The instant camera would spit out little usable prints that might save us some time.

"I'll get on out of your way," Herb said. "You holler if you need anything."

"I'll do that."

With the pack of six fresh pictures curing in the camera bag, I drove north, curious about one more little bit of information. Keeping the Crown Vic booted, just short of sliding into some immovable object, I roared north, past Herb's driveway, past the intersection with NM 17, thumping over half a dozen cattle guards, until I reached the access to the interstate. That took twelve minutes. Add another five or six out the mile and a half of Bender's Canyon, and in somewhere around eighteen or twenty minutes, the kids in the Suburban had reached the interstate. At a hundred miles an hour on that highway, they would have smacked mirrors with Riley Holmes' Cadillac in about fifteen minutes, maybe a little less.

I had heard the crash at 9:17 p.m. The kids had fled their little party in Bender's Canyon sometime close to 8:30. Long shadows by then. A good time to be spooked.

"Three oh eight, three ten." I held the mike, not really expecting an answer. Bob Torrez should have been home, blowing Zs.

"Three ten, PCS. Three oh eight made a run down to the one-hour photo in Deming." Chad Beuler sounded as if he was reading a good book and didn't want interruptions.

"ETA back?"

"Another hour, three ten."

"Ten four. Tell him to contact me the minute he gets back."

"Ten four."

I turned around and headed south, ready to look for other little bits. I could easily understand Deputy Torrez' determination. Too many questions remained unanswered.

Chapter Fourteen

"We're closed." What a cheerful, welcoming greeting. Victor Sanchez glanced up at me as I entered the back door—the kitchen door—of the Broken Spur Saloon, a door with the equally cheerful, welcoming sign, "Keep Out." I knew he wasn't closed. Not at six-thirty in the evening, height of the dinner hour. Victor would think about closing sometime after midnight, when it was time to usher the drunks home.

He couldn't be too busy to talk, since there were only two vehicles out front, a Volkswagen plated to Delaware, the other a long-of-tooth Ford three-quarter-ton hitched to an empty livestock trailer, the whole battered rig licensed to Gus Prescott, a local rancher. I had eased the Crown Vic in behind the building, between Victor's late-model Cadillac and the front steps of his mobile home, then radioed dispatch to tell them where I was.

My entry wasn't a surprise for Victor, since I'd rapped on the door at the same time I turned the knob. At least I didn't catch a colander of reject greens that he was in the habit of pitching out the back door to feed the skunks and peccaries.

Victor stood with his back against one of the big refrigerators, left arm across his comfortable belly with that hand buried in his right armpit, right hand holding a white porcelain cup of coffee. He didn't look especially overworked.

"I got me this fancy front door out there," he said ungraciously. "You lookin' for dinner?"

"As a matter of fact," I answered.

"You're looking for something else, too." He looked me up and down, coming to what conclusion, I didn't know. "Cheeseburger enough?"

It took me a scant second to consider that. "That would be fine. And some of your delectable fries." He made no move toward production, so I launched into it. With Victor, predictability was a losing battle beyond his cranky attitude. Location, location, location. That's what kept customers coming, not his cheerful spirit.

"You probably heard about last night."

"Which part of it?" Victor's big, square face, framed by a thick mane of heavily oiled raven black hair and a newly sprouted little goatee that tried to balance his mustache, showed no surprise or concern.

"We had four kids killed, one of 'em right up here in Bender's Canyon, the other three in an MVA just off the interstate at Posadas. I think—we think—that the four were all together down here at some point." One of his black caterpillar eyebrows lifted a fraction. "Not here, not here in the Broken Spur, but in the canyon," I added.

He pushed himself away from the fridge, pulled open the door, and drew out a stainless steel bowl carrying a couple of pounds of ground beef covered in plastic wrap. He set it on the center butcher block table, and went to the sink where he methodically washed the armpit off his hands, then toweled them dry. Next came a generous handful of frozen fries, snapping and frothing as he placed the basket in the deep fat. My stomach growled.

"Bad place up in there," he finally allowed. But he turned his attention to the construction of a hefty burger. One egg, a generous pinch of chopped onion, salt and pepper, a modest amount of finely chopped green chilé, just enough to draw down through the burger the additional flavors of the strips of the hot chilé peppers with which he'd grace the top.

"Yes, it is. Chris Browning was driving a two-tone blue Suburban. Darlene Spencer and a couple of the Torrez kids were with him." Victor didn't respond. "We're wondering if at any time yesterday evening they might have stopped by here. Maybe to buy soda, chips…anything at all."

"Wouldn't know about that." Deftly, he slapped the burger patty on the hot grill, and without a wasted motion lay two wide strips of green chilé on the side of the grill under lowered heat. He drew a bun out of the bag, touched the down sides with oil, and slid them on the grill. He frowned at his creation, but he apparently wasn't thinking about food.

"You remember Bessie Montoya?" He glanced over at me, face expressionless.

"Sure. Darrel and Marron's daughter." Both parents worked for the state highway department. I knew young Bessie because she had made something of a name for herself, not always lucky enough to make the best choices. Bright enough, she'd graduated from high school near the bottom of her class. She'd tried college for a while, until the state university suggested that she'd be happier somewhere else. "She works for you." The local job meant Bessie lived at home, much to her parents' underwhelming relief.

"*Worked* for me. I fired her ass two weeks ago. I got my niece workin' for me now."

"What went wrong?"

"She sold a twenty-four pack to Darlene Hot Pants. Apparently she thought I never look out the window." He waved a hand at the little serving window that opened from the kitchen to behind the bar where he slid the finished orders. He turned to tend to the burger and its fixings.

"So Darlene bought some beer. Did she have anyone with her?"

"Who knows? Could have been anyone out in the car, waitin'." He waved the spatula at me. "But see, I ain't in the business of sellin' to underage. I find that one of my people did that, and they're history. Gone. My niece took over after Bessie hit the road, and my niece is a smart kid. She wouldn't have sold to Darlene." He plated the fries and the burger, now dressed with the nicely scorched chilé filets, and handed it to me. "We card everybody. If you ever ordered anything other than that black coffee you swill, we'd card you." He almost smiled. "Go talk with her, if you want."

"But this incident with Bessie selling to Darlene was a couple of weeks ago?"

"About that." He jotted on a guest ticket and slapped it on the window shelf, knocking the wooden sill a couple times with knuckle. "She'll get your ticket out front." He turned his back to me, his pleasant way of ending a conversation, and I headed for the swinging door.

"And tell the Torrez kid…" Sanchez added, and I stopped. "…he don't need to hang out in my parking lot. Bad for business."

The Torrez kid? "He was in earlier today?"

"Just tell him to do his paperwork somewhere else. Or his radar. Or whatever the hell he's doing." Victor concentrated on the few dishes and utensils in the stainless steel sink, making more noise than he needed to. "He don't need to be parked in my lot. Or anywhere near me, for that matter."

"I'll mention it to him. Thanks for the burger."

"It's always on the menu."

The saloon proper was dark, naturally cool, thanks to the thick adobe walls, and quiet. An elderly couple sat near the west window, and he glanced up at me as I passed, offered a gold-touched smile, and pointed an index finger of approval at his plate.

"Must be a treat living near this place," he said.

"Oh, it is. Enjoy your travels," I replied amiably. They were clearly tougher than I was, traveling all the way from Delaware in a damn Volkswagen Beetle.

Gus Prescott, the rancher with the pickup and stock trailer, was standing at the glass-topped counter near the register, watching Victoria Sanchez add the numbers.

I headed for the small side room, a path that took me past Gus.

"Do you have a minute or two?" Transferring my heaping plate, I took his offered hand. His grip was firm, hands rough enough that a month's bath in hand lotion wouldn't have made much difference.

"Lemme check my social calendar," he said with a grin, and followed me to the table. Gus was so thin that cancer was either already trimming his bones or about to. What flesh remained on his lanky frame was thoroughly pickled in alcohol. His ranch was east of Herb Torrance's and accessible by a miserable little two-track off of State 56 at Moore. Gus was proud of that driveway. If someone was patient and driving a tough four-by-four, he could follow cow paths out of the east end of Bender's Canyon, and finally end up within view of the Prescott ranch. But then there'd be arroyos to cross, and the jut of a mesa, and by the time he drove up to the Prescotts' front porch, daylight would be gone.

"We had a rough night." I sat down, carefully arranging the plated artistry. As always, I reflected on what Victor's business might be if he was a cheerful, hospitable soul.

"Four kids from town got tangled up in some shenanigans in the canyon, and didn't make it home. Crashed their truck into an interstate abutment."

"Oh, shit." His heavily lined, tan face sagged with sympathy. "Anybody I know?"

"Willis Browning's son, for one. Two of the Torrez kids."

"Well, hell." He adjusted his ball cap. "You was sayin' four…"

"Darlene Spencer was involved somehow."

He shook his head sadly, maybe doing a quick count of his own teenagers, making sure they were all near the nest. "My gosh." He shook his head again. "The Browning boy hunted prairie dogs on the ranch a time or two. He's a classmate of Christine's. I mean, *I* didn't know him or the others, but I guess she would have. Just too damn bad."

"Yes. The evidence suggests that they were engaged in party-hearty time down in the canyon behind Herb's number two windmill. It's looking like they did some vandalism to the mill and tank both. Either they did, or someone else with them took a whole bunch of shots."

He frowned, trying his best not to look at the mound of golden French fries on my plate. I turned the plate so that they were more invitingly within reach, but he didn't take the bait.

"That ain't the first time. Some of these hunters get trigger happy, 'specially if they haven't come across any legit game. Hell, you know that big stock tank I got over by the north gate, just a bit in from the highway? I've had to repair holes in that half a dozen times. Gets so I don't even bother to call you folks. I mean, what can you do?"

"I was wondering if just in the past day or two you've seen anyone else around. See anyone you don't know? Hear any random shooting, or find gates left open—that sort of thing?"

His frown deepened. He crossed one bony knee over the other, lit a non-filtered cigarette, and regarded the plank floor. "You know, it's been quiet around these parts of late. But like I said, that kind of shit happens all the time." He squinted through his smoke, looking speculatively at me. "What do you have goin' on?"

Before I could reply, Victoria arrived with a sloshing cup of coffee for me. She tried her best to smile, but it looked as if she were in pain rather than pleasure.

"Ms. Sanchez, how's your day going?"

"Okay."

I drained the saucer back into the cup. "Busy night last night?"

"Boring."

"Boring is nice sometimes." She looked as if she didn't understand that concept. "Anyone come in to use the phone? Anything like that? Someone with car trouble?"

"Just those guys that broke their truck."

"Those guys…"

"Well, the one guy. But he had somebody with him, 'cause I could hear 'em talking outside. I mean, before he came inside." She looked over her shoulder toward the kitchen, but Victor's surveillance had flagged. Working for her uncle must have been an interesting experience.

"Who did he call?"

She shook her head. "He asked if he could use the phone, and that he needed to see the phone book."

"You didn't hear who he called."

"No. We had other customers. But he was the same guy who came in earlier. He and another guy. They bought a whole bunch of stuff. Mostly beer and a couple bottles of bourbon."

"Earlier in the day, you mean?" She nodded. "Young?"

"No. Old guys."

"Like us?" I grinned at Gus. Victoria blushed.

"No. A little bit younger."

"You'd recognize them if you saw them again?"

"Oh, sure. The guy who bought the package liquor—he's the one who came in later to use the phone. He was kind of a flirt."

"Big guy?"

Victoria frowned. "Not so much." She looked back toward the kitchen again. "Gross fat, though."

"What time would that have been?"

"I wasn't paying attention. Sometime yesterday evening. I think it was already dark, though."

"He reached whoever it was he was trying to call?"

She tried a wry smile and swept back a heavy strand of black hair. That smile was going to take some practice so that it wouldn't make her look like a stroke victim. "I wasn't exactly eavesdropping," she said. "But he said, 'Okay, see you soon,' when he hung up." Victoria started to turn away. "Oh," she remembered, "the tow truck came about an hour later. Maybe a little longer. You know Les?"

"Attawene? Sure."

"He came in and got a cup of coffee to go after they were done hooking up."

The old man near the window caught her eye, raising his cup.

"Victoria, thanks." I had a long list of questions I could ask, but decided to save them for later, lest Victoria earn her uncle's wrath. Les Attawene, the wrecker driver, would have a full log of information about his tow job, right down to the VIN of the rescued truck.

Gus unhooked his leg and recrossed going the other way. He lit another cigarette and shook the pack toward me. I held up a hand in protest…again. "I'm trying to quit," I said.

"That's easy. I've done it hundreds of times." He grinned. "And I guess I should be getting my carcass home."

"Give my best to your spouse."

"I'll do that. And don't be such a damn stranger. We usually got some pie or something layin' around." He pushed himself to his feet and stood for a moment, both hands on the table, the cigarette smoke drifting up into his eyes. "Hell of a thing about that wreck last night. I'll talk to Christine and see what she has to say. She spends enough time on the damn phone, there shouldn't be much about the whole deal she hasn't heard."

I handed him one of my cards, although over the years he'd gathered a fair collection. "If she thinks of something I should know, have her call me."

"I'll do that."

Chapter Fifteen

My handheld radio stood on the table at my elbow while Gus Prescott and I gabbed, but as if it were controlled by some large eye in the sky, it knew when I was alone. The volume was turned down, and Deputy Robert Torrez' voice came across as a whisper.

"Three ten, three oh eight."

"Three ten."

"Ten twenty?"

"Three ten is ten eight at Uncle Vic's."

The briefest of pauses greeted that, a location code that any airhead could crack with a little thought. Still, it discouraged some of our more casual scanner ghouls who tried to keep track of us.

"Ten four. ETA twenty."

And where might you be? "Three oh eight, ten twenty."

"Three oh eight westbound at interstate mile marker thirty-four."

I clicked the transmit button twice and let those little barks suffice as a reply. If Deputy Torrez was twelve miles east on the interstate, he wasn't going to cover that twelve miles, plus another twenty-six or so on State 53, in twenty minutes. An average of even a hundred miles an hour would require a little more than fourteen minutes of travel time. Maybe, hopefully, the young man meant a New Mexican twenty minutes—which could mean anything from just exactly that to next week sometime.

Victoria appeared with the coffeepot, topped off mine, and reached into her apron pocket for my tab. But I had twenty minutes to wait, and needed to put it to good use.

"Victoria, I'd like one of those scrumptious pieces of cherry pie, if you please."

"A la mode?"

"Oh, sure. Why not?" There were actually many reasons why not, including the considerable girth pushing out my gun belt. I might have been able to resist with the help of an after-dinner cigarette, but I'd benefitted from enough of Gus Prescott's second-hand smoke that I held out, even though I could feel the comforting push of the cigarette pack in my shirt pocket.

The pie crust was marginal, the ice cream a little old and cardboardy, but the cherry filling was real, sour, and just wonderful. Halfway through it, a boisterous Mexican family arrived—mom, pop, four youngsters none of whom had become a grouchy teen, and *abuela,* steel-gray hair bun, flinty eyes ever watchful for a child's indiscretions, and the wag of a quick admonishing index finger.

The folks from Delaware listened to the chatter of Spanish for a few minutes, and decided it was time to *vamos.* At the register, he turned to me, forehead puckered. "Would you know how far it is to the nearest gas station?"

"Posadas is northeast, twenty-eight miles. The nearest gasoline in Mexico is Janos. That's about fifty miles. The border crossing closes at eight p.m." I glanced at the clock. "You've got plenty of time yet."

"Closes?"

I made gates out of both hands and swung them shut. "Which direction were you headed?"

"Well, south, maybe. I just assumed…"

"Nope. Janos is a good hop. Road is graded gravel, but it's no boulevard."

"In Regál," and he pronounced it as if he were referring to monarchy, "there's a motel? Best Western or something?"

I smiled my most sympathetic "you're an idiot" grin. "There is nothing in Regál except a Catholic mission and twenty or thirty good folks."

"See?" His wife poked him none too gently in the belly as she said to me, "Rory always thinks that he can wing it. No planning."

"Ah, well." I skidded the last bit of pie onto my fork. "Posadas has gas stations galore, and one good motel, just past the interstate exit."

"Damn." He shook his head in frustration. "I just hate to backtrack. You know what I mean? We just thought…"

"You just thought, Rory," his wife said. I could see tempers were getting a little thin. When they rattled their way back to Posadas, they needed to trade the bug in on a Caddy.

"Well," he sighed. "You're sure?"

"About which part?"

"The crossing actually closes?"

"At eight. Yes. I'm sure."

He looked at the patch on the shoulder of my uniform shirt. "Well, I guess you would know."

"Stop at the Posadas Inn," I said. "Tell the owner I sent you. That's Mr. Patel."

"Patel?" Rory said bleakly.

He looked startled when Deputy Robert Torrez walked through the door, followed by Doug Posey from Game and Fish and RC Markham, a New Mexico State Police officer. Maybe it was because lack of sleep had carved his handsome face, or that he was half a foot taller than either state officer, but Deputy Torrez looked like the ramrod of the outfit.

Sober-faced, he nodded at Rory and his wife; Doug gave the Delaware couple a friendly grin; and RC showed that he'd listened during the last pitch from his superiors that state cops were expected to be ambassadors.

"Evening, folks," he said. Rory gaped at the tiny scorpion preserved in a crystal cube that RC wore hooked into the diagonal Sam Brown strap across his chest. "You folks travel safe, now." He looked across the room at the Mexican family. "Rafael, how you doin'?" RC called, and the father saluted crisply. The trooper turned back to us. "Rafael just left the Marine Corps for us, can you believe that?"

Rory and his wife started to make their exit, and Markham put on a serious face. "That your VW outside? The one with the Delaware tags?"

"Certainly is," Rory said. "All the way."

"You're showing expired. You're runnin' on May."

"Oh, my gosh. The new one is in the glove box. I keep forgetting about it."

Markham grinned, leaning a little closer. His leather gear creaked. "Take a minute and stick 'er on, then. While you're thinking about it."

"See?" his wife said.

"Yeah, yeah. I was waiting for the month to expire, and then I just forgot."

"You can put 'em on early, you know." Markham smiled engagingly. "No days lost."

I scooted around to give all three officers room at the tiny table. A moment later, we heard the wheeze of the VW.

"They're going to make it, you think?" Markham laughed.

"If they don't kill each other first," I said. Torrez had an envelope in his hand. "Get your pictures?"

"Yep." He slid them out and handed the whole pack to me. The photos were sharp, perfectly focused, and presented a nice tour of Herb Torrance's ventilated windmill.

"This all happened at the same time as the girl?" Markham asked.

"We think so."

"And what's your theory, Deputy?"

Torrez reached across and selected a single photo, but held on to it as Victoria arrived with three more cups balanced in one hand, the coffee carafe in the other. She pointed at the creamer and sugar packets in the center of the table, flashed what could have been a smile at Bob Torrez, and quickly retreated. She didn't ask if someone might want food. I saw Victor Sanchez leaning on the serving window. The two of them had a brief conversation, and sure enough, Victoria returned, receipt book in hand. After that effort, she might have been disappointed in the negative response from the trio, but managed to hide it.

When she had returned to the bar, Torrez slid the photo back across to me. The gouge in the windmill's inner wheel band was clear, and the photographer had zoomed in until the mark dominated the frame. He selected another photo, this one appearing to be an artistic landscape. I saw my own image, standing on the old juniper log over in the bushes, far enough from the windmill that I was just a dot.

Without comment, Torrez selected a third photo, this one also showing the landscape, but taken from ground level.

"And so..." Markham prompted as he examined each photo in turn, then passed them to Doug Posey.

Torrez looked at me steadily, as if seeking permission. "And so," I echoed, even though I had already guessed what the young man was thinking. Torrez reached across and touched an index finger to the gouged ring on the windmill.

"I think a bullet ricocheted off here. From here," and he touched the photo taken from the ground, "you can't see the log where you're standin'." He touched the landscape taken from atop the windmill. "You can, from here." He drew a diagonal, downward tilted line, in a slight arc, through the air with one hand. He fell silent.

I pushed my empty plate to one side, pulled the photo enlargements close, and leaned on my elbows to study the images. "All the other holes through the sails are nice and round," I said. "Back sides?"

He slid another photo across.

"Blown out, as we would expect," I said. "And if I had micrometers for eyeballs, I'd guess at about thirty-caliber." I looked at the damage wrought on the support ring. "Can't tell from this, though. It might even be a little bigger."

When the deputy didn't respond, Markham said skeptically, "You're saying that you think a ricochet hit the girl in the eye?"

"Yep." Torrez didn't bother to modify his answer with an "I think that…" or "In my opinion…"

"Perrone recovered the projectile," I said. "That's our next step, then." I reached into my pocket and pulled out the film canister that contained the results of my photography of the stump, but didn't bother to pop the plastic lid. "Interesting thing. Reuben Fuentes heard what might have been a wreck of some kind last night on the county road. Just beyond the turnoff to Herb Torrance's place, there's a sharp, graveled curve. Lots of tire scuffs in the gravel, and a spot where someone bashed their vehicle into an old stump. Herb didn't hear it, but Reuben says that he *did*. Then later in the evening, Miss Victoria isn't sure just when, but not really late, a guy came in here to use the phone…to call a wrecker, Victoria tells me. Les Attawene came down and towed away a damaged pickup. Victoria happened to see it out the window. Pickup, not a car."

Torrez waited, silent. I added, "It's not going to be hard to find that truck, if it was damaged enough to require a tow."

"You have something that ties those guys in with either the tank shooting or with the girl?" Markham asked. A fair question.

"So far, not a thing," I said. "Except they're in the same part of the county—and maybe at the right time." I drained my coffee. "I don't like coincidences. As far as we can determine, the kids had only one firearm with them. And, as far as we can determine, something like three or four *different* firearms took part in the tank party." I leaned back in my chair. "Now, were the tank shooters there at the same time as the kids? We don't know."

"I need to see that truck." Torrez manipulated the eight-by-tens back into the envelope. I looked at the clock over the bar, one of those novelty things shaped like a black cat whose tail swung back and forth as the pendulum. It reminded me that we were moving close to twenty-four hours after the fatal crash, and every minute counted as things cooled down.

"You're right—we need to see the truck. We need to know. In the meantime, *you're* meeting Mears and Garcia at nine with the Luminol," I said. "I'll cruise around and see where the damaged truck turns up." I'd known Les Attawene for years, and he worked closely with us any time there was an MVA that required his services. He'd volunteer information to me that he might not to a rookie whom he didn't know well. However it sounded, Torrez nodded agreement. I turned to Posey. "You're sticking close tonight?"

"You bet."

"I've got until midnight," Markham offered. No overtime for state employees, apparently.

"Who comes on after you?"

"Nobody until seven. Just the guys runnin' the interstate. But their ears are open. There'll always be somebody in the neighborhood." He grinned and pointed. Victor Sanchez had emerged from his kitchen, and he surveyed his domain with a frown. We four cops were his only company, and that didn't make him giggle.

I got up and crossed to the register, gave Victoria what the ticket asked for, and tipped altogether too much on top of that. "Anybody want something to go?"

Torrez, Posey, and Markham all shook their heads, and Victor's frown deepened.

"Victor, thanks for your hospitality," I said. "Great burger."

"'Course it was," Mr. Congeniality huffed.

Chapter Sixteen

On the other hand, Les Attawene didn't sound put out that I was disturbing his evening. Part of his livelihood depended on emergency calls, and circumstances usually dictated that most human mistakes behind the wheel occurred after the sun went down. But he did his best not to sound too eager. He read the VIN and license from his notes.

"That one went to D'Anzo," he said. "He ran off the road into a darn old stump down south. He bent some pieces back away from the wheel by hand, enough to make it back as far as the saloon. That's where he was when he called me."

"Did he say exactly where he had the accident?"

"Somewhere down by Regál, he said. I don't know…maybe that old spur road off the highway right at the top? That's all I can figure. Don't know of any stumps right along the highway."

There was nothing illegal about running off the road and hitting an old stump. If the damage had been done on County Road 14, why bother inventing another tale?

"He hit a hell of a clout," Attawene added. "Drove the bumper back into the wheel, bent a couple of the suspension parts. Carmen said she could scavenge some parts off a couple of wrecks they have. If she don't have it, Florek does."

"Is Carmen D'Anzo who you talked to at D'Anzo's?"

"Yup. She checked 'er in."

"I guess I'll run over that way, then." It was no hardship rendezvousing with Carmen. I'd watched a couple of the high school/community theater productions that featured the young lady's talents, and heard several folks wonder why Carmen was still in Posadas, rather than rich and idolized in Hollywood or on Broadway. Most recently, I'd seen her in a production of *The Crucible*. Her performance had given me goose bumps. But I'd talked to her often enough to know her first love was auto mechanics, and she had sense enough to hold to that.

"You need me to meet up with you there?" He enjoyed talking with Carmen as well.

"I don't think so, Les, thanks. I've got the VIN number and license tag. I'm good to go."

Judge Lester Hobart, on the other hand, wasn't wild with enthusiasm. I called him first, then walked down the hall to his office. His insomnia was as bad as mine, and he had returned to the dark cave of his office to catch up on paperwork in lieu of lying on his back, staring at the bedroom ceiling. He was deep in the statutes, hunting who knew what when I arrived. I explained what I wanted, and his wizened face crumpled in skepticism.

"The only thing that keeps me from just saying 'no' is that you usually don't pester me with nonsense," he groused. "This guy hits a stump, and somehow you're thinking that's related to the girl's death?" He scoffed. "That's what I'm hearing you say, Bill."

"Essentially. But there's a question of *where* and when. This may not be the truck that Reuben heard, or that scarred up the stump on 43. The driver may have gone off the road down by Regál Pass, like he told Les. Two trucks hitting two stumps in one night is a stretch, Judge. If the driver made up the story about Regál…"

"Huh."

"And if it *is* the same truck," I said, "why would he concoct the story about where the accident happened? Lots of folks slide their vehicles off 14. It's a nasty road. Why bother with the yarn?"

"Tell me what you're looking for." Hobart rested his chin in his hand, eyelids heavy.

"Evidence of firearms, for one thing. Whoever ventilated Herb's water tank used several different kinds. The kids had only one with them." I held up both hands and sawed them back and forth. "It's a question of who was where…and when."

"And am I right? You haven't ID'd the projectile that killed the Spencer girl?"

"Not yet. That's coming."

"But if it was fired from a gun other than the one the kids had with them…"

"Then that's a step."

"Either way. Goddamn shame, that accident. Three kids, just like that. And then this thing with the other girl." He shook his head in despair. "You know, I always enjoyed working with Willis. Dying of a broken heart is no way to go."

In another few minutes, I had the warrant.

Chapter Seventeen

As the night deepened, the otherwise quiet village of Posadas became even quieter. A tractor trailer in the distance, dogs in every neighborhood exercising their vocal cords, now and then a car or truck on the main drag. I rolled through the village with the Crown Vic's windows down, maybe touching fifteen miles an hour. This early in the evening, even the six bars were quiet.

D'Anzo's lot was starting to show the pressures of a faltering economy. At one time, a couple dozen cars had graced the front row of the parking lot, with another row of trucks behind that. The inventory was sparse now. The sign still tried to read *D'Anzo Chrysler-Plymouth*, even though the 'L' had dropped off some time ago.

Saul D'Anzo had been dead for years, and neither of his sons had showed much interest in selling cars and trucks. Nick D'Anzo, one of Saul's nephews, managed the business now. In an unusual turn of events, Nick's sister, Carmen, was the shop manager, and she eagerly broke lots of stereotypes.

Nick hadn't sounded super-enthusiastic when he answered my phone call, but reluctantly agreed to haul his shop manager-sister down to the dealership to meet with me. The word "warrant" may have stirred them a little.

Chubby in a rumpled sweatshirt and jeans, Nick arrived first in an aging pickup truck with the dealership's logo on the door.

"Are you going to need inside?"

"I don't think so," I replied. He didn't ask what the evening visit was about, but we chatted about inconsequentials for only a couple of minutes before a dark green Road Runner rumbled in. If you put his Carmen on a game show, not many contestants would guess that she was service manager for a car dealership. Hollywood starlet, maybe. Her ash-blond hair was ponytailed under the *Snap-On Tools* ball cap, and the carefully ironed denim shirt, sleeves rolled to the elbows, did little to hide her astounding figure.

"Yo, Sheriff," she greeted. One hand gave mine a warm shake, while the other rested affectionately on her brother's shoulder. "What's up?" Her voice was a nice, husky alto.

"I was telling your brother that last night, Les Attawene brought in a 1982 Dodge half-ton with right front-end damage." I didn't bother to take the warrant out of my clipboard. "I'd like to take a look at it."

Nick looked at Carmen, and she looked at me…a long, silent, speculating gaze, her green eyes almost hidden under the bill of her cap.

"There's a lot going on, isn't there?" she said. "God almighty, last night. Les said he picked up that Suburban in pieces. That's what I'm hearing."

"Yes."

"I haven't had a chance to talk with Bobby. He must be heartbroken." Her eyes searched my face. "*Both* a brother and a sister. It's hard to imagine that."

"A hard time," I nodded. After our greeting, her hands had settled in the hip pockets of her blue jeans, and they stayed there. But her head tipped one way and then the other, as if judging the scales as they loaded.

"Now what's with the stump truck?" she asked. "All I know is that Les picked it up down at the Spur. The driver didn't ride in with it. Go figure *that.* So I thought he might be stopping by today to sign the work order. But no show. Maybe in the morning. I have the estimate ready for the repair job, if he wants it. It's going to be an expensive stump, even with salvage parts."

I handed her one of my cards. "I'd appreciate meeting the driver myself, if you'd give me a call when he contacts you." I opened my clipboard and reviewed the information that Les Attawene had passed on to me. "So you haven't actually met Mr. Clifton Bailey."

"No, sir. And, Sheriff, we won't start any work on his truck until we do. Les said that Mr. Bailey told him that they're staying with friends, but he didn't say who. He gave Les a verbal work order to forward to us, but that doesn't work for me. No way we're going to put a couple thousand into fixing up the truck, and then have him holler that he never gave us a written authorization." She looked a little disgusted. "He knows where his truck is, so sooner or later he'll show."

"Sooner rather than later, hopefully. I need to see the unit, if I may."

"It's in the back boneyard. Let me turn on some floods so you don't trip over something. Nicky, will you get the gate?"

I retrieved my briefcase and heavy flashlight from the car. After a rattle of keys and chain, Nick D'Anzo pushed the wheeled gate open just far enough for us to squeeze through, and in a moment the yard lights snapped on. There was a time, and not long before, that merchants had burned the watts all night. As times tightened, such luxuries went by the wayside. I'd always thought it odd to leave lights on, since that provided a really helpful assist for vandals and burglars.

The Dodge in question was parked in the front row, its bruised nose facing the street. I set my briefcase down, knelt in front of the truck, and used the flashlight to break the hard shadows from the overheads and what little remained of the sunset.

"It took a pretty good lick," Nick observed.

"Indeed, it did."

"Nobody hurt, though?"

"Not this time. Not that they've admitted, anyhow."

The polished chrome bumper had caught the stump just outboard of the right-front bumper guard, directly under the single rectangular headlight unit. Bumper chrome and juniper had melded, and the stump hadn't given any quarter. The collision had crushed the bumper inward toward the tire and wheel, crushing some of the lower fender around the wheel well far enough to crinkle the upper body work. The narrow chrome strip that bordered the wheel well hung loose. Some work had been done to free the wheel from bodywork, but it was raked out of alignment so badly that even I could see the damage.

"No one hurt in this?" I hadn't heard Carmen's approach.

"I don't think so. Nobody reported it to us, and I haven't had a chance to talk with them. As far as we know, it was just an off-road miscalculation. If he had collision insurance and wants to use it, then he'll need a report from us anyway. They took a hard enough lick that I'm surprised someone's dentures aren't still stuck in the dash."

"I didn't look," Carmen said matter-of-factly. "Maybe they are." She dangled the key ring toward me. She watched as I found a pair of blue latex gloves in the briefcase and pulled them on.

"I know I shouldn't ask this," she said, "but all this just for bumping into a stump out in the boonies? I don't think so."

"And you'd be right on both counts," I said. The door lock opened easily, but the overhead light wasn't working. I reached out and tried the switch on the back of the little fixture, and the light clicked on. I stood still for a long moment, letting the interior fragrance of the truck waft out. Aftershave had a clingy, lingering smell. The truck was three years old, and in that time a lot of skin bracer molecules had found a home inside. To add to the potpourri, the ashtray was hanging open and choked with butts. And mixed in was the one odor that was one of my personal least-favorites, the stale aroma of cheap beer.

An empty rifle rack was mounted behind the seat, a triple rack adequate for an arsenal. I leaned in and popped open the glove box. All the expected paperwork was there, including an envelope of receipts from Discount Tire World in Fort Riley, Kansas. A plastic box containing four archery broadheads with razor-edged hunting tips was nestled among the papers. A box of fuses. A tire gauge. A small box of mints. A roll of antacid tablets.

I frowned and retrieved the box of broadheads, holding the light close for a better look. "Hog Slayers," I read. "Nasty." I put them back in the glove box and slammed the door. I bent down and directed the flashlight beam under the seat. It illuminated the usual clutter that gravity deposits over time and that the vacuum cleaner missed: a few kernels of popcorn, two peanuts, assorted toothpicks, and a crumpled gasoline receipt from Full-Stop Auto Plaza in Fort Riley.

I straightened up and surveyed the cab. Nothing special there. In fact, it appeared as if the cab had been cleaned in anticipation of a long trip. Dust had been wiped off the dash, and the blue scum on the inside of the windshield had been cleaned. Maybe Mr. Bailey had been planning on a little Mexican pig hunting of his own. Maybe he was one of the trio that the border agents had met earlier in the day.

"How about the back?" I said. The brother and sister duo followed me around and watched as I tried the most likely key for the low camper shell. It yawned open, the hinges already protesting from the collection of road dust. A narrow futon was spread in the back, looking comfortable with its pillow, flannel sheets, and blanket.

Ahead of the wheel wells, snugged up against the back of the cab, a steel tool chest fitted securely. It was one of those with the diamond plate pattern on the steel, and in addition to actually being bolted to the truck, the box was secured closed with two padlocks, both on heavy-duty hasps.

I patted the thick futon and regarded the toolbox. Curiosity is a powerful motivator. I edged back out of the truckbed, knees protesting. "Give me a minute," I said, and trudged back to the car. Tucked away in the Crown Vic's trunk with all the other accoutrements of law enforcement was a large set of bolt-cutters. When I returned to the Dodge, I held them up. "And, yes…I do have a warrant," I said when it looked as if Carmen was going to protest.

Despite the warrant, I hesitated. My chain of evidence was pitifully short, and shy of specifics. Judge Hobart had granted a warrant to search the truck, based on his longtime faith that I knew what I was doing. Maybe I did, maybe I didn't. Certainly shy of direct links, I could prove that the Dodge had been in the general vicinity of the Torrance ranch, if I considered the stump out on the county road the "general vicinity" and if I could prove that stump had jumped out in the road in front of this Dodge. No one had seen truck or owner at the windmill site, even though some bullet holes—and maybe slugs recovered from the tank—in due time *might* establish that link.

No one had seen the truck or its owner down in Bender's Canyon, either. The truck *had* been seen at the Broken Spur Saloon. So had other vehicles. Whether or not Victoria Sanchez could positively identify the Dodge after a quick look out the saloon window was open to debate.

But Darlene Spencer's death had changed the rules—at least as far as I was concerned.

If Mr. Bailey squawked about his truck invasion, I might owe an apology and two new locks. At worst, he might sue me on general principles. The padlocks were box-store cheap, and yielded with a crisp snap of the cutters. The cover yawned open. Two ammo cans, one rifle case, one pistol case. A bundle of damaged fiberglass arrows, some missing nocks, some missing heads. Five olive-drab dried military meals, their heavy plastic wrapping guaranteeing them good for a millennium. A couple of emergency space-blankets, folded tightly in their original foil. And snuggled against the front of the toolbox, a handi-man jack and a spade.

"Well," I muttered, and reached in carefully to unzip the short rifle case. The little carbine inside had a hell of a bore, chambered for .44 magnum. I gently picked up the gun, nestled the butt against my thigh, left index finger right at the muzzle and pulled the bolt back with my index fingertip, just far enough to view the chamber. Both it and the tube magazine were empty. Even though I was still wearing the surgical gloves, I handled the gun with care, avoiding smearing any prints that might already be on the smooth, black metal. I took a long, deep inhale at the muzzle. Sure enough, the gun had been busy. I began to feel like a gambler who had drawn ten-jack-queen and was about to flip over the last two in the run.

I jotted down a note recording the carbine's serial number before replacing it in the case. The companion revolver was a brute of a thing, particularly heavy since it was fully loaded. Its owner was evidently not a believer in the old frontier edict of one empty chamber carried under the hammer. All six ports carried .44 magnum jacketed hollow-points.

Mr. Bailey didn't mess around with little wussy calibers. Both guns—carbine and revolver—were excellent choices for pig hunters, hunts that often turned up close and personal. And since both guns used the same ammunition, it made for simple packing. If he had gone to Mexico, he was smart to leave the guns behind. The carbine would have been okay, but not the revolver. And certainly neither of them, if they'd had a Mexican archery tag.

After making a note of the revolver's serial number, I zipped it back up. The two military ammo boxes contained just that—ammo, and lots of it. One can included empty brass, the other included six unopened boxes of Remington .44 mag ammo. Mr. Bailey came prepared.

I sat back on my haunches. "Tell you what I'm going to do," I said, more to myself than to Nick and Carmen. "I really need to talk to Mr. Bailey ASAP, and you may see him before I do. So…" I made sure the two cased guns were lying as I had found them, then lowered the lid of the toolbox.

"I'd hate to have somebody heist this hardware after I conveniently removed the security locks," I explained. "That'd be embarrassing as hell." I glanced at Nick. "Although I guess your boneyard is fairly secure."

"Only fairly," Nick offered.

"And a thief could jimmy the camper lock with a pocketknife." I nodded back at the storage box. "I need a series of photos, so I'll be calling our department photographer out. I'm going to put a sheriff's lock and seal on the box here, and I'll leave one of my cards on the steering wheel, and one on top of this box. That kind of guarantees that Mr. Bailey will want to talk with me the minute he shows up."

Carmen looked confused. "There's nothing illegal about storing those firearms in there, is there?"

"Nope."

Her lovely, thick eyebrows damn near met in the middle. "Then what's the deal?"

I slid out of the truck. "Maybe it's just me, being overcautious." I smiled at her. "But that's okay. I can take the flack for that." I held up the truck keys. "I'm going to keep these until I talk with Mr. Bailey. I'm going to call our camera wizard, and until we have the series of photos to record all this, I'd appreciate it if one or both of you would stay around. I know that's inconvenient for you, but it can't be helped."

"Eventually we'll find out what's going on?" Carmen asked.

"Yes, you will." I sounded perfectly confident.

Sergeant Avelino Garcia was already pushing the overtime envelope out in Bender's Canyon, as Deputies Torrez and Mears sprayed the countryside with Luminol. We didn't have the manpower to ask a deputy to babysit the truck at D'Anzo's, so I stayed put.

Carmen tried out half a dozen ways of framing her questions, but I good naturedly stonewalled her. If she waited long enough, eventually the tendrils of the community gossip vine would find their way to her, and she'd hear at least one version of Darlene Spencer's death.

After a bit, she and her brother went inside the dealership with a promise that coffee would be forthcoming.

The night hung quiet around me, giving me time to think. I found it puzzling that the owner of an expensive, camper-equipped three-year-old truck would be so cavalier about its repair. He'd managed to drive it from the stump as far as the Broken Spur Saloon, and its wobbly behavior would have told him that repairs were going to be both time-consuming and expensive.

Beyond that, I didn't make much progress, and was astonished when the radio jarred me awake. I wipe my face and blinked, striking the familiar "what was that?" pose.

"Three ten, PCS," dispatcher Chad Bueler said again.

I jerked upright in the seat and fumbled the mike. "Three ten," I croaked.

"Three ten, can you ten nineteen for a phone call?"

"Negative."

"Dr. Perrone would like to conference with you before he heads back to Deming, sir."

"Ask him to swing by D'Anzo's, if he can. I can't leave here just yet. Otherwise I'll have to catch him later."

"Ten four."

And sure enough, about eight minutes later, the good doctor's BMW glided into the parking lot and pulled up window to window.

"Sorry about that, Alan. I'm waiting on Garcia to come take some photos." I pointed at the truck. "These folks were out near Torrance's earlier…probably last night. There's some hardware in the truck that needs documenting."

"That's fine." He relaxed back against the seat, one arm on the windowsill. "No surprises at the Spencer autopsy. Just the one wound in the left eye. The bullet fragment is pretty large… close to nine-point-seven grams."

"And nothing else."

"Nothing else. She hadn't had sex recently, and other than a few inconsequential scrapes and digs from rolling around on the ground, nothing else."

"TOD?"

"I would estimate this morning sometime. Maybe as late as nine or ten o'clock."

Immediately the image came to mind of the girl lying dying while, a hundred yards away, I took my time jawing with Herb Torrance. Alan Perrone saw the expression on my face and interpreted it correctly.

"If she'd been found just ten minutes after she was struck and then immediately transported, I don't think we could have saved her, Sheriff."

"She lived a long time, though."

"Sort of. A strong kid. She would have just drifted out. There's nothing you could have done."

"Yeah, well."

"They're still shooting photos out there?"

I nodded. "Garcia is using both color and black-and-white with filters with the Luminol. He'll develop the black-and-whites tonight, and the color will go to the lab in Deming first thing in the morning."

"My best guess, looking at everything, is that she found herself a spot to urinate, had just about finished, and got found by a ricochet. There're just no signs of anything else going on. No bruises, no nothing. No signs that she tussled with anyone. Certainly no signs of an assault. No torn clothing, no blood except from the head wound. No defensive wounds of any sort. Nothing under the fingernails." He shook his head. "Nothing to suggest she was in a scuffle."

"A ricochet." Bob Torrez had more support in his camp. He'd been an avid, and successful, hunter since he had been old enough to hold a gun. He knew what bullets did, or didn't do.

"Yep, that's what I think. There was nothing about the head wound that would account for the damage to the projectile. What bone it encountered was the thin back wall of the orbit, right around the optic nerve. My bet is that the bullet was deformed before it struck her. Judging from the soft tissue damage, by the time it struck her its velocity had fallen off considerably."

Dr. Perrone fell silent and we gazed at each other, with me thinking that if I thought long and hard enough, all the pieces would jumble together to make sense.

"The recovered bullet and my prelim report are in the morgue file waiting for a certified officer to pick them up," Perrone said. He took his foot off the brake, letting the BMW drift a little. "Holler if there's anything else you need."

"You bet. Thanks, Doctor."

Nine-point-seven grams. A sizeable chunk of lead, that. Conversion charts were filed somewhere in my dusty memory, but the numbers were a blur. Something like fifteen grains to a gram. The arcane grain scale wasn't used by many folks other than those in ballistics. No one counted out seven thousand grains of wheat for a pound any more. But the ammunition industry *did* use the finely chopped grain scale, both for weighing powder and bullets.

The boxes of .44 magnum ammo in the crippled Dodge's toolbox all announced bullet weights of 240 grains...or about fifteen and a half grams.

If my military memory served me correctly, the .30-caliber carbine tossed out little bullets that weighed only 110 grains or so—a bit more than seven grams in the morgue's parlance.

I relaxed back in my seat, letting my thoughts drift. But by ten minutes after eleven, my patience had worn thin.

"Three oh nine, three ten."

Silence greeted me until Chad Beuler's cheerful voice found me. "Three ten, three oh nine is ten forty-two."

Sergeant Garcia is *home?* "What'd he do, retire?"

Chad wisely didn't respond to that lack of understanding on my part.

"PCS, give Sergeant Garcia a call..." I stopped short. "PCS, cancel that." The light was on in one of the dealership's office windows, and from there I could keep an eye on the Dodge and use the D'Anzo's phone.

The showroom door was locked, but Rick saw me coming and hustled over with a jangle of keys.

"I need to use your phone, if I may."

"You bet. How about the one right there in my office? Dial eight to get out."

Garcia's daughter, Valorie, answered with a muted greeting, as if her head was stuffed under a pillow. Maybe it was. She and her husband, Rod, a truck driver up at the Consolidated Mine, lived with their three children in multigenerational bliss with her mother and father, with a maternal grandmother thrown into the mix.

"Sergeant Garcia, please," I said. "Undersheriff Gastner calling."

"He's…" Valorie hesitated, and I could hear a voice in the background. "Just a sec." A hand muffled the phone, and then Avelino Garcia came on the line.

"Yes?"

"Sarge, we need your camera for a bit," I said. "I'm out at D'Anzo's."

A mighty sigh greeted that. "I just stepped out of the shower," he said.

What was I supposed to say? *"Oh, I'm sorry. When would be a better time for you?"* I considered using the shower excuse the next time Sheriff Salcido asked me to attend a County Commission meeting.

"After you dry off, you'll likely need your whole kit," I said pleasantly. "We're shooting the inside of a truckbed toolbox, with a couple of weapons involved. The light is miserable."

"When do you want it? I could run over there first thing in the morning."

"Actually, *now* is just right, Sarge. Rick and Carmen have opened the place up for us, and I'm sure they'd like to go home to bed sometime soon, too." Silence greeted that. Avelino was close to retirement, and I envisioned him counting days on the desk calendar beside his phone. "Judge Hobart gave us a warrant, so we're good to go."

"You said you're at D'Anzo's right now?"

"Yes."

Another pause. "Give me a couple minutes."

"You got it. Thanks, Sarge."

He grunted something and hung up. Headlights blasted through the window, reflecting off the lonely M-bodied Grand Fury posed on the polished showroom floor. Robert Torrez' department ride jarred to a halt beside mine.

"Folks, thank you. We'll be just a few minutes."

"Whatever you need, Sheriff." Carmen and Rick were sitting in her office, her neatly booted feet propped on the corner of her desk. "And the coffee's ready. Help yourself."

"Thank you. That's very kind." I beckoned Torrez and met him at the door.

"It went all right?"

"Yep."

"There's coffee inside. Want some?"

"That'd be good."

We fueled the cups, but I waited until we returned to the vehicles before asking, "So tell me. What do you think? Anything new to change your mind about what happened?"

"Nope. I think that she needed to take a piss, and found that spot away from the others."

"While they stayed at the windmill?"

"Yep."

"And then?"

He opened the door of the Blazer and retrieved his clipboard. He had already attempted a scene drawing, but whatever his other skills might have been, artistry wasn't among them. He pointed with a pencil. "She squatted right here at the end of the log. Got some roots and stuff to lean against. When she finishes, she starts to stand up, turns a little, and pow. The ricochet hits her right in the eye." His pencil traced a line down to another blob he had drawn, with a stick figure of a body. "She tumbles down into that little depression where we found her. Lands flat on her back."

"Cried out? Tried to pull her jeans back up?"

Torrez shrugged. "Don't know what she could do, hurt like that."

"But how do you see it happening? I mean, the windmill—if that's where the ricochet came from—is way over here. She would have had to turn, facing that way."

"Could have. She's standing, sort of, pulling at her jeans, and turns her head to make sure she ain't got an audience."

"And then they find her." The deputy didn't reply to that. Maybe he was running the same mental scenario I was...one of the kids, maybe all three, dash through the brush in response to the cries for help and find the girl, half-dressed, gushing blood, thrashing about. They panic. What teen would keep a cool head during all that?

"Maybe they did," Torrez said quietly. "Or maybe somebody else did."

"You think?"

"There was a lot of shooting going on. At the tank, at the windmill."

"Doc Perrone says the fragment that struck the girl weighed about a hundred-fifty grains. And he agrees with you...he thinks it was a ricochet. The bullet was damaged *before* it hit the girl. That's what he thinks."

"So at a hundred-fifty grains, it wasn't Chris Browning's thirty-carbine. I need to see that piece."

"It's being held in the morgue evidence locker. We need to send it off to the FBI lab for a comparison—when we have something to compare it to."

"I need to see it," Torrez said.

"I hear ya. First things first." I nodded at the Dodge. "Odds are just about one hundred percent that this truck was damaged by ramming a stump, over on the county road just beyond Reuben Fuentes' place. I mentioned that when we met down at the Spur. In fact, Reuben thinks that he heard the crash. The owner made it back to the Broken Spur, and called Attawene's towing. The Sanchez girl remembers seeing them hooking it up. Attawene brought it here. What I think interesting is that the owner, a Mr. Clifton Bailey from Fort Riley, Kansas, had it towed here, but didn't come with it. He didn't make any arrangements with D'Anzo's, other than sending a message with Attawene that he wanted the truck fixed."

I watched Torrez as he glared at the truck as if he could force the answers out of its grill.

"That means Victoria Sanchez is right when she tells us that she saw Bailey with somebody," I said. "She recalls Bailey and a companion coming into the Spur earlier in the afternoon to load up on booze. Now, Bailey didn't come to town with Attawene, so he's out there somewhere, with his buddy. And you know my question."

Torrez looked over at me.

"Were Bailey and his bud the ones out at the tank? Is the bullet that struck Darlene Spencer from one of *their* guns?" The soft crunch of tires announced the arrival of Avelino Garcia's unit. "I don't trust coincidence, Robert. This truck was out in that neighborhood, Victoria saw the occupants at the Spur. And now, we find some interesting guns in their storage box. We need photos of all of that. And those guns may just be the place to start with a ballistic comparison to that fragment that Perrone pulled."

Chapter Eighteen

Deputy Robert Torrez was impatient with the process, but we forced him to a standstill. Despite his earlier resistance, Sergeant Avelino Garcia was unflappably patient now, and no court in the world would fault his procedure.

"Odds are good, Robert, that what we do here *will* end up in court, one way or another," I said. "When we have the time, we take it." The young man crossed his arms across his chest, locking his hands under his armpits. He looked as if he might be listening, so I added, "State prosecutors once blew a Grand Jury case here in Posadas that started with a simple bar fight and ballooned from there. They tried to catch one of the village officers on a charge of intimidating a witness."

I waved a hand to dismiss the rest of the details. "Because it was such a cut-and-dried case—the prosecutor thought—he neglected to provide a simple crime scene drawing of the saloon…one that showed who was where. By the time he was finished mangling the case, the Grand Jury just threw up its hands. No indictment. And they issued a pretty stinging rebuke to the prosecutor. So lessons were learned. No matter what we're doing, we need to think ahead to the resulting court case. That's not always possible, but a surprising percentage of the time it *is* possible. Just like with the windmill. You took careful pictures to support your hypothesis. Ditto with the victim's body. One step at a time."

Garcia gadgeted up, and then walked off across the dealer's lot. His distance shot—an establishing photo—would show the Dodge pickup in the boneyard, with the large D'Anzo Chrysler-Plymouth sign prominent in the far right corner. Even the front of the dealership office was included. That accomplished, he walked back in and took another shot of just the Dodge, framed by the fence.

"Go ahead and open the tailgate," he instructed, and Torrez did so, then stood off to one side. With the strobe held so that its muted light bounced off the interior roof of the camper shell, Avelino Garcia worked to record the position of the storage box in the truck. I could tell Robert Torrez was impatient with each methodical step, despite my lecture. He had every good reason to want to charge ahead.

I handed Garcia the sheriff's lock key, and he slid into the truck. He propped the remains of the twin padlocks that I had cut off on top of the lid, one by each hasp, and recorded that, then cleared the top and opened the lid.

"Okay, we have two gun cases, half a dozen ammo boxes, and what looks like a few of those dried meals we used to get in the Army."

"I need it all in the photo," I said.

Avelino nodded and scrunched around, taking his time to aim the filtered strobe to avoid shadows that would make the photo useless. Torrez knew better than to climb his bulk into the camper, but he rested a hand on the tailgate, a tiny motion that Avelino noticed.

"Don't move the truck," he snapped, and Torrez jerked his hand away as if burned.

"Okay." Avelino relaxed back.

"Now I want photos of the guns out of their cases. I'll want both an overall view and close-up of the serial numbers and the caliber designations." Bob Torrez may have been six-foot, four and close to two-twenty, but he also had twenty-two-year-old agility. "Get yourself a pair of gloves and give him a hand," I said, and to my surprise, the young deputy pulled a pair of clean gloves out of his hip pocket.

Once in instructor's mode, it was hard to stop. "Robert, the handgun is loaded." He glanced back at me, and I shrugged. "Yeah, I've been there already. I touched the muzzle and butt of both, so if you do that as well, we'll preserve any latents."

By the time they had finished—and it took a while in the poor light for Avelino to figure out his exposures—we had a good catalog of the guns, their vital stats, and their storage locations. All in all, if Mr. Bailey was as innocent as fresh snow, we'd achieved a useless invasion of a man's property rights.

"The one-hour color lab opens at nine?" I asked. "Then these and the Luminol prints need to be at the lab by then."

"Tell you what," Avelino said, "I'll do that. The wife needs to do some shopping, and while she's doin' that, I'll see to the color work."

"You'll be with 'em the whole time."

"You betcha." The veteran sergeant didn't need to be reminded of chain of custody issues, but it didn't hurt for Robert Torrez to hear it again.

"Good. Put 'em back and snap our lock back on, Roberto."

He hesitated. "We can't take 'em into custody now?"

"We could. And the warrant does mention firearms as items of interest. But there's a certain presumption of innocence that we're working with here. We'll push a little further and see what we get before we go the confiscation route."

"I was going to do a bullet comparison."

"I understand that you want to do that," I said patiently. "But right now, we have a scarred stump and a smashed bumper, and a witness who saw Bailey at the Broken Spur. We have nothing that connects Bailey with whatever the kids were up to. But I tell you what," I glanced at my watch, "go home, get some rest, and tomorrow bright and early we'll do some comparisons. We'll start with what you recovered during your wading episode in Herb's tank."

It took Torrez a moment to work up a nod of agreement. It must have been hell being twenty-two, eager, and surrounded with patient, cautious old duffers.

Garcia slid gingerly off the tailgate, and I locked it up and smoothed an adhesive Sheriff's Department seal over the tailgate and the camper's swing-down door. "Sarge, thank you." I beckoned to Torrez. "Let's let the D'Anzos off the hook."

As we entered the dealership, Carmen favored us—well, mostly Robert—with a wide smile. "The coffee will just go down the sink if you don't finish it up." Neither the mild flirt nor the offer of beverage made a dent in the deputy's solemn visage.

"We thank you," I said, and held up the truck keys. "The truck is locked front and back with a Sheriff's seal on the gate. We put the lock back on your boneyard gate. I'm taking the Dodge keys with me. If and when Mr. Bailey contacts you, I need to know."

Carmen made a face that looked as if she might burst into tears, all lighthearted flirting vanished. "I was talking to my mom? She said that she heard that Darlene Spencer was found dead down in the canyon, maybe shot to death? That it looked like she'd been assaulted?"

And where did mom hear all this? I wondered. "Your mom is partially correct, Carmen. Miss Spencer was found dead, and there is evidence that she suffered a head wound." I paused. "There is *no* evidence that she was assaulted in any way other than that."

"Oh, my God."

"Is that what the deal is with the truck?" Rick D'Anzo asked.

"We're not sure." I thrust my hands in my pockets. "That's why it's important that *if* you hear from Mr. Bailey, or anyone in his company, we need to know about it ASAP. You have my number, and you know nine one one. Dispatch can always reach me." I reached out and lifted the carafe to top off my cup. "And folks, it would help us tremendously if you didn't discuss any of these events with anyone. If one of your mechanics says something about the truck, just say that you're waiting on owner authorization."

"They'll see the yellow Sheriff's seal."

"If they do, they do. The tighter we can contain all this, the better."

They agreed with that, but unfortunately, not everyone else in Posadas did. By the time we walked into the Sheriff's Office, I saw a couple of *While You Were Out* notes stuck in my mailbox. One was from County Commissioner Arnie Gray, but he could wait.

The other was a phone message from Leo Bailey, publisher and editor of the *Posadas Register.* The similar name drew me up short, but there were many, many Baileys in the world. I had known Leo for a dozen years before, since he had purchased the *Register* from Russell Smiley's estate. The *Register,* still clinging to historic broad-sheet format, leaned heavily on photos to fill the white space around the ads, and that was okay with most folks. Most of them would rather see a photo of three cub scouts standing goofily in a row, holding awards, than they would hard-case investigative reporting.

I'd heard rumors that Bailey was looking to sell the publication, but until I heard it from Leo himself, I assumed the paper was still in aggressive hands. Leo worked hard, and I admired that—even if sometimes he became a pushy pest. The fact that he had called in the dark of night told me that he was paying attention. He would expect a return call. As rampant as the rumor vine grew, maybe he'd heard something I needed to know.

Chapter Nineteen

I took the notes to my office and tossed them on one of the few spots that wasn't cluttered. Dispatch had written 10:02 p.m. on the note, and below that, Chad Beuler had printed, "Info on MVA." I settled into my chair, pulled the phone closer, and was about to dial when I remembered that Deputy Torrez had been at my elbow all evening, and now had vanished like a puff of smoke.

"Ernie?" I called through the open door. Graveyard dispatcher Ernie Wheeler could hear me just fine, and his swivel chair squeaked. In a moment he appeared in my office doorway.

"Sir?"

"Did Bob Torrez leave the office?"

"Yes, sir."

"Did he say where he was going?"

"No, sir, he did not. I was assuming home, but maybe not. He took the Blazer."

I leaned back and looked out the window at the scenic view of the parking lot. Torrez' personal pickup truck was still parked just beyond the gas pumps. Sure enough, the department Blazer he'd been using was not in its slot. With nothing but a few cat-naps for relief during the past hours, I knew how tired I was. Granted, Deputy Torrez was a hale and hearty twenty-two-year-old, motivated by a nearly incomprehensible family tragedy, so that gave him an edge.

What bothered me more was that Torrez appeared to embrace the solitude of his new job to a point where he didn't feel the need to discuss his comings and goings with either me or dispatch. A vintage case of the pot and kettle, but as undersheriff with a good many years under my belt, I suppose I felt that I had earned my solo status. I didn't ask Sheriff Salcido every time I took a step—and there would come a time when I would expect the same from Robert Torrez. But as a rookie during his first week on the job?

I reached out and pushed the intercom button. "Ernie, find Deputy Torrez for me, please."

"You got it, sir."

Leo Bailey's home phone was listed, but first I dialed the office of the *Posadas Register*. The Friday edition of the paper would be printed down in Deming, and Bailey would make that drive at five a.m. so he'd arrive in time to chat with composing room folks and see the page plates made. I knew his habits. On one early morning, I'd stopped him as he drove down Grande Avenue at close to eighty miles an hour. His excuse—and I had let it work for him—was that he had a late-breaking page one story that still needed to be typeset.

"Bailey."

"Hello, Leo."

"Well, for crissakes." I could imagine him swinging around in his antique swivel chair so he was facing me, pencil poised over a notebook. "Are you going to bring me up to speed on all this shit that's going down?"

The clock ticked to one minute past midnight. "Good morning. And probably not."

"I can't wait forever, you know. I have deadlines."

"There's always Tuesday's edition."

"You're uproarious, BG." He was the only person in Posadas County who called me that, as if hinting that our casual relationship might actually run a little deeper.

"I'm too tired to be uproarious."

"So what's going on?"

"Tell me what you have so far, Leo."

"What I have so far…" I heard papers rustling. "We start off with the three kids killed down at the overpass. One of them is the late ADA's son, Christopher Allen Browning, age sixteen. Two passengers, Orlando Ruiz Torrez, age…lemme see. He would have been…just turned seventeen. And Elena Rowina Torrez, she was fifteen. Okay, that's that. The vehicle was a 1984 Chevrolet Suburban, registered to Mr. Browning."

"All of that is correct."

"And I was sorry as hell to hear that Browning died earlier today. What a kick, eh? I can't even begin to count the number of times we've had coffee together. First his son, and then him. What a kick."

I remained silent, absorbing the "kicks," and pondering how much to tell him.

"You still awake?" he prodded.

"I am, sort of."

"So what else do you have for me? Or are you going to let all the metro papers blow me out of the water…*again?*"

"I have no control over when kids die, or when bad guys do their thing, Leo."

"Yeah, yeah. All that, I know. But I'm sittin' here lookin' at the clock, and whatever you tell me, *right now,* I can get into tomorrow's paper."

"Yep." I leaned to one side and maneuvered my notebook out of my hip pocket.

"So, contributing factors?"

"Speed and alcohol. There appear to be other medical issues involved. We're continuing to investigate that."

"Medical issues? What the hell does that mean?"

"I'm not sure yet."

"Christ, what a big help you are. Look, I took a photo of the Suburban through the county fence, and I have photos of the crash site, not that those amount to shit. So they were comin' down the exit ramp way too fast?"

"*Way* too fast. Lost it, and rolled multiple times. Ended up against the interstate support pillar. One occupant, Orlando Torrez, was ejected from the vehicle. We used the jaws to remove the other two."

Leo's officious tone softened a little. "All pronounced there at the scene?"

"Yes. Coroner Sherwin Wilkes."

"Did you ever have the chance to talk with Browning?"

"Yes. In fact he came to the crash scene. I'm surprised that you weren't there." The multiple frequency police scanner in the bookcase immediately behind Leo Bailey's desk scanned everything from police to weather to air traffic control.

"I was out of town. But jeez, what a kick."

"Yep."

"I'm told that two of the kids were related to your new deputy."

"You're told right. Elli…Elena…and Orlando were Deputy Torrez' younger sister and brother."

"That's a sorry state of affairs. I heard he was there. How could that be?"

"Your grapevine is efficient, Leo. Yes. Deputy Robert Torrez was riding with Sergeant Lars Payson…doing a little community familiarization tour before he started his shift."

"I heard it was his first night on the job."

"Hell, you don't need to talk to me, Leo. Just headline it, *"Grapevine says…"*"

"Okay," and Leo huffed with amusement. "Okay. *Was* it his first night on the job?"

"He'd been around some. He did a few tours before he went to the academy. He was lucky and got an early schedule on that, so he didn't have to wait around twiddling his thumbs. He went to academy, got certified, and now he's facing this godawful mess. It ain't easy, Leo."

"It's fair to characterize him as a rookie, though."

"I suppose. Or 'new hire' if you want to be a little more dignified."

"That's not in my genes." I heard a typewriter clatter in the background. "And these kiddos were returning from where?"

I hesitated. "That's something we're still investigating, Leo. We don't have a definite answer yet. Just some good guesses."

"How about giving me your best one of those, then?"

Resting my head back against the chair, I closed my eyes. After a minute, Leo prompted me, "You still there?"

"Yeah, I'm still here. I'm thinking."

"Gets to be this time of night, and us old codgers tend to drift off."

"I'm wishing I could." I saw the images that we had to work with: the carbine abandoned in the bushes, Darlene Spencer's body, the panic that drove the kids in the fleeing Suburban… none of that was guesswork. "We think that the kids were down in the Bender's Canyon area, just off County Road 14."

"That's rugged country. Party time, you think?"

"I would guess so. It's secluded, and we know it's a favorite spot."

"So it's really the same old story, isn't it? Kids out drinkin', and then they overcook it comin' home."

"There is that."

"So what was this other ambulance call today? Down in that same area, wasn't it? I got busy and didn't follow up on that one."

I cleared my throat and read my notes, making an effort to stay as neutral as I could. "The Posadas County Sheriff's Department is investigating the death of a teenaged girl whose body was discovered near Bender's Canyon Thursday morning. Probably cause of death was a single gunshot wound to the head. The victim was identified as Darlene Spencer, seventeen, of Posadas."

There was a long pause, and the clatter of typewriter keys. He stopped typing and breathed, "Holy shit. You're talking about Francine's daughter? I mean, Franny's kid?"

"Yes."

"Damn, how did that happen? Hunting accident? Suicide? Murder? What are we talkin' here?"

"I wish I had an answer for you."

"Oh, come on. Jesus. But they have to be related, right? The girl's death and the partyin' kids? I mean, that's just too close for it to be a coincidence."

"I can't tell you."

"Can't or won't?"

"Well, okay. *Won't.* Not yet. Investigation is continuing." I sighed. "You know, Leo, I'm trusting you on this. This is a difficult case. I'd appreciate it if you'd keep the story as straightforward as possible. No supposition, no assumptions." Before he had a chance to protest, I asked, "What's your deadline for Tuesday?"

"I can take copy as late as…well, this time on Monday night. We print at five a.m., but I can leave a pocket on page one for a late update. The composing room will bitch and holler, but what the hell."

"I'll make sure you have something, then."

"Don't go cutting me out of this, Sheriff."

"I wouldn't think of it. If I haven't called you by eleven p.m. on Monday, call dispatch. They'll know where I am. Salazar's is handling all the funeral arrangements, so you can get family details from them. Give us some time to work this."

Bailey sighed. "Look…just one thing. And you gotta know this. The Spencer girl's wound…back of the head? Temple? Execution style? What?"

"A single wound in the left eye."

He sucked in a breath. "*In* the eye?"

"That's correct."

"Will Perrone talk to me?"

"Of course not, Leo. Everything goes through me or Sheriff Salcido." I looked up as the tall, broad figure of Deputy Torrez appeared in my office doorway. He held the manila clasped envelope with hospital logo and tracking sheet printed on the front.

"Leo, I need to go. I will call you at eleven p.m. Monday—and probably before. Maybe we can do lunch."

"I'm gonna hold you to it."

"You do that."

"Oh...wait, wait, wait." Leo's plea stopped my hand. "Are you still there?"

I made a deep snoring sound.

"One more thing. You got a minute?"

"Just about."

"A little bit ago, one of my neighbors said there was all kinds of activity across the street at D'Anzo's."

I laughed. "How helpful your neighbor is, Leo."

"Hey, you know. So what was goin' on? She saw lots of flashes, like someone was taking a bunch of pictures. Three cop cars. And both Carmen and Rick were in the office. Now *that's* unusual for this time of night, don't you think?"

"It's been an unusual week, Leo."

"Come on, now. What was goin' on?"

"Just insurance photos."

He scoffed. "You gotta do better than that. Insurance photos at eleven o'clock at night?"

"We're a twenty-four-hour outfit, Leo. We fit in stuff like that when we can."

"Impounded vehicle? What'd you have, a hit-and-run or something? Stolen truck?"

"We don't impound at D'Anzo's, Leo. The guy hit a stump. How's that for breaking front-page fodder?"

"Oh. Whoopie."

"You could do a photo feature on the mechanics as they try to straighten out the front bumper. Or a close-up celebrity shot of the owner's face when he sees the invoice. Hard-hitting stuff, all of that."

He chuckled. "Okay. Okay. Don't forget to call me. Or I'll call you. Or something."

"Good night, Leo."

Chapter Twenty

I hung up and grinned at Robert Torrez. "The press." I waved him toward a chair. "Can't live with 'em, can't live without 'em." He held the manila envelope with both hands. "I see you stopped by the hospital."

"I wanted to do a comparison with some of the bullets I recovered from the tank."

I leaned back, steepled my fingers, and regarded the young man for a long moment. "Let me see if I can make this clear to you, Robert." While he pondered that, no doubt wondering what was coming, I got up and walked around my desk to close the office door.

"How long were you in the Coast Guard, Robert?"

"Three years, sir." One eyebrow drifted up in confusion.

"And left with a medical discharge for your knee."

"Yes, sir."

"How'd you happen to wreck that?"

"An overloaded truck capsized, and some of the steel he was carryin' took out my motorcycle."

"You're lucky it was just a knee."

"Yep."

"During those three years with the Coast Guard, did you ever borrow a cutter and take 'er out for a spin?"

"Sir?"

I let my hands relax in my lap. "Why wouldn't you do that? Port Canaveral, right? I mean that's beautiful ocean down there.

Grab a cutter, go out for a romp off the continental shelf. A little informal patrol looking for druggies. Whale-watching. Something like that?"

His black eyebrows furrowed, and he held up the manila envelope as the connection clicked. "I wasn't supposed to do this?"

I kept a straight face. This kid was smarter than the average bear. "Let me just say it outright, then, Robert." I pointed at the parking lot. "That Blazer belongs to Posadas County. When you're in it, you're representing the county."

He nodded slowly.

"And that means, even if you're busy with a thousand other things, if some distraught civilian flags you down begging for assistance, you stop and do what you can—because that's what they expect when they see the vehicle and the uniform."

I nodded toward my office door. "Dispatch controls our traffic. It's important that Ernie, or Chad, or whoever is on duty, knows where you are…where all the deputies are. If there's a call, they make the decision, based on the deputies' twenty, about who is going to respond." I lifted my eyebrows in expectation, and Torrez returned my gaze steadily.

"I appreciate your initiative, Robert. Don't get me wrong on that score. But as you're aware, this is a quasi-military outfit… uniforms, chain of command, all those sorts of things. When you're taking a department vehicle, dispatch needs to know where you're going. Don't just surprise us. If we need you, or the vehicle, we need to know how to contact you."

"Yes, sir."

"So." I held out my hand and he extended the envelope. I took it and laid it on my desk without unfastening the clasp. "When was the last time you had a decent night's sleep?"

He almost smiled. "It's been a while, sir."

I rested a hand on the manila envelope. "We don't want any mistakes. The *first* thing I want you to do is park the Blazer, hang up the keys, take your truck and go home and crash. Hug your folks, talk to the kids, and then get some sleep. We'll do the tests first thing in the morning." I stood up and thrust out my hand. His return handshake was strong. "I'm going to do the same thing. In the meantime, Baker is working graveyard. He understands the deal with Bailey's truck, and will keep his eyes open."

It seemed like such a logical plan, something to sleep on. The folder with the morgue's evidence stayed in my locked file, and, sure enough—Robert Torrez' Chevy took him home. The Blazer stayed in the lot, freshly fueled and ready to go when needed.

My own home welcomed me with deep, dark silence. As the clock crept up on midnight, I shed boots, hat, gunbelt, radio, and all the other junk that cops lug around. I flipped the colorful bedspread to one side—a huge quilt that my eldest daughter had labored over and that my housekeeper kept wrinkle-free and inviting—and I stretched out with a sigh. I think I saw the clock tick over to 12:08. A good solid hour of sleep, and I don't know how many times the phone rang when it finally succeeded in its assault at seventeen minutes after one. I'd been home for a little more than an hour.

"Gastner," I mumbled, burying my face in the pillow.

"Damn it all to hell," Leo Bailey said by way of greeting. "You didn't tell me who owned the Dodge pickup truck you guys impounded."

"You didn't ask." I rolled onto my back.

"Do you *know?*"

"Of course we know. So what do you want at this hour of the morning?"

"Why is my brother's truck locked up in D'Anzo's yard?"

I pulled myself upright in bed and swung around until I could plant my feet on the cool saltillo tile floor.

"Les Attawene tells me that he hauled the truck in from the Broken Spur Saloon."

"Well, then that's probably right." I reached out and nudged the pack of cigarettes that rested on the nightstand, then decided against it. Caffeine first, then vitamin N.

"What's with the Sheriff's seal pasted all over the back? I had to walk all the way around the enclosure to get a look at that."

"Trespassing all the way."

"Oh, Christ. Yeah, right."

"As long as you called, pass the word along to your brother, is it? We need to talk with him."

"He's hunting those mangy pigs down in Mexico with some buddies. You know Artie Torkelson, don't you? Stuart's brother?"

"Sure." Artie and his older brother Stuart somehow managed to make a living selling Posadas County real estate, specializing in breaking up defunct ranchland.

"Him and an Army buddy. The three of them went down to Mangas it was, I think."

"So your brother and Artie Torkelson—who's the third?"

"Fella by the name of Joe Smith. I'm serious. That's his name. Lieutenant Joe Smith, I think. He's an MP or something like that. They got all the paperwork together and went south for a few days. At the same time they were going to scout out some antelope country down by Prescott's ranch. For the fall hunts. So damn," and he took a moment to suck on a cigarette. "What's the SO's interest in Cliff's truck? He miss some parking tickets or something?"

"No." I wasn't about to explain to Leo that his brother may have pranged the pickup while speeding after the teens. In all fairness, that might not have been what had happened at all. But coincidence after coincidence was piling up. If we matched the bullet fragment in Darlene Spencer's brain with any of the bullets from the stock tank, or from either of Clifton Bailey's guns, we'd have a lot more than coincidence.

"Look, Leo…let me tell you exactly what I know for sure. And then you gotta let me get some sleep. I'm about comatose here." I took a deep breath. "Your brother, if that's who it is that owns the Dodge at D'Anzo's, somehow damaged his truck. You saw the damage to the front end?"

"Sure enough."

"Well, he had it towed in to D'Anzo's, but he didn't accompany it. They tell me that he gave verbal instructions to the tow truck driver to have D'Anzo's do the repairs. But he didn't sign a work order, or leave a deposit. So they're not going to work on the truck until he returns and does the paperwork."

"Well, *that's* dumb. Of course, I never claimed that my brother was a rocket scientist, either. But it doesn't explain the Sheriff's seals, my friend."

"I've told you all I can tell you, Leo."

He exhaled a long, fart-like flapping of the lips. "Look, I'll run over and sign for the work."

"Don't bother. The truck's not moving until we release it. And that won't happen until we talk with your brother."

"You're not making sense, Sheriff. There's something else going on here."

"Be patient. If your brother happens to call you, tell him to get his ass back here."

"Like there are phones all over down in that Mexican back country. Look, you know what I'm thinkin'."

"I do?"

"Yeah, you do. That saloon is right down in that area where you say the kids were partying? They speed off and crash comin' off the interstate. My brother's on the same county road, goin' too fast, as usual. What'd you say he hit?"

"I didn't."

"Well, what *did* he hit?"

"An old stump just off the county road."

"Well, wowser. A goddamn stump. Okay, so he crashes into a stump. There's all kinds of little connecting threads floatin' around with all this." Leo Bailey may have sounded like an Midwestern redneck, but he was a perceptive newsman.

"I'll call you with an update Monday night, Leo. Have your brother call me. Or better yet, have him come see me when he gets back from Mexico." Leo grumbled something incomprehensibly profane and hung up.

I hung up and relaxed back on the bed. Stuart Torkelson, mentioned by Leo Bailey as brother to one of the hunting buddies, was one of those "pillar of the community" sorts, a man with membership in a couple service clubs, with one term under his belt on the Board of Education, and a helpful, coordinating volunteer for Toys for Tots. He judged during the local science fair, helped with 4-H, and was a stalwart member of the Church of Christ. More than once, I'd kept him company in the grand-stands during a Posadas Jaguars football game.

His brother, Arthur "Artie" Torkelson, was sort of a shaky pillar. He hit the bottle enough, but hadn't yet learned to do it in the privacy of his own home. That habit had led him to cross paths with us on a fairly regular basis.

That little link chimed in my tired brain. Several weeks before, well after midnight, Deputy Howard Bishop had helped Critter Cop Doug Posey clean up the remains of a mule deer who'd lingered in the middle of State 56 for a few seconds too long. Artie Torkelson's mammoth Ford one-ton diesel crew cab dually smacked the poor creature so hard that she was tossed a hundred yards down the road, ending up in the middle of the oncoming lanes.

Deputy Bishop was promptly on hand because he'd been parked at the intersection of County Road 14 and the state highway, partially hidden behind the state's gravel pile. From there, he could see Artie Torkelson's truck parked at the Broken Spur. The deputy had seen him leave, and pulled out to follow, intending to ticket Torkelson if the man's pickup so much as kissed the highway's dotted center line.

Fur and brains and guts blasted all over the pavement showed that Torkelson hadn't strayed from his lane, and he passed the field sobriety test, steady enough that the deputy hadn't bothered with the breathalyzer.

That deer-icide helped explain for me why Clifton Bailey—perhaps in company with his buddies—had been in the neigh-borhood of the Broken Spur Wednesday evening. They knew the place, and favored it with their patronage. No doubt, over a beer or three, Artie Torkelson had recounted his collision with wildlife.

I meandered into the kitchen and started the coffeemaker. For a long time, I leaned against the counter, watching the pot. My stomach growled, and I looked at the clock. I had three hours before Fernando Aragon would open the back door of the Don Juan de Oñate Restaurant to begin his prepping for the day. He was used to seeing me early, and never groused about the special favors. The pot gurgled and the little light came on, but I was engrossed in thought.

What if the bullet from Darlene Spencer's brain matched one of the slugs recovered from Herb Torrance's cattle tank? And by extension, what if it matched a bullet test-fired from one of Clifton Bailey's guns—either the Ruger carbine or the Ruger Super Blackhawk revolver? That was clearly the path down which we were headed.

But all of that led to another interesting question. If there was a match, who pulled the trigger? Bailey? One of his two friends? Could they have met the partying youngsters and let them have a go with one of the magnums—just the kind of rip-roaring firearm performance that would appeal to the kiddos. Maybe they'd dipped some of the empty beer cans on the rim of the tank, so that the water-filled aluminum containers would have erupted when struck by a bullet—especially one from a large-caliber gun.

And that led to a thought that raised bile in my protesting gut. How could the shooter, after hearing the ricochet whine away into the brush, *not* have been a member of the party who went looking for Darlene? Did she cry out? Had she been at the stock tank, and left the company of friends to go potty? Wouldn't someone notice when she didn't return? How could circumstances be that Darlene had simply been abandoned, to bleed out during the night?

Fitful sleep isn't much good, but fresh coffee helped me grab a few winks until, at five a.m., I forced myself out of bed, showered, shaved, and found fresh clothes. At five-thirty I was checked in with dispatch and parked at the Don Juan de Oñate. The restaurant didn't open until seven, but no matter.

"Breakfast burrito, green, sour cream, all the trimmings," Fernando sang when he saw me open the screen door into the kitchen. I didn't recognize the tune, but he had a good, operatic voice.

"I love ya," I said, nodding.

"Coffee's ready. Right there at the island. You know where it is. Help yourself." He looked hard at me. "Tough night, eh? In fact, this has been a tough couple of days, no?"

"Yep."

"How about an egg on top of that?"

"You bet. Two would be even better." I skirted around him, giving him a paternal pat on the rock-hard muscle of his shoulder.

"Terrible thing," he said. I knew what he was talking about, so I just nodded. "Too many, too young. *Muy trágico.*"

The screen door opened and Aileen, Fernando's daughter, entered, and favored me with a huge smile. This father-daughter combination was quite a contrast with the pair down in the southern corner of the county at the Broken Spur. Aileen was stout, damn-near burly, with short black hair and a sweet face—she looked more like her mother, Adeline, who would arrive at seven.

"Bobby's out in the parking lot," she informed me.

"Bobby?"

"Okay, *Dreamboat Bobbie,*" she corrected. I recalled Carmen D'Anzo's expression when she greeted the deputy and me at the car dealership and offered coffee. I wondered how many other fair damsels in Posadas were going to be breathlessly following Robert Torrez' career, hoping that he'd direct a "yep" at them. "I told him to come in and have some breakfast, but he said he's already eaten."

"Yeah, right. A bowl of cereal, at best. Let me go get him."

Sure enough, Torrez' pickup was parked next to my unit, the dome light on as he read something in his notes. He looked up as I approached.

"We have a meeting inside," I said.

He looked puzzled.

"Look, I have things I need to tell you. And I can't face a day without a decent breakfast. Come on. I'm buying."

It's a challenge to order a monosyllabic breakfast, but Aileen came to the deputy's rescue.

"You want the same, Handsome?" She nodded at my as-yet-empty place setting.

"Yep." He blushed. Robert Torrez actually blushed.

"Red or green?"

"Christmas, thanks," which meant green on the inside, with red adorning the top…or vice versa, chef's choice.

With coffee poured, I leaned forward, elbows on either side of the cup. "Interesting calls last night. Leo Bailey called twice… once to ask what the commotion was over at D'Anzo's. One of his neighborhood spies saw all the lights, and actually saw fit to call Leo in the goddamn middle of the night, while the tip was hot. Apparently Leo didn't buy the explanation that I gave him, and went over to check for himself. He recognized his brother's truck. A brother out of Kansas. That's where his family is from originally."

"Whoa." Torrez' eyebrows shot up.

"Mr. Clifton Bailey, from Fort Riley, Kansas, is indeed Leo Bailey's younger brother."

Torrez looked off across the room. "So what was Bailey doin' down in the canyon?"

"Well, we don't know for sure that he *was* in Bender's Canyon. In all likelihood, we can place his truck on County 14 at the smashed stump, although that's going to take some labwork to do, and we can for sure place him at the Broken Spur, with corroboration from a strong witness."

I leaned back as the burritos arrived. Aileen was finished with the deliveries and casting not-so-furtive looks at the deputy. She didn't try to engage him in conversation—maybe because I was present, or more likely because she knew what kind of answers she'd get.

When she'd finished topping off the coffee and left, I added, "And that's all. So far. I didn't tell Leo anything else. But he's a smart guy, Robert. *He* sees a connection."

For a moment we ate in silence. Whatever bowl of cereal the deputy had started his day with, it hadn't made a dent in his appetite.

"Do you know how to use our sophisticated bullet trap?" That earned a shadow of a smile.

"I guess."

"Then when we're done here, let's do that." He ate a little faster.

Chapter Twenty-one

Our "forensics lab," a laboratory if one had a finely honed imagination, was a low-ceilinged concrete basement room sharing floor space with our darkroom for black-and-white work. The heart of our ballistics lab was a much-used stereoptic microscope we'd purchased for ten bucks during a Posadas Municipal Schools junque sale. One eyepiece was held securely with a carefully molded piece of duct tape, and the coarse focus knob lost track of the teeth now and then. But the main lenses were not bad. We didn't need the unit often, because far better labs—both State Police and FBI—were readily available to us.

Torrez laid out a series of photos, and placed the spent bullet removed from Darlene Spencer's brain on one print of the probable ricochet strike. The photo blowup clearly captured the damage from the bullet strike. The bullet had hit the galvanized cross member that secured the spokes from sail to hub, coming in at a sharp angle from down below. It had blown one of the spokes free and then whined off, looking for another target.

The damage to the bullet that had hit Darlene was sharp-edged, not neatly mushroomed. Torrez grunted something, and moved the bullet a little.

"Could have," he said.

"There's no neat mushroom there," I added.

"Nope. It hit somethin' sharp, like that," and he tapped the photo, "before flyin' on."

A plastic evidence bag held an assortment of bullets from Herb Torrance's cattle tank, collected by both Torrez and myself. He selected one of the larger ones with a moderately mushroomed tip, the sort of results I'd expect to see after the projectile punched through the thin steel wall of the tank, then was cushioned to a stop by the water.

The base of the ricocheted bullet—the Darlene Spencer bullet—was remarkably undamaged, the rifling marks clear for almost a quarter inch toward the severely deformed nose. When it had hit the windmill—if that's what it hit first—the sharp metal of the windmill's sail apparatus had cleaved off a ragged slice of the bullet's nose. On one side, the undamaged marks extended up the bullet as far as the cannelure, that knurled ring around the bullet that provides some grip when the bullet is crimped in the case.

Torrez placed the two slugs butt to butt on the microscope's wide viewing platform, and then, after adjusting the eyepieces, used a dental pick to rock the bullets this way and that. His large hands managed the slender pick as if he were a dental school graduate. The grooves in the bullets, cut by the carbine's sharp lands, carried signature marks.

He selected the more powerful of the two objectives, and fiddled with the focus some more. Then more dental pick adjustment. With a patience I didn't know he possessed, he worked the bullet from the water tank a full revolution, matching its grooves with the one clear imprint on Darlene's slug. And then back again.

My back was starting to scream, and I straightened up and arched my spine, to the accompaniment of loud snappings and poppings. I watched as Torrez placed the pick on the counter, and then clasped his hands behind his back, staring at the image.

"Huh," he said finally, and up came the dental pick again. After another careful adjustment, he straightened up. "See what you think." I was amused that he held onto the pick, as if making sure that I didn't disturb the arrangement.

The FBI lab is proud of showing perfect images when those images are used to support testimony in court—the Feds have the equipment to do so, including photomicrographs made with pricey comparison microscopes that have twin stages, a pair of identical objectives, and a comparison eyepiece—in addition to the photographic apparatus. All of those bells and whistles allow the images of the two bullets to be merged perfectly, butt to butt, so comparisons can be made.

What Torrez was trying to do was make a ballistic match using garage sale junk. On top of which, we had no way to make a photograph of the results.

Still, I could see that the striations left by the gun's rifling on the two bullets could be aligned to appear, as an FBI tech would gloat, "collinear"…the markings of both the lands and grooves in the barrel leaving their characteristic marks on the soft palette of the bullets' brass jackets. I was willing to wager that the bullet from the stock tank had come from the same gun as the bullet in Darlene's brain—not one hundred percent sure, but a good bet. Good bets don't work so well in court.

"I think we have step one," I said. Torrez actually smiled—a full, beaming smile that showed teeth most Hollywood types would pay zillions to match. "Most important at the moment—did you already measure the diameter of these?" I think that I could tell the difference between a forty-four bullet and a forty-five, if both were lying side-by-side in my hand, even though the difference was a mere twenty-two thousandths. But again—court would make its own demands.

"Four-thirty," he said without hesitation. "I measured just ahead of the base upset."

"Point four three zero," I said. "And that is…"

"The bullet diameter of most factory-made forty-four magnum or forty-four special ammo."

"*That's the secret,*" I almost said. "*Ask you something about guns, and we get full, complete sentences in response…*"

Instead, I asked, "Do you own a forty-four?"

"Yep."

"Did your little brother enjoy shooting with you?"

"Sure." The memory brought a flash of anguished memory to his face.

I nodded. "I think we're close enough to establish probable cause to take a much closer look at the two guns from Clifton Bailey's truck. We need to pick them up, do a tank fire, and compare." I held up a hand. "And no matter what we find out, or *think* we've found out, no court in the world is going to accept this rinky-dink arrangement for official comparisons. When we're done, the whole kit and caboodle gets FedExed to the FBI. Then we get a comparison we can use—one that'll stand up to scrutiny in court."

"Okay." He actually sounded a little bit excited.

I looked down at the bullets lying under the microscope. "Too many unanswered questions, Robert."

"Like who pulled the trigger."

I looked at him in surprise. "That's exactly right. When Alan Perrone examined the three accident victims, he didn't perform NAA tests, or even the old-fashioned paraffin tests…there was no reason to expect that the test for gunshot residue might be necessary."

The deputy grimaced again. "The NAA ain't going to show anything this long after."

"If the gun's *owner* pulled the trigger—if he shot the windmill—that's one thing. Suppose that was Clifton Bailey…or either of his two buddies. But just as possible is that the kids were there, and he hands the forty-four to one of them and says, 'Here, give 'er a whirl.' Big gun, big report, big recoil. The expression on their faces would be worth seeing. And see, that could have been any one of the three. We only have evidence of one ricochet. All the other holes were through and through the sails."

Torrez squinted at the microscope, deep in thought.

"You want me to run over and pick up the guns?"

"Actually, no, I don't. I want you go run down to Regál and get a copy of the customs log page that shows dates and times for Bailey's entry into Mexico. Names, dates, times. And anything else either side can give us." I stopped at the sound of footsteps on the old wooden stairway down to our basement darkroom and lab. In a moment, Sheriff Eduardo Salcido appeared, holding the railing tightly with one hand.

He regarded Bob Torrez. "So how are you doing?"

"I'm okay."

The sheriff nodded thoughtfully, and listened attentively while I filled him in. When I finished with the whole recitation, he shook his head, still regarding the specimens under the microscope. For a moment, he chewed on an errant strand of his mustache. Finally, he looked up at Robert Torrez. "This is good for you, *chavalo.*" Torrez didn't blink at the familiarity. To the sheriff, Bobby Torrez was still a kid, a youngster.

"It's good for you to see that it doesn't matter what the people in the town tell you. Or what gossip you hear." He waited patiently, giving the young man time to respond. After a moment or two, when Torrez said nothing, Salcido smiled at me. "Tell me where I'm wrong." The smile left his face, replaced by a painful frown. "If it turns out that Darlene was killed by a ricochet—just a fluke," and he accented that last word as if it were spelled *floook,* "no crime has been committed, no? Is that what you're thinking now?"

"If Clifton Bailey or his friends *knew* that the girl was hurt, and left the scene without rendering first aid, or even calling for help, or failing to report an incident, I'm sure the district attorney would want to think of something. *Especially* since there's some evidence that the girl lay there all night. She didn't die until yesterday morning—maybe shortly before we got there."

The sheriff looked skeptical, so I added, "On top of that, the damages from vandalizing a windmill and tank are easily more than a thousand dollars. That means Darlene was injured…and then died during, or as a result of, the commission of a property damage felony. Not to mention all the other crap—influence and contributing, unsafe shooting…blah,blah, blah."

Salcido mulled that over for a moment. "That was the direction I was hoping you'd take it, Bill." He jabbed a finger toward the microscope. "That's going to the FBI lab, no?"

"ASAP," I said. "What we see here is just enough to give us some guidance, nothing more."

"I like that," Salcido said. "Before we land on somebody with both feet, we want to be sure." His gaze swept around the bare, dungeon-like room. "What's Leo going to say, you think?"

"I really don't care what he thinks. How he handles it is his call."

Salcido nodded. "I'm meeting with Schroeder this afternoon. He wants an update. He wants to know what direction you're taking this. Do you want in on that party?"

"What time?"

"He says two o'clock. That probably means three." Salcido laughed abruptly. "He's more *mañana* than I am."

I turned to Torrez. "You, too. I wasn't there for the Luminol photo session, you were. And I sure as hell didn't climb up on that damn windmill." I stepped around him and gathered up the photos, putting the close-up of the scarred windmill sail on top before handing them to Salcido. He examined them over the top of his glasses.

"And then," and he made a straight out jab with his hand, then cutting it sharply to the left. "It ricochets, and off she goes."

"I think so, sir." Torrez sounded a bit more cautious. Maybe it was just those four stars on Salcido's collar.

"And Perrone thinks so, too." The sheriff handed the photos back to the deputy. "Did you talk to Herb about taking that fan off the windmill?" He grimaced. "That's going to be a job, you know. But if we ever go to trial, it'll look good in court. Otherwise, half of the jurors won't know what you're talking about."

"Of course," I said. "If we have to do that, we've got a deputy who knows how to use the county's cherry picker. And Sergeant Garcia will have the photos from the Luminol session later today, along with the documentation of the guns. I'm headed that way to pick them up right now."

"And all this time," Salcido mused, "this Bailey character is having the time of his life down in Old Mexico, sticking arrows in the pigs." He looked hard at me. "If Leo gives you a hard time, refer him to me."

"He'll be all right."

Salcido hooked his arm through mine. "Take a minute." He started toward the stairway, and I followed. Clear of the basement, he headed right down the hall to his office.

"How's the kid doing?"

"Torrez is handling things just fine."

"He's keeping his mind on his work?"

"Appears to be, Eduardo. I couldn't ask for more."

"Keep the reins very, very tight, my friend. Very tight." His phone rang, but he ignored it. "Remember that at the moment, he has no background to fall back on. No experience to guide him. My biggest fear is that he's running on raw emotion, you know? If it turns out that all this is something more than just a tragic accident, they're—whoever *they* are this week, no?—they're going to want to see justice done. With enough community pressure, it's easy to make mistakes. Bobby is working inside this monsoon of grief right now. He's going to want to pin all this on somebody. You," and he stabbed a finger at me, "you and me do our best to make sure that we do what's right."

"Absolutely."

"Take your time and do everything just right. What's the kid going to do now?"

"He's going to touch bases with the border office in Regál. Their log will show the names, dates, times…all that sort of thing, for when the pig hunters went down to Mexico. We know what time Les Attawene picked up Bailey's damaged truck at the Spur. We know that Bailey and his friends couldn't have crossed into Mexico before six a.m. That gives us some work to do. They may have stayed at the inn, or they may have stayed with relatives. I need to narrow that down. All of that time, we were busy with the crash down at the interstate, and its aftermath. We didn't even find the girl until the next morning. By that time, Bailey may have heard what happened. He may have heard about the three kids."

Salcido linked his hands together as if they were doors closing. "That's good. But let me ask you this...why not just have
Customs and Immigration send you a fax with all that information? Isn't that easier?"

"We could do that. But Torrez needs the face time. Right
now, he's in sort of a monosyllabic mode. I want him to meet
with officers face-to-face. Ask questions. See what they remember
about Mr. Bailey and his buddies."

Salcido pondered that, and finally gave it a nod. "What do
you want me to do?"

"At this point, nothing. You have the rest of the county to look
after. By this afternoon, I should have an update for the DA. For
one thing, we'll have the bullet comparison for him. Granted,
it'll be our own amateur hour version, but it'll give us support."

"That's if they match, my friend."

"True enough. If they don't match...well, I don't know.
Maybe one of Bailey's friends has a forty-four as well. As far as
we know..." and I shrugged, "there are a limited number of
people who were in Bender's Canyon at the time when Darlene
was shot." I counted fingers. "The four kids, and now it's looking
more than likely, the three adults—Bailey and his two buddies.
My gut feeling is that some permutation of those seven people
will give us the shooter."

He nodded and gently shook his fist toward the stairway to
the darkroom. "Tight rein, Bill. Keep him close. You know how
quickly things can go wrong." Then he held up one finger. "Who
went to Deming this morning with film? Was that Avelino?"

"Yes. And Torrez went down yesterday."

He nodded. "When you have a minute," and he smiled suddenly, "I need a firm estimate about how much a colorlab would
cost us. You know, one of those machines like the box stores use
that spits out color prints for you? This driving back and forth
wastes our time and our manpower, no?"

"I agree. But I'm sure they're pricey, Eduardo."

"I'm sure they are. So is our time and manpower. We'd be
ahead in this investigation if we weren't waiting on film, no?"

"Yes, we would be."

"Then…no, you're busy just now. Let me do this. I'll speak with Avelino and see what he wants. Then I'll work up a proposal." He nodded with satisfaction. "That's what I'll do."

The sheriff went back downstairs to talk with Torrez, and I took that opportunity to drive out and secure the two guns from Clifton Bailey's truck. I had hoped to duck in and out of D'Anzo's unnoticed, but Carmen caught me red-handed.

"No word yet," she said as she approached across the parking lot. She pushed her dark glasses up into her thick hair and stood with her back to the sun as she unlocked the boneyard fence. "There's been a string of drive-bys who want to look at this truck."

"They can look all they want, as long as they stay outside the fence."

"Just this morning, I've heard from four different people about Darlene Spencer. Such a sad thing. Everybody is talking about it."

"Sometimes that can be a help, Carmen."

I unlocked the camper window and lowered the tailgate. I wasn't about to duplicate Bob Torrez' coordinated hop up in the truckbed, and Carmen must have noticed my hesitation.

"Can I climb up in there for you, sir?" I couldn't help regarding her sylph-like figure.

"I'd appreciate that, but…" I shook my head. "I need to do this." She looked perplexed. "If some lawyer asks you if you handled the guns, you truthfully need to be able to say no." I grinned as I hoisted my carcass butt-first onto the tailgate and then swung my legs up. "The law is a pain in the ass sometimes."

After unlocking things and making out a receipt that I left in the toolbox, I took both guns in their cases, and one partial box of ammo. There were only twenty-two loaded rounds left in that box, and it seemed reasonable to assume that the fired bullets had come from there. The other five boxes were full, fifty count in each.

"You've never met the truck owner, then?" I slid out awkwardly.

"He didn't come in with the truck, no."

"Have you ever met Mr. Bailey before?"

"I haven't. I've been practicing putting on my most innocent face for when he shows up." She grinned, more than a little apprehension tempering the expression.

"Nine one one," I said sternly. "That's the first thing you do. Nine one one."

"That's easy to remember."

"Yep. Nine one one. That's before you even talk with him or unlock the boneyard gate. Just between you and me, the owner of this truck is Leo Bailey's younger brother. Leo might be with him. And have you ever met Artie Torkelson? Stuart's brother? We're told that Clifton Bailey may be in Artie's company. Stay on your toes. I'm suggesting that if you see any of those fellows, you contact us. Do not give out any information."

She puffed her cheeks out, then said, "I have to tell you, Sheriff. This whole thing is making me very, very nervous."

"That's good. That means you'll be very, very careful. And you and Rick remember." I made a zipper motion with my fingers over my mouth. "Lose lips sink ships." She smiled at that and made a zipping motion of her own. I gathered up guns and ammo and secured them in a black evidence bag, then stowed them in the trunk of my car.

"PCS, three ten."

"Go ahead, three ten." Gayle Sedillos was working dispatch days for the next two weeks, and I liked her clipped, efficient style. Just twenty-one years old, she was turning out to be a quick study.

"PCS, three ten is clear D'Anzo's. I'm ten eight."

"Ten four, three ten."

Posadas Properties was just down the street, behind Posadas State Bank. I took a moment and caught up my log, then told Gayle where I was going. The sky was achingly bright, the sun trying its best to peel the paint off parked cars. I parked on the street that paralleled Pershing Park off Bustos, finding some partial shade under the park's elm trees, all of which looked as if they were on their last roots.

A gush of super-cooled air greeted me as I opened the door to the real estate office. The receptionist awarded me with a wide smile, charming from the nose down. But her eyes were like blue chips of ice. That's one trouble with a small town. Everybody's little secrets are there for the picking. I knew that Sylvia Styles, not yet twenty-four years old, already had one marriage, one divorce, and one charge of domestic violence behind her. Looking at her neat, trim figure and tiny stature, it's hard to imagine that she had broken her ex-husband's nose, fractured his left collarbone, and wrecked his right knee so badly that he was on crutches for a month. She handled a mean golf club. After that temper tantrum, he had divorced her, and taken custody of the two Styles children.

Maybe she was genuinely happy now—it was hard for me to tell. I had been the arresting officer for her golf outing, and she was slow to forgive—even though Judge Hobart had resisted the temptation to jail her shapely little butt. Instead, he'd put her under a restraining order to protect Jake and the kids, and ordered a few hours of community service.

"Ms...." I noticed that her name plaque said *Sylvia Bohanan*. Her husband had dumped her, and she'd dumped the name. "Ms. Bohanan, I need to talk with Stuart."

"Oh," she said with regret. "You know what? He went to an early lunch with Leo Bailey."

"At the Don Juan?"

"Always the Don Juan," she said, rolling her eyes.

"I'll catch up with him there. Thanks."

"You're welcome." The smile reappeared, genuine this time, no doubt because I was leaving.

After the refrigerated air, the heat of a June morning felt delightful. It was six blocks west to the Don Juan at the corner of Twelfth and Bustos. Walking would have done me good, but I needed my office with me. That was my excuse. As I neared the parking lot, I saw Torkelson's massive Ford 4x4—giant trucks ran in the family, apparently. Glossy black from stem to stern, even the grill and cowcatcher on the front were black. Parked next to it was Leo Bailey's little Honda. Evidently, the newspaper publisher had made it back from Deming promptly. Maybe that meant no problems with the newspaper's latest edition. I was curious to see the spin he gave the story.

Chapter Twenty-two

The Don Juan was dark and cool, and Desireé Aragón, one of Fernando's nieces, greeted me. Like all the other Aragóns I'd met, she was shaped from the pro-wrestler mold. And, like all the others, she had been perfectly endowed in the personality department. The clock above the ugly velvet portrait of Don Juan de Oñate, one of Spain's least politically correct explorer/conquerors, said that lunch hour was still an hour away. The lunch crowd would start to filter in shortly before noon, but even so, my favorite table, in the back and partially hidden by the waitress station, was occupied.

Desireé spotted me and held up a menu. As I strode through the empty restaurant, I recognized the back of Stuart Torkelson's head, his bouffant hairdo perfectly in place. Leo Bailey, ever observant, saw me enter and beckoned me over with a minimal flexing of the fingers.

"Early lunch for you?" Desireé asked with that perfect, welcoming smile.

"I'm not sure yet," I said. "How about just coffee for now?"

"Perfect."

As she retreated, I shook hands with both men. "Leo," I said, "I hope everything went well this morning. A folded *Posadas Register* lay under his right forearm, and he pushed it toward me by way of answer. The article on Wednesday night's crash dominated the top right corner of the front page.

The banner headline bellowed, "*Teens Killed in Rollover*," and I scanned the article quickly. Straightforward, no assumptions, no editorializing, it read like a hundred others I'd seen over the years.

Any details that might have been the least bit controversial, like the mention of high speed and possible alcohol consumption, were attributed to me. There was no mention of Orlando Torrez' possible death *before* the crash. Nor had the rumor mill given him any spin on Darlene Spencer's tragedy. As if sensing how thin was the ice on which we all were skating, the story confined itself to details of the Suburban's violent crash. There was no mention of the collision with Riley Holmes' Cadillac. That gave me a small opening.

"Fair enough," I said, handing the paper back to Leo.

"Just awful," Stuart whispered.

"You might want to know that we're currently investigating a minor collision between the kids' Suburban and another vehicle. That happened about ten miles west of here, up on the interstate." I slid my hands together. "A sideswipe that ripped off the other vehicle's driver's side mirror."

Leo scooted over and nodded at the seat. "Take a load off."

"Thanks. Anyway, that collision, just moments before the fatal crash, gives us some valuable information that we didn't have before."

"Like what?" Bailey had his notebook out, food forgotten. My coffee arrived, and I waited until the young lady retreated.

"It's the first hint that something was going on in that Suburban before the crash. We think there was a good reason why the kids were speeding. We just don't know what it was."

She hadn't retreated far. Desireé hovered just out of range, pad in hand.

"I can't, Desireé. Not today. I'll only be here a minute or two." She vanished with a smile, and I turned back to Stuart Torkelson, who up to this point hadn't volunteered a word.

"Stu, are the three hunters staying with you while they're in town?"

"The three…"

"His brother, Clifton." I nodded at Leo. "Your brother, Artie? And Lieutenant Smith? I know they're off sticking pigs in Mexico at the moment, but before and after?"

"Cliff is staying with me," Leo said.

"Okay. And the other two?"

Torkelson nodded. "Sure enough. They're at the house for a bit. I mean, not right *now*. Before they went down to the Rio Mancos country. They're scoping out some of the ranch country around here for the antelope hunts later on this fall. And then for a day or two when they get back." He smiled. "They're hoping to have a bunch of pork to process when they come back."

"They'll use O'Conner?" Jim O'Conner was the only game processor I knew, and even clean roadkills—if that wasn't an oxymoron—kept him busy. "They're just bow hunting down south, though."

Torkelson looked surprised. "Oh, God, yes. It practically takes an act of congress...*their* congress, I mean, to carry firearms across the border. Bows, no problem."

I smiled. "You aren't kidding on that score. On the occasions when I have to drive south, I stash the hardware at the BP office if I'm driving the county car. What, they left all their hardware with you before crossing over?"

"Yep. I could open a gun shop with that arsenal."

Leo Bailey was resting his head on his hand, regarding me steadily. "So what's new with the Spencer girl?" He was adept at making connections.

"Investigation continues."

His eyes narrowed just a bit. "You think my brother was down there? In the canyon?"

"I haven't heard about this," Torkelson said uneasily. "My gosh, now, Darlene? I heard about that, all right. Why would the boys be down there?"

"Good question." I could see that my cryptic answer made Torkelson uneasy.

"Stu, we need to get. Or at least, *I* do," Leo said. "Bill, good to see you. Remember Monday." Looking as if he'd been left out of the conversation, Stuart hesitated, then shook my hand as he rose.

"If I can help in any way?" His grip was clammy.

"I'll let you know. Did the guys say when they're heading back from the hunt?"

"Oh—that was sort of indefinite. But what's today? Friday? I'm thinking probably Sunday or so."

I pushed to my feet "I hope they've had good luck."

"Monday," Leo said again, and pointed a cocked finger pistol at me.

I shook his hand again. "You won't let me forget, Leo."

By the time Bob Torrez returned from Regál, I was ready for him. A quick comparison of the unfired ammo for the forty-four convinced me that the bullets in the tank and from the windmill ricochet were consistent. They were all flat-nosed bullets with the copper jacket covering everything but about an eighth of an inch up front. Apparently Cliff Bailey had been saving the hollow points for later, perhaps for something that made for better eating than galvanized steel.

I heard Torrez' heavy boots on the stairs.

"What's the news?" I asked.

He laid his notebook on the table and unfolded a photo copy of a log page. "Clifton Bailey, Arthur Torkelson, and Joe Smith crossed into Mexico at ten minutes after six *yesterday* morning. That's Thursday."

"Several hours before Darlene was found."

"Yep."

"And at that point, it's likely that she was still alive."

"Yep."

"The officers are going to keep an eye out for us?"

Torrez nodded. "Drivin' an eighty-six Ford Bronco registered to Arthur Torkelson, New Mexico tag TORQUE."

"Cute. Let's see what the bullets tell us."

Our recovery tank was a spectacularly ridiculous gadget that Sergeant Avelino Garcia had fabricated during his first year with the department. It was clumsy, awkward, time-consuming, and worked wonderfully well. Avelino had started with an eight-foot-long section of eight-inch diameter steel drill casing. The "down" end included a watertight cap held in place with four bolts passing through the cap and welded flanges on the pipe.

The "hot" end was welded closed with a three-inch hole with centering guides through which one thrust the barrel of the test weapon. The whole affair sat on sturdy channel-iron legs so that the tube rested at about a forty-five-degree angle. Filled with water, it was massively heavy. And sloppy. A rubber pad hung down over the shooting hole, in an effort to stop some of the backsplash. It almost worked.

Unfortunately, to recover the bullet required emptying the pipe into the floor drain. Since we tested at most two or three guns a year for ballistic matches, the inconvenience didn't matter much.

"Let's do the handgun first," I said, and watched as Torrez readied the tank. He eased the heavy muzzle of the Super Black-hawk onto the tank's barrel guides, and carefully estimated the barrel to tube alignment. Even with earphones, the sound was convincingly loud. And the backsplash soaked the deputy's right arm. He unbolted the end, letting the water drain carefully so that the projectile didn't go into the sewer as well.

The bullet was pristine. Torrez had held the gun steady and centered so that the bullet had never kissed the side of the pipe during its journey. After dabbing the test bullet dry, he spent a long time arranging it on the microscope stand, butt to butt with the bullet recovered from Herb Torrance's stock tank.

When he straightened up and turned to me, his grin was huge. He stood back and let me peer.

"Bingo. Easy match. Even I'm convinced."

"Yep." He looked at me with interest. "No point in doing the rifle, then."

"A negative result is useful evidence," I said. "I picked the handgun to go first because I guessed that's what kids would like to shoot," I said. "The little rifle is just that. A rifle. It doesn't have the macho pizzazz of the big handgun. I figure if you offer 'em side by side, the kids are going to choose the handgun every time. You said yourself that Orlando liked to shoot your forty-four. So…" I looked at the comparison again. "The pond bullet matches the windmill bullet. And now the test slug matches as well. Which means, if we're right, that a bullet from this Ruger Super Blackhawk, the gun taken from Bailey's truck, is the bullet that killed Darlene Spencer."

Torrez' reply to that was a single, whispered groan, and he was no longer smiling. I didn't know what he was thinking, of course—other than that there was the possibility that his eager little brother had fired the fatal bullet.

Chapter Twenty-three

We tested the rifle amid another impressive bang and splash, and it was interesting to see, under the stereo microscope, how dissimilar bullets from two different guns can really be. Even though both guns were Rugers, perhaps from the same factory with the same barrel rifling machines, the imprints scored into the brass hide of bullets were as individual as fingerprints.

"If we're right, we have three witnesses to what happened in Bender's Canyon," I said. "That's where this leaves us. Bailey, Torkelson, and Smith."

"Why'd they leave?"

"Exactly," I said. "You'd think that if three adults came upon an injured girl, they'd do something to help. They could have bundled her into their truck, taken her in to the hospital. Or at least to the Broken Spur to wait for an ambulance. But what did they do…or at least, what did *Bailey* do, assuming that he was the one driving his own Dodge when it slammed into that stump? What was he doing out there on County Road 14?"

Torrez fell silent, as was his habit. He stared at the dusty ceiling.

"Guesses?" I prompted.

The deputy sighed. "Chasin' the kids, maybe. Maybe they saw something and took off."

"Saw what?"

"If they saw Bailey with Darlene…"

"Saw them and came to all the wrong conclusions?"

"Could be."

"Darlene was not carrying a wallet that day," I said. "She wasn't driving, so maybe she wasn't in the habit." Torrez looked sideways at me. "No wallet, no address. How would Bailey know who the girl *was*? Where she lived?"

"Don't matter if he's just takin' her to the emergency room."

"True enough. But I don't buy it. To me, the most logical answer is that the three men didn't know Darlene was down there. Never saw her. Maybe they assumed that when the kids left, she went with them. I can understand the kids finding her, and panicking. I can see that. Double panic, *especially* if Orlando was starting to have troubles with the asthma attack. But I'd expect a little more from three adults—especially when one of them is a lieutenant in the MP's."

"You guys finished shaking the building?" Sergeant Lars Payson stood at the base of the stairs.

"We are. We have a successful comparison. A real preliminary one, but it gives us something."

"Not with that junk, you don't," Payson said skeptically, looking at the pipe apparatus.

"The FBI will confirm it. This gives us a place to start."

Payson looked skeptical. "The DA is here, if you want to meet with him."

"We do."

"I kinda shifted the patrol schedule around. Sisneros is staying central in case something blows up."

"Good. We're at a point where a BOLO should be issued for Clifton Bailey and his pals. They're our primary persons of interest. The Border Patrol has been alerted as well."

"I'll see to that," Payson said.

With the firearms wiped off and secured in their cases, we followed Payson upstairs to the small conference room. District Attorney Dan Schroeder had adopted his usual posture, leaning far back in his chair, one arm looped over the back, the other hand fiddling with a gold ballpoint pen. He was in conversation with Sheriff Salcido, who sat with his hands folded on the table in front of him, looking for all the world as if *he'd* done something wrong.

"Thanks for taking the time, gents." Schroeder flashed his most sincere politician's smile. Sergeant Payson closed the door of the conference room, and we went through the handshaking ritual before taking our seats.

Schroeder ran both hands through his well-oiled blond hair, leaving finger tracks. The pen never left his hand. "Sheriff Salcido has filled me in on most of the details." He straightened the legal pad in front of him and surveyed the chicken scratchings on it. "Let's just take my concerns in order, then, working backward. Tell me if I'm off base.

"Number one," and he tapped the pad with his pen, "we don't know why the excessive speed just before the crash." He tapped the paper again. "We have some reason to believe that something—we don't know what—was going on in the vehicle before the crash that may, or may not, have contributed.

"Number two…the driver was alcohol-impaired. One passenger was apparently not impaired. The third passenger was in the throes of a reaction of some sort, perhaps a combination of asthma meds and alcohol. There is supposition that that passenger may actually have been deceased before the crash." He glanced up at us, a silent, unreactive audience.

"Okay. Number three." I glanced to one side and saw that Payson was taking notes in his elegant architect's printing. "It appears that the youngsters had been down in Bender's Canyon. A fourth youngster, Darlene Spencer, whom we assume was in their company at some point in time, was also in the canyon, and her body was found the next day in the general vicinity of Herb Torrance's windmill and stock tank number two. The medical examiner says death resulted from a single bullet wound through the eye to the forebrain with massive hemorrhage."

Schroeder heaved a sigh. "Number four. *Preliminary* evidence shows that three other men were also present in the canyon, *perhaps* concurrent with the four children. That evidence suggests that all present were in some way or another involved with vandalizing both a stock tank and windmill owned by Herbert Torrance with repeated gunshots from a variety of firearms, and that the bullet that struck Darlene Spencer was fired during that time, perhaps ricocheting off the windmill structure." He stopped reading and picked up one of the photographs that Deputy Torrez had taken—the close-up of the windmill's sail. "Wow." He examined the photo for a moment, then dropped it back on the table.

"Number five. A vehicle belonging to Clifton Bailey, currently domiciled in Fort Riley, Kansas, struck a juniper stump off County Road 14, *perhaps* while pursuing, or following, the youngsters who had departed the scene in their Suburban." He looked up at me. "We don't actually know yet why Bailey was on County Road 14, do we?"

"No, sir."

He nodded, and waited for me to elaborate, and when I didn't, nodded again and continued on. "Number six. No effort was made by any parties present to remove the injured Darlene Spencer from the canyon location, nor to summon first aid for her. According to the medical examiner, it's *probable* that Darlene Spencer survived through much of the night, although most likely comatose." He paused. "And thank God for being comatose.

"Number seven. Do we have a number seven?" He flipped a page of his legal pad. "Yup. Number seven. It is not known who fired the shot that ricocheted, striking Miss Spencer. Evidence suggests that she had left the immediate area in order to find a spot to relieve herself, and was struck during that time.

"Number eight. At this point, the District Attorney's office is interested in pursuing charges of felony property vandalism," and he held up fingers to count them off, "reckless endangerment with a firearm of a child leading to death, failure to report an incident, and…" he looked up at us, letting his gaze come to rest on Robert Torrez' impassive face, "whatever else I can dream up." He tossed the legal pad on the table and straightened up, clasping his hands together in front of his face. "What am

I missing? We have four of our community's best and brightest gone. What am I missing?"

"What *we're* missing is any information from Clifton Bailey, whom we feel was clearly involved somehow."

"Somehow," Schroeder interjected. "We're really in the dark about what the hell actually happened down in that canyon."

"That's correct. The ballistics tests we just completed down-stairs lead us to believe that one of Mr. Bailey's guns—one that we recovered following the search of his truck—is the weapon that fired the fatal bullet."

Schroeder wrote diligently on his pad for a moment before looking up. "The FBI will confirm that?"

"Yes."

"You're being very careful to avoid saying that Clifton Bailey is the person who *fired* the fatal shot."

"Yes."

"Yes, he did, or yes, you're being careful?"

"I'm being careful. It appears that any of *six* people could have fired it. Everyone *except* Darlene Spencer, of course."

"Ah." He rested his chin on his hands. "So…what resources do we need that we currently don't have?"

"Ballistics tests from the FBI to support our own conclusions. Those are being arranged. We need to talk with Mr. Bailey and his two companions, who, as far as we know, are still in Mexico on a pig hunt. At the moment, those three are our only witnesses."

"Do you expect any others to come forward?"

"Not for the actual shooting incident. Reuben Fuentes prob-ably heard the crash into the stump that involved Mr. Bailey's truck."

"Probably. But he didn't witness it?"

"No."

He grimaced. "Herb never talked to any of these individu-als? The kids or any of the three adults? I mean, he's right down there in the thick of it."

"No."

"Have you been in touch with Mexican authorities? I mean, is that an avenue for us? You have contacts down there, I know."

"Yes, we do."

"But…" he prompted.

"If we go that route, we're talking all the bureaucratic red tape that we're all so familiar with. Official requests, along with a whole litany of reasons, then extradition proceedings, then this, then that." I saw the crow's-feet deepen at the corners of Schroeder's close-set eyes.

"What do you suggest, then?"

"The only newspaper coverage so far could lead the three to believe that we're not looking beyond the kids to place blame for Miss Spencer's death. The metro papers have just picked up the initial skeleton story from the *Register,* so that helps. They *might* think, at this point, that they're in the clear. And you know, there's every possibility that the three don't even *know* about Miss Spencer's death." I held up both hands in surrender. "They may never have seen the body, they might be totally in the dark about what happened. And now they're hunting in a relatively remote area of Mexico, down by the Rio Mancos, so they may not have had word."

"What about Leo?"

"Leo Bailey knows we're looking at a connection. He knows we searched his brother's truck. What else he's been able to figure out, or what he plans to do about it, is anybody's guess."

"He's not involved in any way, though?"

"We don't think so."

"Could he have tipped off his brother?"

"In Mexico? I don't think so."

"I think," Sheriff Salcido said slowly, stretching out the word into a sing-song, "that it's best to meet these men at the border, no? We hear that they're probably coming back Sunday." He shrugged. "If that's the case, it's faster to do that, rather than trying to run circles around all the bureaucratic hurdles that the Mexican government will throw up, even with Lieutenant Naranjo's help." The sheriff glanced across at me, eyebrows raised.

"A good point," I said. "Tomás Naranjo has been most cooperative in the past. I think he should be advised, but that's as far as it should go, at this point. We also are issuing a BOLO for all three men. So any border point is going to be on the watch. They'll take them into custody for us. On our side of the fence."

"Does Bailey have a family?" Schroeder asked. "Besides his brother?"

"I have no idea. I've never talked with him. I've never talked to Leo about that."

"If he has no family, it may not be to his advantage to return to the U.S.," Schroeder said. "At least, certainly not at the Regál crossing."

"A BOLO should snare him, no matter where or when," I said.

"Maybe." Schroeder didn't sound particularly enthusiastic, but he nodded agreement. "I'll be glad when all three are in custody, and are answering questions."

He gathered his papers and looked at each one of us. "Any questions for me?"

"I don't think so," I said.

"Deputy Torrez," Schroeder said, "this has to be a hard time for you. I'm truly sorry—and I know that doesn't count for much. But rest assured that all of this will be resolved somehow. And I know that doesn't bring your brother and sister back, or Chris Browning, or Darlene Spencer. Or my old friend Willis Browning." He looked hard at me. "Enough's enough. Be careful about how all of this goes down."

I caught Sergeant Payson at the door. "Will you work with Torrez to get the bullets packed up for shipment to the FBI lab? They need to go out today. I don't think he's ever done that before, and you can give him pointers, help him talk to the right people. I'll take care of the BOLO." I felt a hand on my elbow, and turned to see Sheriff Salcido. He nodded his head toward his office, and I joined him there.

"You'd tell me if you were entertaining any plans to head down into Mexico," he said softly.

"Of course. I'm not. I don't see what that would accomplish. I'm not going down there to chase three guys through the brush."

"I'm glad to hear that." He nodded as if to say, "That's that."

Chapter Twenty-four

I left the office an hour or two before six, and rendezvoused at the Don Juan with Sergeant Lars Payson and Officer Doug Posey of the New Mexico Game and Fish Department. I had missed my chance with lunch when I met with Stuart Torkelson and Leo Bailey, so it seemed high time for a proper dinner. Lars had no particular home life, having split with his wife a dozen years before. They'd had no kids, and neither had ever remarried.

At Posadas Jaguars basketball games, Lars and his ex still sat with each other and shared popcorn.

Doug Posey, just twenty-three years old, was a swinging bachelor—not that there was a whole lot of swinging going on in Posadas County. One of his favorite hobbies was trying to talk me into going with him on a fishing trip to Alaska. I'd agreed to do that when Alaska eliminated their mosquito, no-see-um, and horsefly populations.

Both Payson, who was then forty-two, and the four-years-removed-from-being-a-teenager Doug Posey, were good dinner company, taking my mind off the awful events of the past few days.

Sheriff Eduardo Salcido was over visiting with Modesto and Ariana Torrez. Deputy Torrez had gone off duty at four that afternoon, but when I left the office shortly after five, he was still on the premises.

Deputy Tom Mears was working swing, and because this was a Saturday night, the shift sergeant, Howard Bishop, was also working, Mears was working the area around María, famous for its active saloon whose back door was mere yards from the barbed-wire border fence. Sergeant Bishop, never particularly quick to get rolling unless it was lights-and-siren time, was working in his cubbyhole of an office, just down the hall from dispatch. State Police Officer TC Markham was up on the interstate, keeping tourists and truckers honest.

My own portable radio was sitting on the table beside me at the Don Juan. We had just ordered, and Posey had launched into a tale of his latest arrest featuring a Texas man who didn't think that he needed a license to shoot feral hogs. Posey patiently explained that the little guy he'd blown practically to bits with a .338 LaPua was a *javelina,* not a feral hog. I didn't hear how the tale ended, because Ernie Wheeler's voice interrupted. Wheeler was my dispatcher of choice for a busy weekend swing shift.

"Three zero one, PCS. Ten twenty?"

"Three oh one is ten-ten at Madrid's," Mears replied.

"Three zero one, be advised…" and Wheeler halted his transmission. He started again after clearing his throat, finger still depressing the transmit bar. "Be advised that a civilian reports that the subjects of the BOLO are being detained in Regál at the moment."

Wheeler hadn't finished his broadcast when I was on my feet, followed closely by Payson. I dropped a twenty and a quick apology at the register, and dashed outside into the heat of late afternoon.

"PCS, three ten. Ten nine?" The 310 cranked a few times too many before it rumbled to life, leaving a gathering cloud of blue smoke as I pulled out of the parking lot.

"Three ten, we have a phone call from Gus Prescott down at the Spur. He says the guys you BOLO'd are out in the parking lot."

"That's negative on Regál? They're at the Spur?" Surely, Wheeler knew that the Broken Spur Saloon was actually eight long miles across the pass from Regál.

"Three ten, roger that."

"PCS, you said *'detained.'* Who's responded?" As far as I knew, Bishop was still in the office. Mears was in María. Even as Wheeler ruminated about that, I shot through the intersection of Bustos and Grande, turned right so hard that the Crown Vic groaned and tried to push its nose up on the sidewalk. I corrected and we headed south, Payson just yards behind me.

"We're not just sure. It was a civilian who called. No radio communication."

"Three ten and three oh three are in route," I said. "ETA twenty minutes."

That was a stretch, I knew. The Spur was twenty-six miles southwest from the interstate underpass in Posadas. If I held a steady hundred miles an hour, it would take us sixteen minutes, more or less, depending how many critters or tourists we had to avoid. With a newer car, Payson could go faster, and probably would.

A rich stink rose from the floor of my aging Crown Vic as I accelerated out of town on State 56. The oil pressure needle wavered just below center. It seemed like an eternity ago that I'd fielded questions from County Commissioner Randy Murray about the state of the Sheriff Department's fleet. Too bad he wasn't riding with me at this moment.

"Three oh three, go ahead. I've got some problems," I radioed.

"Affirmative. You're smokin' pretty good." Payson's two-year-old patrol car pulled into the left hand lane and accelerated past. A quarter mile back, Doug Posey was flogging his Chevy state truck in an effort to keep up.

"PCS, three oh one is responding. ETA forty minutes."

"Uh, roger that."

Mears would arrive in time to clean up the mess. The advantage was that if the richly complaining 310 crapped out completely, I could hitch a ride with him. Posey pulled close to my back bumper, the wiggle-waggles in his grill frantic.

"You're smokin' pretty good," he echoed as the pickup slid by.

"Ten four." I raised a hand in salute as he passed. But I wasn't giving much thought to the smoking.

The Border Patrol had assured us that they'd take Bailey and his buddies into custody when they tried to cross...but somehow, that hadn't happened. There were dozens of ways the situation could have been gone south. Someone might have come on shift who hadn't read the BOLO. Someone just forgot. Whatever. Obviously, the trio weren't being pursued by customs agents. If they had been, and were stopped at the Spur, there was no reason for Gus Prescott to call us. He would have just sat with his face in his beer, enjoying the show.

The Crown Vic seemed willing to give me eighty-five miles an hour, the rich, blue vapor trail spreading out behind. The Rio Salinas Arroyo came and went, and as the intersection with Forest Road 122 out to Borracho Springs appeared, I was coaxing maybe seventy-five out of the hemorrhaging Ford.

"PCS, three ten, three oh three is ten six Spur."

"Ten four, three oh three."

The highway passed over the Rio Guijarra arroyo, a deep cut that hadn't carried anything other than gravel in a dozen years, and I could see the flashing lights up ahead in the Spur parking lot. My approach was down to fifty miles an hour by the time I spiked the brakes and felt the hard shimmy of some other auto part announcing its resignation.

Victor's parking lot was full, but my attention was drawn to two vehicles in particular. A late model blue and white Ford Bronco with a pop-up camper hitched behind was pulled in at the side of the saloon, and angled in behind it, blocking its exit, was a regular cab 1973 Chevy pickup, sort of battered bronze in color, that I knew well. Sergeant Payson's patrol car, lights ablaze, formed a chevron with Doug Posey's state truck beside the camper unit, further blocking it in. Off to the left, Gus Prescott's pickup was flanked by two sedans, both with out-of-state plates. My attention was drawn to the bronze Chevy.

Bob Torrez hadn't been able to resist doing a little hunting of his own.

Chapter Twenty-five

The trouble with arriving at a scene with lights flashing is that those very lights can escalate an otherwise calm situation. The deputy had corralled four men. This didn't look like one of those, "Say guys, do you have a minute to chat?" moments. Still, it had been a helpful civilian who called the cops, not the deputy radioing for backup.

Torrez' audience wasn't happy, and when I saw who the moderator was, neither was I. It wasn't just four men that the deputy had collected. It was three men and Victor Sanchez. The group offered enough belligerent body English to hint that this wasn't a friendly gab fest. And predictably, Victor's stubby index finger was jabbing at the center of Deputy Robert Torrez' chest without actually making contact. The deputy may have been driving his own truck, but he hadn't gone home and changed into civilian clothes. He was in uniform.

As physically imposing as young Torrez might have been, the four-to-one odds weren't in his favor. Apparently unperturbed by his riled audience, the new deputy held a fistful of documents that he arranged on top of his aluminum clipboard.

I walked across the parking lot, taking my time to survey the men gathered around Victor Sanchez…two were on the youthful side of middle-age, but significantly overweight…both of them bruisers. The third young man looked as if he had just stepped off a military recruitment poster—neat, close-cropped pate, no facial hair, icy blue eyes and strong jaw, and shoulders so square that you could use him as a carpenter's tool.

Sometimes it's hard to pick a target on which to focus opening remarks, sometimes it's easy. In this case, Victor Sanchez did the job for me. The owner of the Broken Spur saloon was certainly turning the air blue. I suspect as each police car pulled into his parking lot in turn, the color in his face rainbowed. He pivoted just enough to glare at me as I approached, fists balled on his hips. Just on the margin between burly and fat and a head shorter than the deputy, Victor combined nasty and ugly in fair proportions.

I didn't mind Victor's motormouth, especially if he kept it leashed to the confines of his establishment. But his belligerent nonsense was clearly adding to the men's bravado.

"Someone in the saloon called us," I said. "So here we are." Now that I was present, Sergeant Payson was drifting around to peer into the windows of the Bronco, his right hand relaxed on the butt of his holstered revolver. He hummed a little tune, as if enjoying the prospect of thumping some heads. He was behind the trio, all of whom faced Torrez. Doug Posey, who looked as if he must have been somebody's teenaged son, stood directly behind the camper.

"Wasn't a bit of trouble until this kid," and Victor jerked his thumb at Deputy Torrez, "decided to show up and start throwin' his weight around." I could imagine Torrez doing that, all right. Yep. Victor turned—at least he did that—and spat with the wind. "Every time you damn guys are in the neighborhood, you cost me business. You *got* no business here. This is private property."

I'd heard this same litany from Victor a dozen times, and to his credit I would be the first to admit that the saloon owner generally solved his own troubles with the occasional hunter, cowboy, or construction worker who swam too deeply in the sauce. As Sheriff Salcido was fond of saying, with considerable admiration, "That Victor—he's quick with the frying pan." I'd seen more than one drunk prostrate on the saloon's wood floor, skull bruised by a quick bash of cast-iron.

As if inflated by support from the saloon owner, the fat guy with a pillow hanging over his belt put his hands on his hips and took his turn glowering at me. I knew well enough what he saw…an over-the-hill guy whose own avoirdupois was not in tight control, with close-cropped gray hair, thin mustache, and casual clothes. My weekend uniform included basic blue jeans and a white shirt with one Posadas County Sheriff's Department shoulder patch and my name tag over the right breast pocket. It was enough to suggest "cop," enhanced by the badge that rode on my belt between buckle and holster.

"This isn't your affair, Bud," he said. Despite the blubber, despite the fisherman's hat pulled right down until it bent his ears, I saw enough family resemblance that I pegged him as Leo Bailey's brother…same shape of skull, same deep-set ice chips for eyes, and probably the same square build before gravity took over. At the moment he was fueled with so much liquor that I could smell it on his breath. Unless they'd been working on their own stash in the Bronco, they'd crossed the border early enough to hit up the Spur for refreshment…and maybe carried a nice cargo of imported Mexican booze as well.

"Do I know you?" I asked, centering on him. I didn't like being called "Bud," but before the man could reply, Deputy Torrez extended a driver's license toward me with his left hand. He kept the heavy metal clipboard in his right hand, a handy swatter. I took the license, saw it was a Kansas issue, and turned slightly to keep the glare off the plastic.

"This is bullshit, man," Victor growled. "When you're finished with all your shit, you can get out of my parking lot. He has no right to come bargin' in my personal place of business." Mr. Gracious turned on his heel and stalked off toward the side door of the saloon—his private entrance to the kitchen.

"Mr. Clifton Bailey," I read. "Fort Riley, Kansas." It listed his weight at two hundred fifteen, a lie by about fifty pounds. He stood flat-footed now, his weight on his heels. A good push would send him rolling backward like a jelly donut. When he extended his hand for the license, I shook my head and handed it back to Torrez. The man's eyes narrowed, burying themselves in a puffy face made even more so by too much alcohol and not enough sleep. "Your brother is a little worried about you, Mr. Bailey."

"My brother?"

"Leo, our local newspaper man. I guess he's wondering how he's going to be able to keep your picture and the family name out of the newspaper. "

"Lieutenant Joseph Allen Smith," and Torrez handed me a Tennessee driver's license and a military ID as he explained, "is—was—in possession of a concealed handgun in a liquor establishment."

I looked at the license. In typical fashion, the MVD camera managed to make the handsome young fellow look like a scruffy convict. But he'd clean up okay, and in full uniform might even be impressive. Clarksville, his listed hometown, was an Army town, home of the Army's 101st. I examined the military ID. The faded vestige of my own still rode in my wallet.

Now, I was impressed. Rookie Deputy Torrez had thought to collect all the necessary paperwork. They'd apparently surrendered the documents without a fight, maybe the smartest thing they'd done all day, and that was a hopeful sign.

"What's your assignment at the base, Lieutenant?"

"Sir, Military Police, sir." He snapped the answer out and then clammed up.

"Ah. Then you know better." I could see the bottom inch of his belt holster beneath the hem of his light cotton shirt, but couldn't tell if the handgun was still in his possession.

"Yes, sir."

"You probably noticed the sign on the saloon door that warns patrons. Concealed or not, in New Mexico, it's illegal to carry firearms into a liquor establishment unless you're a law enforcement officer in pursuit of his duties." Like lunch. Or a cool break. The posted warning was required by the state, but I knew that tacking the paper to the wall was the extent of Victor's compliance.

"You fellas are lucky you weren't stopped down in Mexico. You'd still be making yourselves at home in a Mexican prison."

"Look, look," Clifton Bailey interrupted, holding up a none-too-steady but placating hand. The sudden bonhomie coincided with Lars Payson's appearance from behind the truck. Sergeant Payson stood behind Torrez, just off to one side. "We're just out here doing some camping, and some scouting for one of the fall hunts. We were down across the border camping for a little while, hunting javelina down Mancos way. We had all the right paperwork, anyway. Joe is on leave, and I guess it's fair to say that the past couple of months haven't been much of a picnic for him over in Bosnia." He tried a wry, ingratiating smile, as if I was going to melt when I heard the international trouble spot mentioned. "We're sorry about this mix-up with the gun in a bar. He's just so used to carryin' it…"

I ignored that and reached out for the next offering from the deputy.

Torrez handed me the remaining driver's license. "Mr. Arthur Edward Torkelson, far from his home in Posadas, New Mexico." I nodded at the short, porky version of Stuart Torkelson, his older brother. I could smell Artie's sweat halfway across the parking lot. His arms were crossed across his chest, the denim shirt plastered to his body in half a dozen places. He rested his elbow on the rear window frame of the camper, elbow to elbow with Bailey. The one free hand picked nervously at the rubber window frame.

I handed the licenses back to Torrez. Movement caught my eye, and I saw Victor Sanchez standing by the back corner of his saloon, just outside the kitchen door. I grinned at him and touched two fingers to my forehead. He ducked back inside.

"So," I said to the rookie deputy, "I have to wonder if these fellows have given any thought to finding designated drivers to take this fancy rig back to town."

"Attawene needs the business," Torrez said.

"Christ almighty," Bailey said. "How's that going to be…" and promptly got stuck on the next word. He burped some air and settled for "…necessary?"

"Maybe the breathalyzer will prove us wrong," I said. "But the sauce has been flowing pretty heavily here, seems to me." Torrez handed me the registration certificate for the truck, showing Torkelson as owner.

Bailey hung on a smug expression that made me want to write him a bale of tickets then and there. "We ain't *driving,*" he announced triumphantly. He tried to stand a little straighter, but misplaced a foot and staggered just enough to put a lie to anything he said. "Hell, we wasn't even *in* the vehicles when this young fella high-balls into the parking lot, raisin' all kinds of dust. Then he comes right into the saloon like he owns the place. But hell I know...he's just workin' the quota. I know how it works. He followed us inside just so he could give Joe a hard time about the gun."

"It's good that we understand each other then," I said. "Mr. Bailey, where's your vehicle?"

"Up at that flea trap motel in Posadas."

I turned and regarded him for a moment. "You sure?"

"Hell, yes, I'm sure." His eyes skated back and forth like pinballs.

"You think D'Anzos have finished repairing it already?"

"Ah, shit, man," Artie Torkelson muttered dejectedly.

"Mr. Bailey, let's cut to the chase. As you probably know, we're investigating an unfortunate incident that started right in this neighborhood a day or two ago. We had some kids partying, and one thing led to another. Next thing we know, they've driven off the interstate up in town, and collided with the overpass support pillar."

I could see from his wandering eyes that he was having trouble following me. "Now, it seems that sometime that same evening, someone managed to run into a stump along County Road 14, damaging his truck. That truck was towed to D'Anzo's in Posadas, where it sits, waiting for repair authorization. MVD tells us that it's your truck. The wrecker driver remembers you well when he hooked up with you right here, in this parking lot, Wednesday evening."

Cliff Bailey was beginning to look more like a stroke victim than a bruising drunk. His face first flushed and then went pasty-pale.

"The truck is not parked at the motel, and I have to wonder why you would tell us that."

"I didn't...I...you..." He gulped and one hand clutched at his chest. "No. Look." But an explanation wasn't forthcoming. Instead he looked wildly at first Smith and then at Torkelson. His partners didn't look as if any great, creative ideas had occurred to them.

I watched him struggle, and it was the young Army lieutenant who tried to help him out.

"Cliff, what's going on? Sheriff, we don't know what you're talking about."

"Let's try this, then. Someone blew all kinds of holes in one of Herb Torrance's windmills and cattle drinkers, just out of the canyon," I said. "We know that four youngsters from the area were there in the canyon, and we know that the three of you were there." That was a stretch, but the trio didn't need to know that at the moment, our evidence was shaky. "We know that the kids left the area, and possibly you may have chased them for a ways up the county road. Until you overcooked it and hit a stump."

"Cliff..." the lieutenant appealed.

"I wasn't *chasin'* them," he blurted, his face exploring various shades of purple. His vascular system was amazingly artistic in its use of color. "My God, what do you think? One of 'em was having a seizure of some sort, and they took off like...like crazy people. I mean, we heard just a little bit ago what happened with that crash up in town. I was readin' the local paper inside, here, just now. Yeah, we saw 'em, and maybe we all did some shooting. But I didn't chase 'em anywheres. I didn't have *nothin'* to do with their wreck up in town. Nothin'."

"All four of 'em took off?"

"Yeah, all of 'em. I mean," and he looked confused, "well sure. All of 'em."

"Then you would be surprised to learn that one of those youngsters was struck by a ricocheting bullet and lay out in that country all night, all by herself, to eventually die of her wounds sometime the next morning. About the time you three took off to Mexico to hunt pigs, there she was."

He tried vainly to make all that work in his mind, and failed. "Three of those kids were killed in the crash, my friend," I added. "The fourth died right over there." I nodded at the rough country north of the Broken Spur.

Maybe that was the wrong thing to say, because Clifton Bailey looked as if someone had slammed a door in his face. "I want a lawyer." His chin jutted out pugnaciously, the alcohol doing the talking. He shifted his considerable weight, glaring first at me, then at the impassive Robert Torrez, then swiveled to take in Sergeant Payson and Officer Posey. I remained silent, giving him time to let the attack of belligerence pass. Drunk as he was, as used to bullying folks as he might have been, even his frazzled brain could see that the odds weren't good.

"Fair enough. Lawyers are a good idea just about now. We'll all adjourn this meeting and convene in town. How's that?" I didn't give him time to reply. "Sergeant Payson, will you transport Mr. Bailey in your unit? Officer Posey, I know it's a squeeze, but can you transport Lieutenant Smith? Mr. Torkelson…" I stopped as Deputy Tom Mears, hot off the trail from María, braked hard into the parking lot. "Ah, Doug, you're off the hook. Lieutenant Smith will ride with Deputy Mears."

"But we…I mean, you can't just haul us in without arresting us. I mean, on what charge?" Bailey cried.

"Let's start with felony damage to property. That's a place to start. And then we can tack on public intoxication. And contribution to the delinquency of minors. And at this point, reckless endangerment leading to great bodily harm of a child," I said. "So, yes, you have the right to remain silent, gentlemen," and I went through the rest of the litany. My invitations about the various rides back to town sounded more hospitable than they were. The only person who expected the handcuffs was Lieutenant Smith.

Chapter Twenty-six

A quick arraignment was to our advantage, and District Judge Lester Hobart agreed to see the whole gang at ten the next morning. That delay would accomplish a couple of important things. First, there was some serious sobering up needed. Just as important, it gave us the opportunity to talk with the men individually—and both Lieutenant Smith and Artie Torkelson seemed willing, lawyer or not.

With separate rides to Posadas, and then separate accommodations in the village lockup, they hadn't had the opportunity to talk to each other, and that made their situation a challenge. They'd had no chance to rehearse a joint tale of innocence.

No other detainee was in our county lockup at the moment, so Lieutenant Smith enjoyed one of the cells in the juvenile "wing," the short hallway that included only two cells, while Bailey had tried to find some comfort in one of the women's cells on the first floor. Torkelson had been sure that his brother would come up with whatever bail was set, but surprise…bail wouldn't be set until the arraignment with Judge Hobart in the morning. Until then, Artie was given the opportunity to enjoy our hospitality for the night.

During the drive back to town, my Ford capped out at forty-five miles an hour with a symphony of dying parts grinding themselves further to pieces. Officer Posey followed us, just in case we should be forced to become pedestrians. I was transporting Artie Torkelson, who remained silent for the trip. Once in a while, I'd glance in the rearview mirror and see him looking at the handcuffs, and once in a while he'd give a little shake of the head as if he didn't believe the direction his life had taken.

A little after eight that evening, Sheriff Salcido met with me, Sergeant Payson, and Deputy Torrez in our small conference room. We had decided to meet with Lieutenant Smith first, since he was clearly the most sober of the bunch. He had refused a lawyer. Cuffs removed, he sat carefully, gratefully accepting a cup of fresh coffee.

"Lieutenant Joseph Smith, currently on active duty at Fort Campbell, residence in Clarksville, Tennessee," I announced for the benefit of the tape recorder.

"That's correct, sir."

I smiled at him. "Relax, Lieutenant."

He took a deep breath. "I can't, sir. Jail time does that."

"Do you understand why you're here?"

"I think so."

"Let's start with just the simple time line. The evening of June fourth."

Smith picked at a scuff of skin raised on his wrist by the cuffs. "We spent the day out looking for good antelope habitat."

"The 'we' being?"

"Artie Torkelson, Clifton Bailey, and myself."

"Sometime during the day, you stopped by the Broken Spur to tank up?"

"Once that afternoon, and again a little after six p.m., when we had some dinner there." He smiled ruefully. "We talked to some of the locals, and one of 'em told us about that canyon as a spot we could maybe do some shooting and stuff."

"Stuff?"

He shrugged. "Cliff and Artie seemed determined to tie one on. I didn't much, because I knew we were headed for Mexico the next day, and I didn't want to be feeling lousy for that. I know what their roads are like." He shifted in his chair. "Anyway, we tried to go in the canyon road, but it was too narrow, so we went on up a ways and drove in a two-track that Artie said belonged to one of the local ranchers. He said he wouldn't mind. We drove in as far as a water tank and windmill."

"What started you shooting at the tank?"

He groaned and looked heavenward. "Shit. We put up a bunch of bottles and cans on the rim of the tank and started poppin' 'em."

"With what?"

"I had my nine millimeter Beretta…the one I surrendered to the deputy. And a Marlin thirty-thirty. My pig gun. Stuart had his three oh eight and a forty-five. Bailey had a couple forty-four mags and a little twenty-two pistol."

"That tank ended up with a lot of holes in it, Lieutenant."

"Yeah, it did. Stuart was tryin' to hit one of the bottles on the rim, and missed. This geyser of water goes up, and, I don't know. I guess we thought that was hilarious. Then he pulls a shot at the side of the tank facing us, and that's even more hilarious, 'cause Cliff said it looked like it was pissing, you know. This jet of water arcing out." He fell silent.

"Things degenerated into a real shoot-fest, then?"

He nodded. "I guess."

"Did anyone else show up? Did the rancher come down to see what all the shooting was about?"

"Nope. But we were going on toward sunset, and we did hear voices. First thing we know, here's four kids coming up the hill out of the canyon. One of 'em has a rifle."

"Did you recognize the weapon?"

"Sure. A little M-1 carbine."

"Four kids, though."

"Yes, sir. Two boys, two girls."

"What happened then?"

"Oh, we just shot the breeze, talkin' about the country, about this and that. Clifton offered 'em beers all around. One of the girls didn't seem much interested, but the others took 'em. We were talkin' guns and hunting, stuff like that. You know. Just chitchat. They were all locals."

"Did they bring beer or other alcoholic beverages with them?"

Smith hesitated, no doubt as a cop himself recognizing that this is where the shit was going to get really deep. "I didn't see any."

"So you provided."

"Cliff did, I guess."

"You guess. And then?"

He drew himself up in his chair. "And then? The one kid—skinny little Mexican kid—he's impressed by Bailey's handgun... the forty-four? He says his brother has one just like it. So Bailey says something like, 'You any good with it?' And the kid says he is, and Bailey asks him if he wants to shoot it, and I can see what Bailey is thinking. All big talk. The recoil of that hand cannon is going to scare the daylights out of him. But the kid's game, and he says sure."

"So the youngster shoots the forty-four. At what?" During this whole conversation, Deputy Torrez gaze was trying to bore holes through Smith's skull. Torrez' hands were folded one atop the other on the table, but his knuckles were white.

"He shoots once and blows one of the cans off the rim, then turns around to look at us with this big shit-eating grin. Like 'I did it! My ears are going to be ringing for a week!' He was real excited."

"At that point," I said, "who was there?"

Smith looked puzzled. "Like I said...us three, and the kids. Well, the one girl went back down to get something out of their car. So she wasn't there just at that moment. But the other three were...the blond kid, Chris, I guess they called him. The little Mexican kid, and another girl. The way they were talking, I guess she was his sister."

"So one went back down into the canyon?"

"Yes. Good-lookin' kid. I heard the Chris guy call her Dari? Something like that."

"She left the area, then."

"Yes."

"Was that the only shot that the boy took with the magnum?"

"Nope. And then Bailey says, 'Well, let's try a movin' target,' and he points up at the windmill. It's just kind of lazy spinning, you know."

"Facing which way?"

He frowned and looked off into the distance at nothing. "The breeze, what there was of it, was comin' down off the hill behind us. So the tail of the mill would be pointin' southwest, maybe."

"You didn't make an effort to talk them out of it? The vandalism to the mill?"

"No, sir."

"Why not? You must have known that this whole mess could be big trouble for you."

"Just a...shit, I don't know. I could have said something, but I didn't."

I slid a piece of clean copier paper across to him. "Sketch it out for me."

He did, with a few erasures to make corrections. Sure enough, it would have been easy to draw a little 'x' in a line downhill from the windmill, where Darlene would spend her last night. I left the drawing with him. "So the kid shoots at the spinning mill?"

"Yeah. He let go three or four rounds, trying to shoot real fast? But the gun jumps so bad he has to change his grip each time. Then Chris says something like, 'Well, I can do that,' and he racks that little carbine and lets fly. He had to try a couple times, because he kept getting jams. Finally, he empties it, and Bailey asks if he can have a go. With the kid's gun, I mean. Chris says that he's out of ammo, but he's got some down in the truck, down in the canyon. He'll go get it. So off *he* goes."

"Did he take the carbine with him?"

"I think he did."

"And in the meantime?"

"Cliff shot some more. He punched the tank a few times, to see if the forty-four would go through both sides."

"And did it?"

"No, it didn't. Only one or two places above the waterline. And that's when the kid looks like he's gettin' sick."

"The kid?"

"The youngster who shot the magnum. I don't remember his name. But he's startin' to wheeze, like he can't get any air. His sister asks him if he's got his inhaler with him, and he starts with that. At one point, she turned to me…I don't know why me, you know…and she says, 'We gotta go.' And she starts down the hill with her brother. He was in *bad* shape."

"So you saw them walking away, toward the canyon? In the same direction as Chris went when he was looking for more ammo?"

"Yes. Artie says we should give 'em a ride or something. Make sure they get back to town. I mean, they'd had a lot to drink."

"And did you?"

"Well, at one point we heard lots of screaming…shouting, more like. Artie says something like, 'You think they'll be all right?' I said we ought to check, so I jogged down toward the canyon, to make sure they were okay—not getting stuck in the arroyo bed or something like that.

"Were you able to make out what was said?"

"No." He shrugged. "Then they drove off. I saw the ass end of the Suburban as they went out past all those rocks."

"Could you tell who was in the truck?"

"No. The light was bad by then."

I sat back and looked across at the other officers. Sheriff Salcido rose, went to the coffee urn and filled his cup. "You know, I'm confused on something," he said softly. He returned to the table, set the cup down carefully, and leaned forward on his elbows.

"You tell us that this one girl went down to the Suburban to 'get something.' She didn't return?"

"No, sir."

"So you don't know if she 'got something' or not."

"No, sir. I don't."

"I want to be clear," the sheriff persisted. "The girl—Dari, you called her—left the group. When was the next time you saw her?"

Smith looked puzzled. "I didn't We didn't. She didn't come back."

"So you assumed…"

"Well, she had to have been in the Suburban when they left. When the kids left the canyon."

"Had to have been," Salcido said softly.

"When you gentlemen left the area, where did you go?"

"I was riding with Artie, and Cliff took his own truck. He wanted to drive up the dirt road a ways to make sure the kids got to the interstate all right. Artie and me went down to the Spur, where Cliff was going to meet up with us."

"And that's what happened?"

"Well, sort of. Cliff said he slid off the dirt road at some point and took out a tree or something. He came back to the saloon with a bent truck, all dirty and pissed at himself."

"What did he say about the kids?"

"Just that he guessed they'd be all right. They took off to the north."

I reached out and popped the tape out of the recorder and slipped in a new one. "All right. Let's listen to this tale of woe again." I nodded at Sergeant Payson. "You do the honors this time."

We listened to Lieutenant Smith's tale about four times, and nothing much changed. By the time we were finished, both Torkelson and Bailey were snoring so loudly it sounded as if they might blow their cell doors off.

"Seven o'clock, tomorrow," I announced. "Same time, same station. They'll both be sober by then."

Chapter Twenty-seven

District Judge Lester Hobart was sixty-three years old, and looked ninety. "Wizened" could have been the word invented just for him. Maybe his favorite pastime was sun-bathing. He had to know that we lived in the UV capital of the Western Hemisphere, but his skin was bronzed beyond metallic, damn near to mummy. Wrinkles had become crevasses. Freckles had morphed into sludgy scabs along his jawline, and across the wide band of unprotected scalp on the dome of his skull.

Still, he was irascible enough that melanoma probably went elsewhere to pick on easier prey.

The black judicial robe hung like a pole-less tent on his spare frame, and because he also hosted the early stages of Parkinson's Disease, he held the court papers in both hands, plastered tight against his desk, his rheumy gray eyes absorbing every word. He plodded through all depositions, including the one Clifton Bailey had recited after a change of heart come dawn.

"So…if this isn't the damnedest thing I've ever read." It wasn't—Hobart had been sitting the bench for centuries, and probably would for a century more. He'd adjudicated his share of hair-raising cases. The three shootists stood before the judge, trying to look respectable…as respectable as anyone can after spending the night in the can—even a jail as down-home as ours. It had been a long evening of depositions and interviews, with a long morning of more of the same after that.

Another warrant made it easy to swing by Stuart Torkelson's residence and pick up the other firearms that the hunters had left there in anticipation of their trip down into Mexico. Bob Torrez was eagerly anticipating a long session comparing bullets from the tank with the various weapons.

Judge Hobart glared at the trio, his old head oscillating from right to left. Being bothered on a Sunday morning didn't add to his bonhomie. "All right. So you all have a reunion of sorts. You come over to Posadas for a little recreation with your buddy, here, Mr. Torkelson." He nodded sagely and lifted the pack of papers we had supplied him. "I'm sure it's in here, but tell me anyway." He squinted at the first sheet. "Mr. Clifton Bailey. Why are you here?"

Bailey tried to stand a little straighter. "They're claiming…"

The judge cut him off with an impatient wave of the hand. "I know what *they're* claiming. What's your connection with Posadas County? How'd you come to choose us for your handiwork?"

The man's voice diminished to a hoarse whisper. "My brother, Leo, lives here. We've hunted here from time to time. That's what we were doin', is scouting some country for a fall hunt."

"Are you in the news business, too?"

"No, Your Honor."

"Then what do you do?"

"I'm a district sales manager for Griffon Home Products. They're a hardware wholesaler."

Hobart nodded abruptly. "Mr. Torkelson, you're a native of sorts. How do you come to know Mr. Bailey?"

"Oh, I've known him for years, Your Honor."

Hobart almost smiled. "I don't think that's what I asked," and Torkelson looked confused. "How did you two meet?"

"I guess the first time was when we shared a campground down in Carlsbad. We got to talking of an evening, and you know. One thing led to another."

"Where are you working now?"

"I work for my brother's real estate firm, here in town."

"How nice." Hobart drew a deep breath. "Lieutenant Smith?"

"I was married to Mr. Bailey's wife's sister, sir."

"Was?"

"No longer."

"And what do you do for Uncle Sam?"

"Military Police, Fort Campbell, out of Clarksville, Tennessee."

Judge Hobart picked up the paperwork and leafed through. The corners shook in his unsteady hands.

"Well, this is a mess, gentlemen. Now, we could pontificate all day about how stupid your behavior was, but I think you already know. At least it's refreshing that all of your stories are substantially the same. *Substantially.*" He paused, surveying the various forms of contrition on the three faces. "So, let's not waste any time. This is the way it's going to be." He laid down the paperwork and folded his hands on top of it.

"The most important thing, the most grievous thing to me, is that this community is still struggling with the tragic loss of four of its best and brightest. Now it seems to me, Mr. Torkelson, Mr. Bailey, and Lieutenant Smith, that as adults you should have provided some guidance for these four youngsters, rather than engaging them in this," and he looked at the paperwork, and then several of the photos, "this *outrageous* and nonsensical behavior.

"Hell, I'm not sure who, if any of you, is telling the whole truth. So we're not going to engage in a lawyer fest at this arraignment. Four youngsters have died as the direct result of your actions." He rapped the desk with his gavel. "I set bail at fifty thousand dollars each, cash only, and turn this over to the Grand Jury for consideration. Let those good folks figure all this out. You'll be receiving target notification from the Grand Jury in due course, along with a court calendar of their proceedings. That letter will inform you that you *may* testify during that process, but I strongly suggest that you do not. This is a good time to talk with your lawyers. Otherwise, just continue with your lives as best as you can."

"Your Honor…" Artie Torkelson started to plead, but Judge Hobart cut him off.

"This isn't a question-and-answer session, my friend, nor the time for legal advice. Find a lawyer, and find a good one." He rapped his gavel, then looked at me. "Our taxpayers are hosting this crew at the moment?"

"Yes, Your Honor."

"Good. Let 'em make as many phone calls as they need to get the job done. Have any of 'em started the process of finding a lawyer?"

"It's my understanding that they have, Your Honor."

"Well, good. The sooner the better. We're going to be pushing Schroeder to get rolling with the Grand Jury. Let them try and sort out this mess. You all are dismissed." He waved his fingers as if shooing flies away. "Undersheriff Gastner, stay for a moment, please."

The three men, again cuffed and escorted by Deputy Torrez and Sergeant Payson, left chambers looking as if they'd been whipped. Judge Hobart leaned back in his chair and watched them leave.

"Bill, it's my understanding that most of this happened on your watch?"

"I guess so."

He smiled. "You *guess* so. I'm also told that the young deputy started his first day on the job by responding to the accident that killed his brother and sister?"

"That's more or less correct, Judge. Deputy Torrez was riding with Sergeant Payson the night of the crash. He had been scheduled to officially start work the next day. He was just doing a community familiarization run with the sergeant."

"He's lived here all his life," the judge said. "What's he need familiarization for?"

I smiled. "The way a cop looks at a community is different from what the average numb civilian sees, sir."

Hobart nodded. He shuffled some of the paperwork. "I see his name on several of these documents and depositions."

"Yes."

"Turning into quite the bull dog, isn't he?"

"He's a motivated young man, that's for sure."

"Look," Hobart said, "I just wanted to say this. The Grand Jury *needs* to indict these three boneheads, although we don't know what charges the DA is going to settle for yet. But the success of that jury is going to depend a great deal on the testimony of one Robert Torrez. That boy has zero experience in front of a Grand Jury, he seems taciturn as hell, and I don't know what sort of temper he has. No doubt Schroeder will handle him with kid gloves, but coach him a little, will you? Hell, you've been around since the Ice Age. You know it isn't what the DA asks that matters during the proceedings…it's what the *jurors* ask. So prepare this kid, all right?"

"I'll do my best, Your Honor."

"It's too easy for them to think that the young man is just out to settle accounts."

Chapter Twenty-eight

District Attorney Daniel Schroeder loved Grand Juries. He loved being in the spotlight. It was just him, the jurors, the stenographer, and whichever witness Schroeder decided to call. No judge, no audience, no press. The three targets—Schroeder was going after all of them—had gotten the life-changing letter that informed them that they were the targets of a Grand Jury investigation. The letter explained in no uncertain terms that the Grand Jury was *not* charged with determining guilt or innocence—that was the turf of the petit jury trial if an indictment was issued.

It had been my experience that most folks didn't understand that...and Stuart Torkelson was one of them. During the weeks before the proceedings, he pestered me a dozen times on behalf of his brother. "What are they doing? What's Schroeder doing? Should I talk with him?" And on and on. I would patiently explain to him that the Grand Jury's *only* duty was to determine if enough evidence existed for a trial. That was all. And no—he couldn't sit in and listen, much less participate as a character witness.

The proceedings were closed—secret. The theory was that if a no bill was returned—not enough evidence for a trial—the various potentially damaging testimonies would not be bandied about the community, ruining a person's reputation. I had never known that to work, though. The community grapevine is powerfully invasive.

And all of that is *if* the target of the Grand Jury kept his or her mouth shut. But by motor-mouthing at the wrong time to the wrong people, the target has the latitude to do as much damage as he wishes to family and reputation. Lawyers would tell their clients *not* to appear before the jury, who had an absolute talent for asking unexpected or embarrassing questions to which the answers might be incriminating.

"But I have to tell that jury what *really* happened," the client might blurt, forgetting that his version of what *really* happened was already recorded in black and white in depositions with the police. Like a kid with his grubby paw caught in the cookie jar, some clients really believed that all they had to say was, "Yeah, I was lying then, but honest…I'm telling the truth now!"

Clifton Bailey demanded that he be given a chance to appear before the Grand Jury. His lawyer, Susan Eskildsen, tried to talk him out of it. *Posadas Register* publisher and editor Leo Bailey, who knew exactly how Grand Juries worked, tried to talk his brother out of it. I tried. Even Sheriff Salcido tried. His ex-wife *might* have tried. Mr. Bailey was absolutely convinced that his golden, impassioned tongue would educate that jury, would sway the jury, would make them see the light. It would be as easy as selling hardware.

What Mr. Bailey really didn't seem to understand was that seventeen-year-old Darlene Spencer was dead, killed by a forty-four bullet in the brain fired by his gun. He was going to have a hard time mining pity from the jurors.

Dan Schroeder, who was going after a whole battery of counts, especially wanted an indictment on charges of reckless abuse of a child resulting in death, and contributing to the delinquency of a child. With that in mind, he didn't want to risk Deputy Robert Torrez testifying first. He had a hundred examples of how I might behave in court—and none for Torrez.

The small courtroom in the county building was air-conditioned to arctic standards that late July day, which was good considering that the outside temperature touched 102 degrees by ten a.m. Schroeder had spent a small fortune on photographic blowups. I'd known prosecutors who'd blown what I thought were easy cases by simply doing a lazy preparation—missing simple things, like explaining the crime scene crystal clearly for the jurors.

This time, the whole scenario was there in fourteen-by-twenty color prints—windmill, cattle drinker, a pathetically small, covered body. Supported by an easel built out of two-by-four lumber was the eight-foot sail removed from Herb Torrance's windmill.

I shifted in the old wooden witness chair, trying to find a soft spot. The clock ticked to 11:05—it had taken Schroeder more than an hour to seat, orient, and instruct the jury, seven women and five men. I knew all of them. Each had a notebook and pencil, and watched Schroeder expectantly. The DA pulled off his wire-rimmed glasses, rubbed his eyes, and then resettled.

"Would you state your name for the jury, please."

"William K. Gastner."

"And your occupation?"

"Undersheriff of Posadas County."

"Undersheriff. That means you're second in command over there?"

"Yes."

He plodded through my background, education, and experience. "Sheriff," and he made a show of organizing his legal pad, "tell us about the night of June fourth, nineteen eighty-six."

"The Sheriff's Department, with the assistance of the New Mexico State Police, investigated a fatal motor vehicle crash at the intersection of Grande Avenue and the Interstate exchange in Posadas."

Schroeder lifted a large, beautifully rendered diagram of the intersection in question and touched the bright dot from his laser pointer to the point where the exit ramp left the interstate. "Would you explain what happened?"

I did, and as I narrated, he moved the little dot down the ramp, squiggled it some to indicate the rollover, and pegged it against the interstate's center support.

"And passengers in the vehicle were?"

I listed the names and ages, and saw a couple of the jurors grimace.

"Were any of the occupants ejected?"

"Yes. Orlando Torrez was."

"All killed instantly?"

"Probably. There is some evidence that Orlando Torrez might have died some moments *before* the crash."

He looked at the jurors. "We'll be talking with Dr. Perrone about that," he said. He led me through the incident, one skid mark at a time, and worked his way back to the collision with the sideswiped Cadillac.

"Was it your professional opinion that the Suburban was traveling at a high rate of speed?"

"Yes."

"The driver of the Cadillac says in his deposition that his cruise control was set at eighty miles an hour. Yet he says the Suburban blew right by him. Is that your understanding?"

"Yes."

He paused to consider his next question carefully. He had left out the testimony of the Holmeses, whose carefully crafted deposition could offer only shaky testimony about the possible activities inside the Suburban when it charged past them.

"Mr. Gastner, were you able to determine *where* the youngsters had been before the crash?"

"Most likely the general area of Bender's Canyon, east of County Road 14." Even as I spoke, Schroeder lifted another large map and put it in place. Again the excited little laser dot flashed out.

"Were you able to ascertain what they might have been doing there?"

"Partying, I suppose. Or thinking about it." *OBJECTION!* If this were a petit jury trial, with both defense and prosecutors, the objections would be flying thick and fast. But a Grand Jury doesn't waste its time trying to establish "beyond a reasonable doubt." Schroeder was merely trying to eventually illustrate for jurors that there was cause—enough evidence, however slim—to go to a full trial.

The DA looked puzzled, and placed yet a third map on the easel, this one showing the entire western side of the county. "Did anyone *tell* you that the teens had been partying in Bender's Canyon?"

"No. We were told that they might have been in Lordsburg at a 4-H event. We determined that was not the case."

"Just something they told their parents, maybe?"

"That could be."

"What led you there, then? To the canyon? What led you to believe that they had been in that location?"

"The day after the crash, I responded to what I thought was an unrelated vandalism complaint by an area rancher, Herb Torrance." I looked at the jury. "Life goes on. We had other complaints besides that late night crash." Schroeder's laser dot swung up to the cluster of dots representing Herb's property. "Someone had shot one of his stock tanks and windmills full of holes," I said. "Deputy Robert Torrez and I were able to recover several slugs fired into the tank."

"At that point, you had no obvious suspect for the vandalism?"

"No."

"Did Mr. Torrance put a value on the damage?"

"Certainly more than a thousand dollars."

"How did you then make the connection between the two incidents? Between the crash in the village on the one hand, and the tank vandalism on the other end of county?"

"In the course of investigating the area, Deputy Robert Torrez found a thirty-caliber carbine, abandoned in a brushy area southwest of the drinker and windmill."

"A rifle? A gun? Just lying there on the ground?"

"An M-1 carbine. World War II vintage."

"This was a firearm that you recognized?"

"No. I didn't recognize it at first, but Deputy Robert Torrez did." I watched the District Attorney heft the carbine, still in its evidence bag.

"Do you recognize this?"

"Yes. That's the carbine that Deputy Torrez found."

He looked at it skeptically. "Good heavens. Of all the guns in the world, how did the deputy chance to recognize that one?" As he waited for my answer, he presented the wrapped carbine to the jury.

"He told me that he'd looked at that particular carbine closely when it was for sale in Payton's Gun Shop in Posadas. He didn't buy it. During his examination of the gun, he noticed a couple of irregularities—just little things, but that detracted from the historical value. Willis Browning *did* purchase the carbine, and out of habit kept it in a case in the Suburban. He even qualified with it during a Sheriff's Department shoot."

"So this wasn't recovered at the scene of the crash?"

"No. The case that Mr. Browning carried the carbine in was present, but not the carbine itself."

"So at the time of the crash, this firearm—you're referring to it as a *carbine*—was *not* in the Suburban, but was laying in the bushes out in Bender's Canyon."

"I can't say that for sure. It was found out there the next day. I can't testify where it spent the night."

Schroeder looked pained and referred once again to his legal pad. "Now, you said that Deputy Torrez found this rifle while surveying around the general area of the water tank. And he was doing that survey *because* of the obvious vandalism to the tank and windmill."

"Yes."

Schroeder nodded and walked one of the color prints over to the jury, a portrait of the leaking tank. A black arrow had been drawn to each bullet hole.

"How many times was the tank struck, Sheriff?"

"Thirty-one."

He repeated that, and let the number sink in for a moment, then slid a photo of the windmill into place on the display easel. He leaned back against the jury box railing so he could regard both the photo and the huge windmill sail displayed on its custom stand. Black adhesive arrows feathered out from the sails, each one pointing at a bullet hole.

"And how many strikes to the windmill itself?"

"Fourteen."

"Fourteen. Was all of the damage consistent with a single firearm?"

"No. At least two guns were used."

"Were you able to match any of this damage to a particular gun?"

"Deputy Torrez was able to collect sixteen spent casings from the area, where they had most likely been ejected when fired. Those had characteristic marks that the FBI laboratory identified as consistent with being fired from that particular carbine, the one we found on site. No bullets matched back to the carbine were recovered from the tank."

"So…this gun, and perhaps others, played a tap dance all over that tank and windmill."

I didn't respond, since it wasn't a question.

"During the survey of the area, did you or the deputy find anything else out of the ordinary?"

He made it sound like such an uneventful, sunny summer's day, but I understood the jolt he wanted the jurors to feel.

"A moment or two later, Deputy Torrez discovered the body of a young woman whom both of us recognized as Darlene Spencer."

He took his time finding the photograph he wanted. It was not one of the photos that Avelino Garcia had taken later, when a drape provided some protection for the girl's privacy. I saw several of the jurors wince.

He turned to one of the maps, leaving the photo of the dead girl on the easel. "At this point, two things." He shook his head, obviously moved by the contents of the photograph of the dead girl. He placed both hands on the rail and glared at the jurors.

"Understand that there will be times, like this, when we will be displaying photos that are highly disturbing. That just can't be helped. I'm deeply sorry, because these are distasteful images that you'll carry in your memories for a long time." He held up two fingers. "But number two, ladies and gentlemen, remember the Grand Jury instructions that I discussed earlier with you. This is a *secret* proceeding." He took the time to make eye contact with each juror in turn.

"You will *not* discuss what you see or hear in this proceeding with *anyone* outside of this room. Not with husband or wife, not with your children, not with a close friend, certainly not with the press." Several heads nodded, and more than a tear or two was dabbed.

At this point, DA Dan Schroeder interrupted his line of questioning and took the time to poll each juror. "Mrs. Albertson, do understand these instructions I have just given?" And he went down the list, until all twelve had responded verbally for the record. He nodded with satisfaction at his efforts to chop off the rumor vine at its base.

"Good. Now, Sheriff Gastner, I draw your attention to the map on the easel. Does this fairly represent the location of the young woman's body when you and your deputy found her?" A little stick figure had been drawn on the rendering, and I nodded.

"Very close, yes."

"The body was located how far from the windmill and tank?"

"We measured one hundred ninety-two feet from the southwest corner of the windmill's base to the body."

He paused, deep in thought. "Now, Undersheriff Gastner, you have been in law enforcement for a long time. Upon discovery of the body, what opinion did you form as to her injuries?"

"The only injury we could see was what appeared to be a single wound in the left eye. Bullet wounds are often characteristic, depending on a whole textbook of circumstances, but this one was irregular, almost jagged in nature."

"No other wounds that you saw?"

"No."

He placed an enlarged photo of Darlene's left eye, then looked at the jury. "Again, ladies and gentlemen, you will hear detailed testimony from the medical examiner's office after a little while.

But Sheriff Gastner, let me ask you. In your experience, have you ever seen gunshot wounds to the skull?"

"Yes."

"The wounds from large-caliber rifles—hunting guns, perhaps. Aren't they *likely* to be through and through?"

"Likely, but it depends on a host of circumstances."

"If such a large caliber gun was held close to the skull and fired, would the wound be through and through, most likely?"

"Most likely."

"This was not, however."

"By no means."

He nodded and stood regarding the grizzly photos. "Upon first seeing her, did you assume, from the condition of the body, that Darlene Spencer had been assaulted in some fashion?"

"No, I did not."

"Yet, as the photo clearly shows, the victim's clothing was in disarray, the lower portion of her body exposed. That didn't cause you to reach any preliminary conclusions?"

"No."

"And why is that?"

"There were no other signs of assault, Mr. Schroeder. No defense wounds, no bruises, nothing under the nails, nothing of that sort. No other clothing was disturbed."

Again, he regarded the photo for a long moment. "None of the upper clothing was disturbed?"

"No, it was not."

"So what did you think?"

"I thought that the medical examiner should be called to the scene ASAP."

"And was he?"

"Of course."

"Did Deputy Torrez offer any conclusions of his own?"

"He did not."

"Did there come a time when both of you formed conclusions about what might have happened?"

"Medical Examiner Perrone performed a thorough examination of the body *in situ,* and then conducted an autopsy later. He determined that a bullet had struck Miss Spencer, penetrating the left orbit, lacerating the optic nerve and its pathway, and lacerating two major arteries deeper in the brain."

"And Dr. Perrone will testify in detail, of course. But I'm interested right now in the conclusions that you and Deputy Torrez might have developed at this point."

"When he saw the bullet that the medical examiner recovered from the victim's skull, he said that the remains of the slug looked like a ricochet to him. I don't know what he thought *before* seeing the recovered projectile."

"Well, *after* seeing the projectile, then. How is it that he would come to view it as the result of a ricochet?"

"He mentioned to me only that the sharp edges of the deformed bullet appeared consistent with striking something sharp during the trajectory. Normally soft-nosed bullets mushroom, sometimes quite evenly, when striking tissue. This bullet was clearly damaged by striking something sharp first."

"And did the deputy develop a hypothesis about that?"

"He did."

"What was his hypothesis?"

"I can tell you what he *did,* Counselor. What his thought processes were, you'd have to get from him."

Schroeder smiled benignly. "And what did he do?"

"He climbed the windmill and examined the sails. What some folks call the blades."

The DA moved the large portrait of the windmill front and center. "He climbed up here?"

"Yes. To the maintenance platform below the transmission housing."

"And the purpose of that expedition was?"

"He examined each sail in turn."

Schroeder glanced at the jury. "And his determination?"

"The sails had been peppered with small-caliber bullet holes— eleven of them. And three from a larger-caliber gun."

"Did any particular damage draw the deputy's attention?"

"Yes. One of the bullet strikes appeared to have hit one of the cross members." I nodded at the large schematic of the windmill sail that Schroeder put on the easel. "That's where the wheel arms bolt to the inner wheel band, to support the set of sails."

Schroeder stepped across to the displayed sail, and pushed the heavy castered easel carrying the windmill sail closer to the jury rail. "It would be helpful if you would all step down here for a closer look at this to understand what Sheriff Gastner means." He beckoned them down, and they milled about the sail, peering at the damage.

When they returned to their seats, Schroeder slid the contents of an evidence bag into his hand.

"Sheriff, do you recognize this?"

"Yes, I do."

"Would you describe it, please."

"That's the bullet that Dr. Perrone removed during autopsy from Darlene Spencer's brain."

Schroeder placed the heavy, deformed fragment in a small white plastic dish and handed it to the jury. "Were you able to determine the caliber of that projectile?"

"Yes. It was measured at four hundred-thirty-thousandths at the base. What would be termed forty-four caliber."

"Forty-four? Why is a bullet that measures four-thirty referred to as forty-four, Sherifff?"

"A historical issue, Mr. Schroeder. A thirty-eight is not a thirty-eight, a forty-four is not forty-four. It's an inaccurate reference that's been with us for more than a century."

"I see. Anyway, you determined that this was fired from a forty-four-caliber gun."

"Yes."

"Did there come a time when you were able to establish specifically *which* gun?"

"Yes. We recovered two forty-four-caliber firearms from a truck owned by Clifton Bailey."

"Where was the truck parked when you did this?"

"D'Anzo Chrysler-Plymouth, here in Posadas."

At this point, Schroeder slipped an enlarged photo of the pickup onto the easel. "Do you recognize this vehicle?"

"Yes. That's the vehicle in question, owned by Clifton Bailey."

"And where were the two firearms?"

"In a locked toolbox inside the rear camper shell." More photos were lined up showing the interior of the camper shell, the toolbox, and the box lid raised to show the guns in place.

"You said that this truck was stored at the dealer's here in Posadas. What prompted you to investigate here?"

"We had evidence that a vehicle had been involved in a collision with a stump near Bender's Canyon. We talked to a witness who may have heard the crash. He did not see it happen, but he's sure he heard it. The truck made it back as far as the local saloon, where Mr. Bailey called a wrecker. The waitress at the saloon recalls that incident."

"I see." He placed an FBI photo montage on the easel. "Ladies and gentlemen, I would like to call your attention to exhibit B-thirteen. Sheriff, will you explain what we're looking at, please?"

"That's a series of comparison photos showing the bullet fragment from the victim's skull compared with a bullet that Deputy Torrez recovered from a test tank, fired from one of Mr. Bailey's firearms, in this case a Ruger Super Blackhawk, forty-four magnum revolver."

Schroeder hefted the revolver. "Would you identify this exhibit, please."

"That's the forty-four magnum just mentioned, owned by Clifton Bailey."

"And the results of the comparison?"

"I am convinced that both bullets were fired from the same gun."

He looked at me quizzically. "Were you present at these tests?"

"Yes." *And they were performed by a rookie deputy just days on the job,* I wasn't tempted to add. If this case ever went to trial, however, a good defense lawyer would have a field day.

"So…" He stood with a hand on his jaw, thinking. "And this third comparison?"

"That's one of the slugs recovered from Herb Torrance's stock tank. Tests showed that that bullet also was fired from Mr. Bailey's forty-four-caliber handgun."

He frowned. "So in your opinion, we have a match, then. The deformed bullet removed from the victim, the bullet recovered from the stock tank, and the bullet fired during your department's own laboratory testing. All from this revolver."

"Yes."

"Mr. Gastner, returning to an earlier question. In your career, have you had occasion to investigate the results of a magnum-class bullet wound to the head?"

"Yes. Both human and livestock."

"And in those cases—any of them—was the damage inflicted similar to that suffered by the victim, Darlene Spencer?"

"No."

"How did they differ?"

"In every case, the magnum round exited the skull. In all cases but one bovine incident, the rounds blew away large portions of the skull caps."

"But that is *not* consistent with the damage to Darlene Spencer's skull, is it?"

"No, it's not. The damaged bullet you've shown the jury did not exit the skull."

"Enough to kill instantly, however."

Schroeder had planted that grim question just right. When I answered, "No, it did not," the jury visibly flinched.

"Again, we'll be talking to Dr. Alan Perrone shortly, but it's your experienced opinion that death was *not* instantaneous?"

"There's reason to believe that the victim probably lived through the night."

"Lived through the night, alone and hurt," Schroeder echoed. I glanced at the jury, and the magnitude of Clifton Bailey's mistake in demanding an opportunity to testify was clearly written on their faces. At that moment, they would gladly have supplied the rope for a lynching.

He turned and looked at the site schematic. "It appears…no strike that." Schroeder turned to look at me. "One hundred and ninety feet, more or less. Why was Darlene Spencer almost two hundred feet away from the scene of the shooting, apparently concealed in brush and shrubs?"

"Tests with Luminol suggest that she had walked some distance away in order to go to the bathroom." Schroeder put a large, bizarrely patterned photo on the easel.

"Can you explain what we see here, Sheriff?"

"That's a photo taken at night, showing the images produced when Luminol touches bodily fluids. On the right is an area where we're quite sure that the victim first urinated. The amount of urine present suggests that. When finished, she stood up, or started to stand up, and was struck. The area on the left is where she fell, and where her body remained until she was discovered the next day."

"You said that you believe she was conscious most of the night."

"No, I didn't say that, Counselor. I said that she was *alive* until sometime the next morning."

Schroeder nodded his acceptance of the correction. "But then, no one—not the youngsters, or for that matter any of the adults present in the canyon—no one made any attempt at rendering first aid to the victim?"

"I don't know the answer to that, Counselor. The three adults all claim that they did not know she was there and hurt. They *did* know that she said she was going to the Suburban, which was in that general area. By that time, the light was failing. We do know that when everyone eventually left the area, Darlene Spencer was left behind."

Chapter Twenty-nine

There were some looming tangles to this case, though—and I think that Dan Schroeder knew that. Maybe even Clifton Bailey knew it. But Schroeder wanted the power of a Grand Jury indictment, so he didn't touch the tangles. But Lewis Bennett did.

Bennett, juror number 8, a young welder employed by Consolidated Mining, looked sideways at me, his brow wrinkled like a prune. "According to what we've heard," Bennett said slowly, "there were *seven* people in the canyon that evening." He held up seven fingers. "How do we know who actually fired the bullet that ricocheted off the windmill and then struck Darlene Spencer? *She* didn't shoot it, so that leaves six, right?"

"Correct," I said. "Unless there was someone else in the canyon that night that we don't know about."

He waved a hand at the windmill. "If the bullets match, it doesn't really matter that it was a ricochet or not, right?"

"Correct," I said. "Unless issues of intent are considered."

Schroeder started to speak, but Bennett charged ahead, undaunted. "So even if we narrow it down to a bullet from Mr. Bailey's gun, do we know which one of the six, or which ones… do we know who fired the fatal bullet?"

I looked at Schroeder, as if to say, "Do you want me to answer that?" He gave a little nod.

"Other than material in the depositions of the three men, no, we don't."

"Do we get to see those depositions?"

"Most certainly you do," Schroeder said. "Most certainly." He straightened up and pushed away from his lectern. "And that brings us to an important point. Sheriff Gastner, were the three men tested for blood alcohol at some point during the night of the shooting?"

"Yes."

"And the results of those tests?"

"Mr. Bailey tested one-point-nine. Mr. Torkelson tested one-point-eight. Lieutenant Smith tested at one-point-one."

"Did they have alcohol in their possession?"

"Yes. They had made a stop at the Broken Spur Saloon to purchase a significant amount of alcoholic beverages. Empty cans and broken bottles that carried their fingerprints were inventoried at the scene."

"And the four children?"

"There is evidence that three of them had not consumed any significant amount of alcohol before the shooting incident, but certainly did during the incident. After the crash in Posadas, only Elena…Ellie…Torrez tested absent for alcohol."

"So we can imagine that the alcohol flowed freely that night."

I didn't reply, but could imagine the defense attorney, in the heat of trial, blanching as she leaped to her feet to object. I suspect that Dan Schroeder knew that as well. Part of his arsenal, perhaps saved for just such a moment, included the impressive inventory of beer cans and liquor bottles.

"Sheriff, during your long career, you have served at one time or another as a firearms instructor, have you not?"

"Yes."

"Both with children and adults?"

"Yes."

"And here we have a situation where three adults have apparently joined four youngster for a shoot-fest of some sort. It is usual to include alcoholic beverages at such an event?"

"Of course not."

"Would you, as an experienced, certified instructor, call the mixing of alcoholic beverages with the shooting sports grounds for a charge of criminal negligence?"

"Yes."

Schroeder nodded with satisfaction. "Is shooting *at* private property condoned by certified instructors such as yourself?"

"Of course not. Vandalism with a firearm is a serious crime."

"And finally, is there some sort of tenet that exhorts people engaged in the shooting sports to be certain of the backstop when they shoot?"

"Yes."

This time, Schroeder moved to the railing and rested his balled fists on the polished wood. "What we have here is an instance where the targets of this Grand Jury violated every circumstance of *common sense* possible." He held up a thumb. "They were most likely under the influence of alcohol, as were the youngsters in their company. They were engaged in vandalism, destroying ranch property located *on* private property. They fired carelessly, so much so that, when one of the children left the group to relieve herself, she was struck by a ricochet." By this time, he was holding up a whole handful of fingers. "And most puzzling of all, no one rendered no first aid for the victim." He paused. "If by some fluke they didn't *know* that she had been hurt, we can only say that *they should have known.*"

He paused to let it all sink in. "Did they know she was down in that canyon? Yes, they did. Were they shooting, or allowing one of the children to shoot, in that general direction? Yes, they were. I want you to remember each of those points as we continue with the rest of the witnesses."

In a moment he turned to me. "For the moment, let's recess." He looked at each juror in turn. "When we return in thirty minutes, we'll hear from State Medical Examiner Dr. Alan Perrone and from Deputy Robert Torrez. During the break, do not discuss the case among yourselves, and most certainly not with anyone else. You're welcome to use the jury commons to stretch and get some air." He smiled. "See you back in thirty minutes."

The DA beckoned to me, and we used Judge Hobart's chambers for privacy. He held up a small notecard.

"Susan is asking for a plea," he said as I closed the door behind us.

"Oh? I'm not surprised, I guess." Susan Eskildsen was a seasoned defense trial lawyer, and she would know a crap shoot when she saw one. It was her luck to draw all three as clients.

"Well, see, here's the deal. Two of the depositions agree. Both Smith and Torkelson recount that it was actually Orlando Torrez who fired at the windmill, several times, using Bailey's revolver, while Bailey stood beside him, hands over his own ears. Nobody recounts hearing the ricochet whine off, so it could have been any of the three shots that struck Darlene. But after a time, both Smith and Torkelson remember that Orlando started having breathing difficulties. Smith even remembers it was just after Chris walked down to the Suburban to get more ammo."

"And Darlene didn't scream, or shout, or anything," I said. "They claim that Chris Browning went back down into the canyon to get another box of carbine ammo from the Suburban...and that's when he found Darlene. If he was going to take a leak and dump some beer, that grove of shrubs was a good spot. And from there he could see Darlene's body."

"That's right. That's a possibility. And we may never know the real answer." He sat on the corner of the judge's desk. "Look, I know that we have some holes that we may not be able to repair. Like why didn't the kids load the wounded girl into the Suburban? Panic time, is my guess. The kid sees the hole in her head, and then on top of that, Orlando is turning purple, so they get him in the car. And off they go. The three men claim they never saw Darlene's body, assumed that she'd left with the other kids...and Clifton claims that they were concerned for Orlando...that's why Bailey claims he chased them for a ways with his truck. To see if they could help somehow."

Schroeder shrugged. "I see an easy indictment. But lots of legwork for the trial."

"What's Eskildsen want?"

"She says Bailey wants to plea to reckless endangerment of a child—there's no way around that. A slam dunk, and he knows it. He wants no charges brought against his buddies, except them taking their share of the restitution for the vandalism."

"That's ridiculous. What's all that going to net Bailey?"

"I'm predicting Hobart will give him ten years. I'm *hoping* that he will. Eskildsen is going for two years. He'll have a felony on his record, so no firearms ownership ever again after he's released. And he'll lose everything he owns to the Spencers after the civil suit finishes with him. It's my guess the civil case will hit both Smith and Torkelson as well."

I nodded.

"Hell of an expensive bullet, huh?" Schroeder said. "What's your take?"

"I want jail time for all of them," I said. "Anything else, anything less, is nonsense. And they share equally in any full restitution to Herb."

"I was going to call Susan back right now, and if she agrees to the plea, there's no point in wasting more Grand Jury time. We can let these good people go."

"Eskildsen can be convincing," I said. "She has to convince the trio to take very real jail time, and Bailey isn't going to be able to protect his friends. They go down with him. Anything less… to hell with it. If they don't agree to that, I say we go to trial."

"The jury will be relieved," Schroeder said, but I wasn't sure yet whether or not *I* was relieved.

Chapter Thirty

July matured, bringing with it the blank blue skies and broiling sun we were used to. It felt good to sit inside the Don Juan de Oñate, bathed in the frigid air conditioning, and be able to look out and see the traffic passing by on Bustos, tires cutting squishy grooves in the overheated asphalt. The green chilé-smothered burrito had been up to snuff, and I lingered in my corner, sipping coffee and enjoying the last cigarette I had vowed to have that day.

"Three ten, PCS. Ten twenty." Gayle Sedillos was working dispatch days now, and I enjoyed hearing her on the radio—a nice mix of sweetness and clipped efficiency. She gave the "r" of *three* just the faintest hint of a trill, and said *twenty*, with two clear t's, instead of *twenny*.

I exhaled patiently and leaned forward to pick up my hand-held radio.

"Three ten is ten eight, Don Juan."

"Three ten, can you speak with the owner of the Spur? He called with a complaint and wants to see you."

And why me, I thought, although I knew why. Sergeant Payson was cruising north and east, and the rookie, Robert Torrez, was somewhere down south. Victor Sanchez didn't like either one of them. Of course, he also didn't like me—he probably didn't like any person wearing a uniform.

"PCS, ten four. ETA about thirty."

"Ten four, three ten."

Traffic on New Mexico 56 was not exactly bumper to bumper...a car or truck every two or three miles northeast bound. My faithful 310 was in the shop, the mechanics trying to decide if it was worth saving. If not, it'd be wholesaled out, hauled by the *burros* to Mexico, and no doubt spend its last miles thumping over dusty Mexican roads. I drove my own vehicle, and relaxed as the Blazer purred south on 56, air conditioner just right. Just beyond the Rio Guigarro, my radio came to life again.

"PCS, three oh eight is stopping Virginia tag eight-oh-eight baker alpha echo."

"Ten four, three oh eight." In a moment, I saw the light display on the south side of the road, Deputy Torrez' county unit snugged in behind a dark blue Chevy Caprice with two bicycles strapped to the roof rack. Torrez hadn't dismounted yet, but waited patiently for the NCIC response. And Gayle was prompt. Just as I passed, she radioed what he needed to hear. "Virginia tag Three oh eight, baker alpha echo should appear on a 1985 Chevrolet, color blue, no wants or warrants."

"Ten four." In the rearview mirror I saw Torrez exit the vehicle. In another few minutes, I pulled into the Broken Spur's parking lot. It seemed to be the day for livestock trailers. I found a space between two of them, got out, and—I think just because I knew it irritated him—strolled around to the kitchen door, disregarding the signs that proclaimed, *EMPLOYEES ONLY, NO ADMITTANCE WHATSOEVER.*

"Good afternoon, Victor," I said as I entered the kitchen. He was presiding over a grill full of burgers, onions, and potatoes, and he glanced up for the fraction of a second it took to see who had invaded his domain. His son Victor Junior was working at the sink, and daughter Eileen had her head in the big double-doored fridge, rooting around for something.

Victor waved his spatula at me. "I don't know how many times I got to tell you this," he said. "You got that hotshot out there runnin' traffic right at my front door. I don't appreciate that."

He turned four burger patties deftly and then mashed them so that the fat spat and sizzled. "He's got the whole county to work. He don't need to sit on my doorstep."

"I'll absolutely tell him that," I said with an understanding nod. "Business looks like it's picking up."

"Yeah, well."

I watched the kid wash a fistful of knives as if they were the king's cutlery. I guess they were. Eileen closed the fridge doors and carried an armload of tomatoes to the central table. She beamed at me, and wrinkled her nose at the back of her father's head.

"Is the deputy what you called about, Victor?"

He glanced at me as if seeing me for the first time. "Yeah, that's why I called." He whacked the spatula edge against the cast-iron grill rim. "If he don't stop, I'm going to the county."

"That's the best idea," I said agreeably. "Give Randy Murray a call."

That earned another sideways glance. "*That* useless son of a bitch," Victor muttered to the sizzling potatoes. And then he surprised the hell out of me, sounding actually civil as he did so.

"You heard who bought the paper?"

"The *Register?* Some outfit back in Kansas. That's all I know."

"Bailey got tired of writing about family, I guess." His brother was enjoying eight years at the taxpayers' expense, his two buddies looking at the same. Schroeder had turned down the plea deal, but their next mistake may have been waiving their right to a jury trial. Hell, they knew the evidence was there. Judge Hobart hadn't seen any reason to differentiate the sentences based on any kind of extenuating circumstances, and swatted all three hard...probably about the limit he could go without intent being proven.

"Well, Leo has been thinking of retiring for a long time."

"They'll use that as an excuse to raise ad rates. You watch and see."

"No doubt." I rapped my knuckles on the butcher-block table. "Look, I need to get. I'll talk with the deputy."

"You do that. He puts three good customers in jail, and now he thinks he's ruling the world."

"He'll age, like the rest of us, Victor. Age and season." I turned to Victor's daughter. "Eileen, you have a nice day." She smiled and nodded, and Victor Junior looked the other way.

The sun was brutal, and as I walked across to my Blazer I saw that Torrez had finished with Virginia eight-zero-eight. He'd parked back down the highway, across from the intersection of County 14, his unit tucked in behind the state's pile of gravel—a productive spot to lie in wait.

I pulled in window-to-window.

"How's it going, Robert?"

"Kinda slow right now," he said, and tossed his clipboard/ logbook onto the passenger seat.

"Victor called us."

"Huh. Well, he don't like me much."

I laughed. "Roberto, Victor doesn't like *anybody* much."

"Nope."

"Well, you keep up the good work." He nodded. "I'm going to pick up Reuben and go down with him to see how his project at the church is coming along. Good day to sit in the shade by the river."

"Even if it don't have water in it," Torrez said, and managed a smile.

"Keep sharp," I said, and pulled the Blazer into gear. Heading up County 14 toward Reuben's place, I radioed dispatch. "PCS, three ten will be ten seven, Tres Santos."

"Ten four, three ten." Gayle paused. "Three oh eight, PCS. Ten twenty?"

"That's good," I said aloud. "You keep close track of him."

To see more Poisoned Pen Press titles:

Visit our website: poisonedpenpress.com/
Request a digital catalog: info@poisonedpenpress.com

CPSIA information can be obtained
at www.ICGtesting.com
Printed in the USA
BVOW09s0245111017
497288BV00002B/2/P